The Prophet Speaks:

'Drawn by I know not what, I went where men had not yet been. With a piece of chalkstone picked from the rubble, I marked my path; but that was well-nigh the last glimmer of ordinary human sense in me, as I drew kilometer by kilometer nearer to my finality.

'I found it in a room where light shone cool from a tall thing of whose simplicity my eyes glided; I could only see that it must be an artifact, and think that most of it must not be matter but energy. Before it lay this which I now wear on my head. I donned it and –

' – there are no words, no thoughts for what came –

'After three nights and days I ascended; and in me dwelt Caruith the Ancient – the Savior of Aeneas. . . .'

Poul Anderson

The Day
of Their Return

CORGI BOOKS

A DIVISION OF TRANSWORLD PUBLISHERS LTD

THE DAY OF THEIR RETURN

A CORGI BOOK 0 552 10770 0

First publication in Great Britain

PRINTING HISTORY
Corgi edition published 1978

Copyright © 1975 by Poul Anderson

This book is set in 10/10½pt Times

Corgi Books are published by Transworld Publishers Ltd,
Century House, 61–63 Uxbridge Road,
Ealing, London, W.5.
Made and printed in Great Britain by
Hunt Barnard Printing Ltd., Aylesbury, Bucks.

TO Marion Zimmer Bradley,
my lady of Darkover

Now a thing was secretly brought to me, and mine ear received a little thereof. In thoughts from the visions of the night, when deep sleep falleth on men, fear came upon me, and trembling, which made all my bones to shake. Then a spirit passed before my face; the hair of my flesh stood up: it stood still, but I could not discern the form thereof: an image was before mine eyes, there was silence, and I heard a voice. . . .

— JOB, iv, 12–16

I

On the third day he arose, and ascended again to the light.

Dawn gleamed across a sea which had once been an ocean. To north, cliffs lifted blue from the steel gray of its horizon; and down them went a streak which was the falls, whose thunder beat dim through a windless cold. The sky stood violet in the west, purple overhead, white in the east where the sun came climbing. But still the morning star shone there, the planet of the First Chosen.

I am the first of the Second Chosen, Jaan knew: *and the voice of those who choose. To be man is to be radiance.*

His nostrils drank air, his muscles exulted. Never had he been this aware. From the brightness of his face to the grit below his feet, he was real.

– O glory upon glory, said that which within him was Caruith.

– It overwhelms this poor body, said Jaan. I am new to resurrection. Do you not feel yourself a stranger in chains?

– Six million years have blown by in the night, said Caruith. I remember waves besparkled and a shout of surf, where now stones lie gaunt beneath us; I remember pride in walls and columns, where ruin huddles above the mouth of the tomb whence we have come; I remember how clouds walked clad in rainbows. Before all, I seek to remember – and fail, because the flesh I am cannot bear the fire I was – I seek to remember the fullness of existence.

Jaan lifted hands to the crown engirdling his brows. – For you, this is a heavy burden, he said.

– No, sang Caruith. I share the opening that it has made for you and your race. I will grow with you, and you with me, and they with us, until mankind is not only worthy to be received into Oneness, it will bring thereunto what is wholly its own. And at last sentience will create God. Now come, let us proclaim it to the people.

He/they went up the mountain toward the Arena. Above them paled Dido, the morning star.

II

East of Windhome the country rolled low for a while, then lifted in the Hesperian Hills. Early summer had gentled their starkness with leaves. Blue-green, gray-green here and there the intense green-green of oak or cedar, purple of rasmin, spread in single trees, bushes, widely spaced groves, across an onyx tinged red and yellow which was the land's living mantle, fire trava.

A draught blew from sunset. Ivar Frederiksen shivered. Even his gunstock felt cold beneath his hand. The sward he lay on had started to curl up for the night, turning into a springy mat. Its daytime odor of flint and sparks was almost gone. A delphi overarched him; gnarled low trunk, grotto of branches and foliage. Multitudinous rustlings went through it, like whispers in an unknown tongue. His vision ranged over a slope bestrewn with shrubs and boulders, to a valley full of shadow. The riverside road was lost in that dusk, the water a wan gleam. His heart knocked, louder than the sound of the Wildfoss flowing.

Nobody. Will they never come?

A flash caught his eye and breath. An aircraft out of the west?

No. The leaves in their restlessness had confused him. What rose above Hornbeck Ridge was just Creusa. Laughter snapped forth, a sign of how taut were his nerves. As if to seek companionship, he followed the moon. It glimmered ever more bright, waxing while it climbed eastward. A pair of wings likewise caught rays from the hidden sun and shone gold against indigo heaven.

Easy! he tried to scold himself. *You're nigh on dis-minded. What if this will be your first battle? No excuse. You're ringleader, aren't you?*

9

Though born to the thin dry air of Aeneas, he felt his nasal passages hurt, his tongue leather. He reached for a canteen. Filled at yonder stream, it gave him a taste of iron.

'Aah – ' he began. And then the Imperials were come.

They appeared like that, sudden as a blow. A part of him knew how. Later than awaited, they had been concealed by twilight and a coppice in his line of sight, until their progress brought them into unmistakable view. But had none of his followers seen them earlier? The guerrillas covered three kilometers on both sides of the gorge. This didn't speak well for their readiness.

Otherwise Ivar was caught in a torrent. He didn't know what roared through him, fear, anger, insanity, nor had he time to wonder. He did observe, in a flicker of amazement, no heroic joy or stern determination. His body obeyed plans while something wailed, *How did I get into this? How do I get out?*

He was on his feet. He gave the hunting cry of a spider wolf, and heard it echoed and passed on. He pulled the hood of his jacket over his head, the nightmask over his face. He snatched his rifle off the ground and sprang from the shelter of the delphi.

Every sense was fever-brilliant. He saw each coiled blade of the fire trava whereon he ran, felt how it gave beneath his boots and rebounded, caught a last warmth radiated from a giant rock, drank in the sweetness of a cedar, brushed the roughness of an oak, could have counted the petals a rasmin spread above him or measured the speed at which a stand of plume trava folded against the gathering cold – but that was all on the edge of awareness as was the play inside of muscles, nerves, blood, lungs, pulse – his being was aimed at his enemies.

They were human, a platoon of marines, afoot save for the driver of a field gun. It hummed along on a gravsled, two meters off the road. Though helmeted, the men were in loose order and walked rather than marched, expecting no trouble on a routine patrol. Most had connected the powerpacks on their shoulders to the heating threads in their baggy green coveralls.

The infrascope on Ivar's rifle told him that. His eyes told of comrades who rose from bush and leaped down the hillsides, masked and armed like him. His ears caught raw young voices, war-calls and wordless yells. Shots crackled. The Aeneans had double the number of their prey, advantage of surprise, will to be free.

They lacked energy weapons; but a sleet of bullets converged on the artillery piece. Ivar saw its driver cast from his seat, a red rag. *We've got them!* He sent a burst himself, then continued his charge, low and zigzag. The plan, the need was to break the platoon and carry their equipment into the wilderness.

The cannon descended. Ivar knew, too late: *Some kind of dead-man switch.* The marines, who had thrown their bodies flat, got up and sought it. A few lay wounded or slain; the rest reached its shelter. Blaster bolts flared and boomed, slugthrowers raved. The Aenean closest to Ivar trembled, rolled over and over, came to a halt and screamed. Screamed. Screamed. His blood on the turf was outrageously bright, spread impossibly wide.

A new Imperial took the big gun's controls. Lightning flew across the river, which threw its blue-whiteness back like molten metal. Thunder hammered. Where that beam passed were no more trees or shrubs or warriors. Smoke roiled above ash.

Blind and deaf, Ivar fell. He clawed at the soil, because he thought the planet was trying to whirl him off.

After a fraction of eternity, the delirium passed. His head still tolled, tatters of light drifted before his vision, but he could hear, see, almost think.

A daggerbush partly screened him. He had ripped his right sleeve and arm on it, but was otherwise unhurt. Nearby sprawled a corpse. Entrails spilled forth. The mask hid which friend this had been. How wrong, how obscene to expose the guts without the face.

Ivar strained through gloom. The enemy had not turned their fieldpiece on this bank of the river. Instead, they used small arms as precision tools. Against their skill and discipline, the guerrillas were glass tossed at armor plate.

Guerrillas? We children? And I led us. Ivan fought not to vomit, not to weep.

He must sneak off. Idiot luck, nothing else, had kept him alive and unnoticed. But the marines were taking prisoners. He saw them bring in several who were lightly injured. Several more, outgunned, raised their hands.

Nobody keeps a secret from a hypnoprobe.

Virgil slipped beneath an unseen horizon. Night burst forth.

Aeneas rotates in twenty hours, nineteen minutes, and a few seconds. Dawn was not far when Ivar Frederiksen reached Windhome.

Gray granite walled the ancestral seat of the Firstman of Ilion. It stood near the edge of an ancient cape. In tiers and scarps, crags and cliffs, thinly brush-grown or naked rock, the continental shelf dropped down three kilometers to the Antonine Seabed. So did the river, a flash by the castle, a clangor of cataracts.

The portal stood closed, a statement that the occupation troops were considered bandits. Ivar stumbled to press the scanner plate. Chimes echoed emptily.

Weariness was an ache which rose in his marrow and seeped through bones and flesh till blood ran thick with it. His knees shook, his jaws clattered. The dried sweat that he could taste and smell on himself stung the cracks in his lips. Afraid to use roads, he had fled a long and rough way.

He leaned on the high steel door and sucked air through a mummy mouth. A breeze sheathed him in iciness. Yet somehow he had never been as aware of the beauty of this land, now when it was lost to him.

The sky soared crystalline black, wild with stars. Through the thin air they shone steadily, in diamond hues; and the Milky Way was a white torrent, and a kindred cloud in the Ula was our sister galaxy spied across a million and a half light-years. Creusa had set; but slower Lavinia rode aloft in her second quarter. Light fell argent on hoarfrost.

Eastward reached fields, meadows, woodlots, bulks that were sleeping farmsteads, and at last the hills. Ivar's gaze fared west. There the rich bottomlands ran in orchards, plantations, canals night-frozen into mirrors, the burnished shield of a salt marsh, to the world's rim. He thought he saw lights move. Were folk abroad already? No, he couldn't make out lamps over such a distance . . . lanterns on ghost ships, sailing an ocean that vanished three million years ago . . .

The portal swung wide. Sergeant Astaff stood behind. In defiance of Imperial decree, his stocky frame bore Ilian uniform. He had left off hood and mask, though. In the unreal luminance, his head was not grizzled, it was as white as the words which puffed from him.

'Firstlin' Ivar! Where you been? What's gone on? Your mother's gnawed fear for you this whole past five-day.'

The heir to the house lurched by him. Beyond the gateway, the courtyard was crisscrossed with moon-shadows from towers, battlements, main keep and lesser building. A hound, of the lean heavy-jawed Hesperian breed, was the only other life in sight. Its claws clicked on flagstones, unnaturally loud.

Astaff pushed a button to close the door. For a time he squinted until he said slowly, 'Better give me that rifle, Firstlin'. I know places where Terrans won't poke.'

'Me too,' sighed from Ivar.

'Didn't do you a lot o' good, stashed away till you were ready for – whatever you've done – hey?' Astaff held out his hand.

'Trouble I'm in, it makes no difference if they catch me with this.' Ivar took hold of the firearm. 'Except I'd make them pay for me.'

Something kindled in the old man. He, like his fathers before him, had served the Firstmen of Ilion for a lifetime. Nevertheless, or else for that same reason, pain was in his tone. 'Why'd you not ask me for help?'

'You'd have talked me out of it,' Ivar said. 'You'd have been right,' he added.

'What did you try?'

'Ambushin' local patrol. To start stockpilin' weapons. I don't know how many of us escaped. Probably most didn't.'

Astaff regarded him.

13

Ivar Frederiksen was tall, 185 centimeters, slender save for wide shoulders and the Aenean depth of chest. Exhaustion weighted down his normal agility and hoarsened the tenor voice. Snub-nosed, square-jawed, freckled, his face looked still younger than it was; no noticeable beard had grown during the past hours. His hair, cut short at nape and ears in the nord manner, was yellow, seldom free of a cowlick or a stray lock across the forehead. Beneath dark brows, his eyes were large and green. Under his jacket he wore the high-collared shirt, pouched belt, heavy-bladed sheath knife, thick trousers tucked into half-boots, of ordinary outdoor dress. There was, in truth, little to mark him off from any other upper-class lad of his planet.

That little was enough.

'What caveheads you were,' the sergeant said at last.

A twitch of anger: 'We should sit clay-sort for Terrans to mold, fire, and use however they see fit?'

'Well,' Astaff replied, 'I would've planned my strike better, and drilled longer beforetime.'

He took Ivar by the elbow. 'You're spent like a cartridge,' he said. 'Go to my quarters. You remember where I bunk, no? Thank Lord, my wife's off visitin' our daughter's family. Grab shower, food, sleep. I've sentry-go till oh-five-hundred. Can't call substitute without drawin' questions; but nobody'll snuff at you.'

Ivar blinked. 'What do you mean? My own rooms –'

'Yah!' Astaff snorted. 'Go on. Rouse your mother, your kid sister. Get 'em involved. Sure. They'll be interrogated, you know, soon's Impies've found you were in that broil. They'll be narcoquizzed, or even 'probed, if any reason develops to think they got clue to your whereabouts. That what you want? Okay. Go bid 'em fond farewell.'

Ivar took a backward step, lifted his hands in appeal. 'No. I, I, I never thought –,'

'Right.'

'Of course I'll – What do you have in mind?' Ivar asked humbly.

'Get you off before Impies arrive. Good thing your dad's been whole while in Nova Roma; clear-cut innocent, and got influence to protect family if Terrans find no sign you

14

were ever here after fight. Hey? You'll leave soon. Wear servant's livery I'll filch for you, snoutmask like you're sneezewort allergic, weapon under cloak. Walk like you got hurry-up errand. This is big household; nobody ought to notice you especially. I'll've found some yeoman who'll take you in, Sam Hedin, Frank Vance, whoever, loyal and livin', offside. You go there.'

'And then?'

Astaff shrugged. 'Who knows? When zoosny's died down, I'll slip your folks word you're alive and loose. Maybe later your dad can wangle pardon for you. But if Terrans catch you while their dead are fresh – son, they'll make example. I know Empire. Traveled through it more than once with Admiral McCormac.' As he spoke the name, he saluted. 'The average Imperial agent who saw would have arrested him on the spot.

Ivar swallowed and stammered, 'I . . . I can't thank – '

'You're next Firstman of Ilion,' the sergeant snapped. 'Maybe last hope we got, this side of Elders returnin'. Now, before somebody comes, haul your butt out of here – and don't forget the rest of you!'

III

Chunderban Desai's previous assignment had been to the delegation which negotiated an end of the Jihannath crisis. That wasn't the change of pace in his career which it seemed. His Majesty's administrators must forever be dickering, compromising, feeling their way, balancing conflicts of individuals, organizations, societies, races, sentient species. The need for skill – quickly to grasp facts, comprehend a situation, brazen out a bluff when in spite of everything the unknown erupted into one's calculations – was greatest at the intermediate level of bureaucracy which he had reached. A resident might deal with a single culture, and have no more to do than keep an eye on affairs. A sector governor oversaw such vastness that to him it became a set of abstractions. But the various ranks of commissioner were expected to handle personally large and difficult territories.

Desai had worked in regions that faced Betelgeuse and, across an unclaimed and ill-explored buffer zone, the Roidhunate of Merseia. Thus he was a natural choice for the special diplomatic team. In his quiet style, he back-stopped the head of it, Lord Advisor Chardon, so well that afterward he received a raise in grade, and was appointed High Commissioner of the Virgilian System, at the opposite end of the Empire.

But this was due to an equally natural association of ideas. The mutiny in Sector Alpha Crucis had been possible because most of the Navy was tied up around Jihannath, where full-scale war looked far too likely. After Terra nevertheless, brilliantly, put the rebels down, Mersia announced that its wish all along had been to avoid a major clash and it was prepared to bargain.

When presently the Policy Board looked about for able people to reconstruct Sector Alpha Crucis, Lord Chardon recommended Desai with an enthusiasm that got him put in charge of Virgil, whose human-colonized planet Aeneas had been the spearhead of the revolt.

Perhaps that was why Desai often harked back to the Merseians, however remote from him they seemed these days.

In a rare moment of idleness, while he waited in his Nova Roma office for the next visitor, he remembered his final conversation with Uldwyr.

They had played corresponding roles on behalf of their respective sovereigns, and in a wry way had become friends. When the protocol had, at weary last, been drawn, the two of them supplemented the dull official celebration with a dinner of their own.

Desai recalled their private room in a restaurant. The wall animations were poor; but a place which catered to a variety of sophonts couldn't be expected to understand everybody's art, and the meal was an inspired combination of human and Merseian dishes.

'Have a refill,' Uldwyr invited, and raised a crock of his people's pungent ale.

'No, thank you,' Desai said. 'I prefer tea. That dessert filled me to the scuppers.'

'The what? – Never mind, I seize the idea, if not the idiom.' Though each was fluent in the other's principal language, and their vocal organs were not very different, it was easiest for Desai to speak Anglic and Uldwyr Eriau.

'You've tucked in plenty of food, for certain.'

'My particular vice, I fear,' Desai smiled. 'Besides, more alcohol would muddle me. I haven't your mass to assimilate it.'

'What matter if you get drunk? I plan to. Our job is done.' And then Uldwyr added: 'For now.'

Shocked, Desai stared across the table.

Uldwyr gave him back a quizzical glance. The Merseian's face was almost human, if one overlooked thick bones and countless details of the flesh. But his finely scaled green skin had no hair whatsoever, he lacked earflaps, a low serration ran from the top of his skull, down his back to the end of the crocodilian tail which counter-balanced his big, forward-leaning body. Arms and hands were, again, nearly manlike; legs and clawed splay feet could have belonged to a biped dinosaur. He wore black, silver-trimmed military tunic and trousers, colorful emblems of rank and of the Vach Hallen into which he was born. A blaster hung on his hip.

'What's the matter?' he asked.

'Oh . . . nothing.' In Desai's mind went: *He didn't mean it hostilely – hostilely to me as a person – his remark. He, his whole civilization, minces words less small than we do. Struggle against Terra is just a fact. The Roidhunate will compromise disputes when expediency dictates, but never the principle that eventually the Empire must be destroyed. Because we – old, sated, desirous only of maintaining a peace which lets us pursue our pleasures – we stand in the way of their ambitions for the Race. Lest the balance of power be upset, we block them, we thwart them, wherever we can; and they seek to undermine us, grind us down, wear us out. But this is nothing personal. I am Uldwyr's honorable enemy, therefore his friend. By giving him opposition, I give meaning to his life.*

The other divined his thoughts and uttered the harsh Merseian chuckle. 'If you want to pretend tonight that matters have been settled for aye, do. I'd really rather we both got drunk and traded war songs.'

'I am not a man of war,' Desai said.

Beneath a shelf of brow ridge, Uldwyr's eyelids expressed skepticism while his mouth grinned. 'You mean you don't like physical violence. It was quite an effective war you waged at the conference table.'

He swigged from his tankard. Desai saw that he was already a little tipsy. 'I imagine the next phase will also be quiet,' he went on. 'Ungloved force hasn't worked too well lately. Starkad, Jihannath – no, I'd look for us to try something more crafty and long-range. Which ought to suit your Empire, *khraich*? You've made a good thing for your Naval Intelligence out of the joint commission on

18

Talwin.' Desia, who knew that, kept silence. 'Maybe our turn is coming.'

Hating his duty, Desai asked in his most casual voice, 'Where?'

'Who knows?' Uldwyr gestured the equivalent of a shrug. 'I have no doubt, and neither do you, we've a swarm of agents in Sector Alpha Crucis, for instance. Besides the recent insurrection, it's close to the Domain of Ythri, which has enjoyed better relations with us than with you – ' His hand chopped the air. 'No, I'm distressing you, am I not? And with what can only be guesswork. Apologies. See here, if you don't care for more ale, why not artfberry brandy? I guarantee a first-class drunk and – You may suppose you're a peaceful fellow, Chunderban, but I know an atom or two about your people, your specific people, I mean. What's that old, old book I've heard you mention and quote from? Rixway?'

'Rig-Veda,' Desai told him.

'You said it includes war chants. Do you know any well enough to put into Anglic? There's a computer terminal.' He pointed to a corner. 'You can patch right into our main translator, now that official business is over. I'd like to hear a bit of your special tradition, Chunderban. So many traditions, works, mysteries – so tiny a lifespan to taste them – '

It became a memorable evening.

Restless, Desai stirred in his chair.

He was a short man with a dark-brown moon face and a paunch. At fifty-five standard years of age, his hair remained black but had receded from the top of his head. The full lips were usually curved slightly upward, which joined the liquid eyes to give him a wistful look. As was his custom, today he wore plain, loosely fitted white shirt and trousers, on his feet slippers a size large for comfort.

Save for the communication and data-retrieval consoles that occupied one wall, his office was similarly unpretentious. It did have a spectacular holograph, a view of Mount Gandhi on his home planet, Ramanujan. But otherwise the pictures were of his wife, their seven children, the

19

families of those four who were grown and settled on as many different globes. A bookshelf held codices as well as reels; some were much-used reference works, the rest for refreshment, poetry, history, essays, most of their authors centuries dust. His desk was less neat than his person.

I shouldn't go taking vacations in the past, he thought. *God knows the present needs more of me than I have to give.*

Or does it? Spare me the ultimate madness of ever considering myself indispensable.

Well, but somebody must man this post. He happens to be me.

Must somebody? How much really occurs because of me, how much in spite of or regardless of? How much, and what, should occur? God! I dared accept the job of ruling, remaking an entire world — when I knew nothing more about it than its name, and that simply because it was the planet of Hugh McCormac, the man who would be Emperor. After two years, what else have I learned?

Ordinarily he could sit quiet, but the Hesperian episode had been too shocking, less in itself than in its implications. Whatever they were. How could he plan against the effect on these people, once the news got out, when he, the foreigner, had no intuition of what that effect might be?

He put a cigarette into a long, elaborately carved holder of landwhale ivory. (He thought it was in atrocious taste, but it had been given him for a birthday present by a ten-year-old daughter who died soon afterward.) The tobacco was an expensive self-indulgence, grown on Esperance, the closest thing to Terran he could obtain hereabouts while shipping remained sparse.

The smoke-bite didn't soothe him. He jumped up and prowled. He hadn't yet adapted so fully to the low gravity of Aeneas, 63 percent standard, that he didn't consciously enjoy movement. The drawback was the dismal exercises he must go through each morning, if he didn't want to turn completely into lard. Unfair, that the Aeneans tended to be such excellent physical specimens without effort. No, not really unfair. On this niggard sphere, few could afford a large panoply of machines; even today, more travel was on foot or animal back than in vehicles, more work done by hand than by automatons or cybernets. Also, in earlier periods – the initial colonization, the Troubles, the slow climb back from chaos – death had winnowed the unfit out of their bloodlines.

Desai halted at the north wall, activated its transparency, and gazed forth across Nova Roma.

Though itself two hundred Terran years old, Imperial House jutted awkwardly from the middle of a city founded seven centuries ago. Most buildings in this district were at least half that age, and architecture had varied little through time. In a climate where it seldom rained and never snowed; where the enemies were drought, cold, hurricane winds, drifting dust, scouring sand; where water for bricks and concrete, forests for timber, organics for synthesis were rare and precious, one quarried the stone which Aeneas did have in abundance, and used its colors and textures.

The typical structure was a block, two or three stories tall, topped by a flat deck which was half garden – the view from above made a charming motley – and half solar-energy collector. Narrow windows carried shutters orna-mented with brass or iron arabesques; the heavy doors were of similar appearance. In most cases, the gray ashlars bore a veneer of carefully chosen and integrated slabs, marble, agate, chalcedony, jasper, nephrite, materials more exotic than that; and often there were carvings besides, friezes, armorial bearings, grotesques; and erosion had mellowed it all, to make the old part of town one subtle harmony. The wealthier homes, shops, and offices surrounded cloister courts, vitryl-roofed to conserve heat and water, where statues and plants stood among fishponds and fountains.

The streets were cramped and twisted, riddled with alleys, continually opening on small irrational plazas. Traffic was thin, mainly pedestrian, otherwise groundcars, trucks, and countryfolk on soft-gaited Aenean horses or six-legged green stathas (likewise foreign, though Desai couldn't offhand remember where they had originated). A capital city – population here a third of a million, much the largest – would inevitably hurt more and recover slower from a war than its hinterland.

He lifted his eyes to look onward. Being to south, the University wasn't visible through this wall. What he saw was the broad bright sweep of the River Flone, and ancient high-arched bridges across it; beyond, the Julian Canal, its tributaries, verdant parks along them, barges and pleasure boats upon their surfaces; farther still, the upthrust of modern many lesser but newer canals, the intricacy of buildings in garish colors, a tinge of industrial haze – the Web.

However petty by Terran standards, he thought, that youngest section was the seedbed of his hopes: in the manufacturing, mercantile, and managerial classes which had arisen during the past few generations, whose interests lay less with the scholars and squirearchs than with the Imperium and its Pax.

Or can I call on them? he wondered. *I've been doing it; but how reliable are they?*

A single planet is too big for single me to understand.

Right and left he spied the edge of wilderness. Life lay emerald on either side of the Flone, where it ran majestically down from the north polar cap. He could see hamlets, manors, water traffic; he knew that the banks were crop-lands and pasture. But the belt was only a few kilometers wide.

Elsewhere reared worn yellow cliffs, black basalt ridges, ocherous dunes, on and on beneath a sky almost purple. Shadows were sharper-edged than on Terra or Ramanujan, for the sun was half again as far away, its disc shrunken. He knew that now, in summer at a middle latitude, the air was chill; he observed on the tossing tendrils of a rahab tree in a roof garden how strongly the wind blew. Come sunset, temperatures would plunge below freezing. And yet Virgil was brighter than Sol, an F7; one could not look near it without heavy eye protection, and Desai marveled that light-skinned humans had ever settled in lands this cruelly irradiated.

Well, planets where unarmored men could live at all were none too common; and there had been the lure of Dido. In the beginning, this was a scientific base, nothing

22

else. No, the second beginning, ages after the unknown builders of what stood in unknowable ruins . . .

A world, a history like that; and I am supposed to tame them?

His receptionist said through the intercom, 'Aycharaych,' pronouncing the lilting diphthongs and guttural *ch*'s well. It was programmed to mimic languages the instant it heard them. That gratified visitors, especially non-humans.

'What?' Desai blinked. The tickler on his desk screened a notation of the appointment. 'Oh. Oh, yes.' He popped out of his reverie. *That being who arrived on the Llynath-awr packet day before yesterday. Wants a permit to conduct studies.* 'Send him in, please.' (By extending verbal courtesy even to a subunit of a computer, the High Commissioner helped maintain an amicable atmosphere. Perhaps.) The screen noted that the newcomer was male, or at any rate referred to himself as such. Planet of origin was listed as Jean-Baptiste, wherever that might be: doubtless a name bestowed by humans because the autochthons had too many different ones of their own.

The door retracted while Aycharaych stepped through. Desai caught his breath. He had not expected someone this impressive.

Or was that the word? Was 'disturbing' more accurate? Xenosophonts who resembled humans occasionally had that effect on the latter; and Aycharaych was more anthropoid than Uldwyr.

One might indeed call him beautiful. He stood tall and thin in a gray robe, broad-chested but wasp-waisted, a frame that ought to have moved gawkily but instead flowed. The bare feet each had four long claws, and spurs on the ankles. The hands were six-fingered, tapered, their nails suggestive of talons. The head arched high and narrow, bearing pointed ears, great rust-red eyes, curved blade of nose, delicate mouth, pointed chin and sharply angled jaws; Desai thought of a Byzantine saint. A crest of blue feathers rose above, and tiny plumes formed eyebrows. Otherwise his skin was wholly smooth across the prominent bones, a glowing golden color.

23

After an instant's hesitation, Desai said, 'Ah . . . welcome, Honorable. I hope I can be of service.' They shook hands. Aycharaych's was warmer than his. The palm had a hardness that wasn't calluses. *Avian*, the man guessed. *Descended from an analog of flightless birds.*

The other's Anglic was flawless; the musical overtone which his low voice gave sounded not like a mispronunciation but a perfection. 'Thank you, Commissioner. You are kind to see me this promptly. I realize how busy you must be.'

'Won't you be seated?' The chair in front of the desk didn't have to adjust itself much. Desai resumed his own. 'Do you mind if I smoke? Would you care for one?' Aycharaych shook his head to both questions, and smiled; again Desai thought of antique images, archaic Grecian sculpture. 'I'm very interested to meet you,' he said. 'I confess your people are new in my experience.'

'We are few who travel off our world,' Aycharaych replied. 'Our sun is in Sector Aldebaran.'

Desai nodded. 'M-hm.' His business had never involved any society in that region. No surprise. The vaguely bounded, roughly spherical volume over which Terra claimed suzerainty had a diameter of some 400 light-years; it held an estimated four million stars, whereof half were believed to have been visited at least once; approximately 100,000 planets had formalized relations with the Imperium, but for most of them it amounted to no more than acknowledgment of subordination and modest taxes, or merely the obligation to make labor and resources available should the Empire ever have need. In return they got the Pax; and they had a right to join in spatial commerce, though the majority lacked the capital, or the industrial base, or the appropriate kind of culture for that – *Too big, too big. If a single planet overwhelms the intellect, what then of our entire microscopic chip of the galaxy, away off toward the edge of a spiral arm, which we imagine we have begun to be a little acquainted with?*

'You are pensive, Commissioner,' Aycharaych remarked.

'Did you notice?' Desai laughed. 'You've known quite a few humans, then.'

'Your race is ubiquitous,' Aycharaych answered politely. 'And fascinating. That is my heart reason for coming here.'

'Ah . . . pardon me, I've not had a chance to give your documents a proper review. I know only that you wish to travel about on Aeneas for scientific purposes.'

'Consider me an anthropologist, if you will. My people have hitherto had scant outside contact, but they anticipate more. My mission for a number of years has been to go to and fro in the Empire, learning the ways of your species, the most numerous and widespread within those borders, so that we may deal wisely with you. I have observed a wonderful variety of life-manners, yes, of thinking, feeling, and perceiving. Your versatility approaches miracle.'

'Thank you,' said Desai, not altogether comfortably. 'I don't believe, myself, we are unique. It merely happened we were the first into space – in our immediate volume and point in history – and our dominant civilization of the time happened to be dynamically expansive. So we spread into many different environments, often isolated, and underwent cultural radiation . . . or fragmentation.' He streamed smoke from his nose and peered through it. 'Can you alone, hope to discover much about us?'

'I am not the sole wanderer,' Aycharaych said. 'Besides, a measure of telepathic ability is helpful.'

'Eh?' Desai noticed himself switch over to thinking in Hindi. But what was he afraid of? Sensitivity to neural emissions, talent at interpreting them, was fairly well understood, had been for centuries. Some species were better at it than others; man was among those that brought forth few good cases, none of them first-class. Nevertheless, human scientists had studied the phenomenon as they had studied the wavelengths wherein they were blind . . .

'You will see the fact mentioned in the data reel concerning me,' Aycharaych said. 'The staff of Sector Governor Muratori takes precautions against espionage. When I

25

first approached them about my mission, as a matter of routine I was exposed to a telepathic agent, a Ryellian, who could scarcely sense that my brain pattern had similarities to hers.'

Desai nodded. Ryellians were expert. Of course, this one could scarcely have read Aycharaych's mind on such superficial contact, nor mapped the scope of his capacities; patterns varied too greatly between species, languages, societies, individuals. 'What can you do of this nature; if I may ask?'

Aycharaych made a denigrating gesture. 'Less than I desire. For example, you need not have changed the verbal form of your interior dream. I felt you do it, but only because the pulses changed. I could never read your mind; that is impossible unless I have known a person long and well, and then I can merely translate surface thoughts, clearly formulated. I cannot project.' He smiled. 'Shall we say I have a minor gift of empathy?'

'Don't underrate that. I wish I had it in the degree you seem to.' Inwardly: *I mustn't let myself fall under his spell. He's captivating, but my duty is to be cold and cautious.*

Desai leaned forward, elbows on desk. 'Forgive me if I'm blunt, Honorable,' he said. 'You've come to a planet which two years ago was in armed rebellion against His Majesty, which hoped to put one of its own sons on the throne by force and violence or, failing that, lead a break-away of this whole sector from the Empire. Mutinous spirit is still high. I'll tell you, because the fact can't be suppressed for any length of time, we lately had an actual attack on a body of occupation troops, for the purpose of stealing their weapons. Riots elsewhere are already matters of public knowledge.

'Law and order are very fragile here, Honorable. I hope to proceed firmly but humanely with the reintegration of the Virgilian system into Imperial life. At present, practically anything could touch off a further explosion. Were it a major one, the consequences would be disastrous for the Aeneans, evil for the Empire. We're not far from the border, from the Domain of Ythri and, worse, indepen-

26

dent war lords, buccaneers, and weird fanatics who have space fleets. Aeneas bulwarked this flank of ours. We can ill afford to lose it.

'A number of hostile or criminal elements took advantage of unsettled conditions to debark. I doubt if my police have yet gotten rid of them all. I certainly don't propose to let in more. That's why ships and detector satellites are in orbit, and none but specific vessels may land – at this port, nowhere else – and persons from them must be registered and must stay inside Nova Roma unless they get specific permission to travel.'

He realized how harsh he sounded, and began to beg pardon. Aycharaych broke smoothly through his embarrassment. 'Please do not think you give offense, Commissioner. I quite sympathize with your position. Besides, I sense your basic good will toward me. You fear I might, inadvertently, rouse emotions which would ignite mobs or outright revolutionaries.'

'I must consider the possibility, Honorable. Even within a single species, the ghastliest blunders are all too easy to make. For instance, my own ancestors on Terra, before spaceflight, once rose against foreign rulers. The conflict took many thousand lives. Its proximate cause was a new type of cartridge which offended the religious sensibilities of native troops.'

'A better example might be the Taiping Rebellion.'

'What?'

'It happened in China, in the same century as the Indian Mutiny. A revolt against a dynasty of outlanders, though one which had governed for considerable time, became a civil war that lasted for a generation and killed people in the millions. The leaders were inspired by a militant form of Christianity – scarcely what Jesus had in mind, no?'

Desai stared at Aycharaych. 'You *have* studied us.'

'A little, oh, a hauntingly little. Much of it in your esthetic works, Aeschylus, Li Po, Shakespeare, Goethe, Sturgeon, Mikhailov . . . the music of a Bach or Richard Strauss, the visual art of a Rembrandt or Hiroshige . . . Enough. I would love to discuss these matters for months, Commissioner, but you have not the time. I do hope to

27

convince you I will not enter as a clumsy ignoramus.'

'Why Aeneas?' Desai wondered.

'Precisely because of the circumstances in which it finds itself, Commissioner. How do humans of an especially proud, self-reliant type behave in defeat? We need that insight too on Jean-Baptiste, if we are not to risk aggrieving you in some future day of trouble. Furthermore, I understand Aeneas contains several cultures besides the dominant one. To make comparisons and observe interactions would teach me much.'

'Well –'

Aycharaych waved a hand. 'The results of my work will not be hoarded. Frequently an outsider perceives elements which those who live by them never do. Or they may take him into their confidence, or at least be less reserved in his presence than in that of a human who could possibly be an Imperial secret agent. Indeed, Commissioner, by his very conspicuousness, an alien like me might serve as an efficient gatherer of intelligence for you,'

Desai started. *Krishna! Does this uncanny being suspect –? No, how could he?*

Gently, almost apologetically, Aycharaych said, 'I persuaded the Governor's staff, and at last had a talk with His Excellency. If you wish to examine my documents, you will find I already have permission to carry out my studies here. But of course I would never undertake anything you disapprove.'

'Excuse me,' Desai felt bewildered, rushed, boxed in. Why should he? Aycharaych was totally courteous, eager to please. 'I ought to have checked through the data beforehand. I would have, but that wretched attempt at guerrilla action – Do you mind waiting a few minutes while I scan?'

'Not in the slightest,' the other said, 'especially if you will let me glance at those books I see over there.' He smiled wider than before. His teeth were wholly nonhuman.

'Yes, by all means,' Desai mumbled, and slapped fingers across the information-retriever panel.

Its screen lit up. An identifying holograph was followed

by relevant correspondence and notations. (Fakery was out of the question. Besides carrying tagged molecules, the reel had been deposited aboard ship by an official courier, borne here in the captain's safe, and personally brought by him to the memory bank underneath Imperial House.) The check on Aycharaych's bona fides had been routine, since they were overworked on Llynathawr too, but competently executed.

He arrived on the sector capital planet by regular passenger liner, went straight to a hotel in Catawrayannis which possessed facilities for xenosophonts, registered with the police as required, and made no effort to evade the scanners which occupation authorities had planted throughout the city. He traveled nowhere, met nobody, and did nothing suspicious. In perfectly straightforward fashion, he applied for the permit he wanted, and submitted to every interview and examination demanded of him.

No one had heard of the planet Jean-Baptiste there, either, but it was in the files and matched Aycharaych's description. The information was meager; but who would keep full data in the libraries of a distant province about a backward world which had never given trouble?

The request of its representative was reasonable, seemed unlikely to cause damage, and might yield helpful results. Sector Governor Muratori got interested, saw the being himself, and granted him an okay.

Desai frowned. His superior was both able and conscientious: had to be, if the harm done by the rapacious and conscienceless predecessor who provoked McCormac's rebellion was to be mended. However, in a top position one is soon isolated from the day-to-day details which make up a body of politics. Muratori was too new in his office to appreciate its limitations. And he was, besides, a stern man, who in Desai's opinion interpreted too literally the axiom that government is legitimatized coercion. It was because of directives from above that, after the University riots, the Commissioner of Virgil reluctantly ordered the razing of the Memorial and the total disarmament of the great Landfolk houses – two actions which he

29

felt had brought on more woes, including the lunacy in Hesperia.

Well, then, why am I worried if Muratori begins to show a trifle more flexibility than hitherto?

'I'm finished,' Desai said. 'Won't you sit down again?'

Aycharaych returned from the bookshelf, holding an Anglic volume of Tagore. 'Have you reached a decision, Commissioner?' he asked.

'You know I haven't,' Desai forced a smile. 'The decision was made for me. I am to let you do your research and give you what help is feasible.'

'I doubt if I need bother you much, Commissioner. I am an evolved for a thin atmosphere, and accustomed to rough travel. My biochemistry is similar enough to yours that food will be no problem. I have ample funds; and surely the Aenean economy could use some more Imperial credits.'

Aycharaych ruffled his crest, a particularly expressive motion. 'But please don't suppose I wish to thrust myself on you, waving a gubernatorial license like a battle flag,' he continued. 'You are the one who knows most and who, besides, must strike on the consequences of any error of mine. That would be a poor way for Jean-Baptiste to enter the larger community, would it not? I intend to be guided by your advice, yes, your preferences. For example, before my first venture, I will be grateful if your staff could plan my route and behavior.'

A thawing passed through Desai. 'You make me happy, Honorable. I'm sure we can work well together. See here, if you'd care to join me in an early lunch – and later I can have a few appointments shuffled around –'

It became a memorable afternoon.

But toward evening, alone, Desai once more felt troubled.

He should go home, to a wife and children who saw him far too little. He should stop chain-smoking; his palate was chemically burnt. Why carry a world on his shoulders, twenty long Aenean hours a day? He couldn't do it, really, for a single minute. No mortal could.

30

Yet when he had taken oath of office a mortal must try, or know himself a perjurer.

The Frederiksen affair plagued him like a newly made wound. Suddenly he leaned across his desk and punched the retriever. This room made and stored holographs of everything that happened within it.

A screen kindled, throwing light into dusky corners; for Desai had left off the fluoros, and sundown was upon the city. He didn't enlarge the figures of Peter Jowett and himself, but he did amplify the audio. Voices boomed. He leaned back to listen.

Jowett, richly dressed, sporting a curled brown beard, was of the Web, a merchant and cosmopolite. However, he was no jackal. He had sincerely, if quietly, opposed the revolt; and now he collaborated with the occupation because he saw the good of his people in their return to the Empire.

He said: ' – glad to offer you what ideas and information I'm able, Commissioner. Cut me off if I start tellin' you what you've heard *ad nauseam*.'

'I hardly think you can,' Desai responded. 'I've been on Aeneas for two years; your ancestors, seven hundred.'

'Yes, men ranged far in the early days, didn't they? spread themselves terribly thin, grew terribly vulnerable. Well. You wanted to consult me about Ivar Frederiksen, right?'

'And anything related.' Desai put a fresh cigarette in his holder.

Jowett lit a cheroot. 'I'm not sure what I have to give you. Remember, I belong to class which Landfolk regard with suspicion at best, contempt or hatred at worst. I've never been intimate of his family.'

'You're in Parliament. A pretty important member, too. And Edward Frederiksen is Firstman of Ilion. You must have a fair amount to do with him, including socially; most political work goes on outside of formal conferences or debates. I know you knew Hugh McCormac well – Edward's brother-in-law, Ivar's uncle.'

Jowett frowned at the red tip of his cigar before he answered slowly: 'Matters are rather worse tangled than

31

that, Commissioner. May I recapitulate elementary facts? I want to set things in perspective, for myself as much as you.'

'Please.'

'As I see it, there are three key facts about Aeneas. One, it began as scientific colony, mainly for purpose of studyin' natives of Dido – which isn't suitable environment for human children, you know. That's origin of University: community of scientists, scholars, and support personnel, around which mystique clusters to this very day. The most ignorant and stupid Aenean stands in some awe of those who are learned. And, of course, University under Empire has become quite distinguished, drawin' students both human and nonhuman from far around. Aeneans are proud of it. Furthermore, it's wealthy as well as respected, thus powerful.

'Fact two. To maintain humans, let alone research establishment, on planet as skimpy as this, you need huge land areas efficiently managed. Hence rise of Landfolk: squires, yeomen, tenants. When League broke down and Troubles came, Aeneas was cut off. It had to fight hard, sometimes right on its own soil, to survive. Landfolk bore brunt. They became quasi-feudal class. Even University caught somethin' of their spirit, givin' military trainin' as regular part of curriculum. You'll recall how Aeneas resisted – a bit bloodily – annexation by Empire, in *its* earlier days. But later we furnished undue share of its officers.

'Fact three. Meanwhile assorted immigrants were trick-lin' in, lookin' for refuge or new start or whatever. They were ethnically different. Haughty nords used their labor but made no effort to integrate them. Piecewise, they found riches for themselves, and so drifted away from dominant civilization. Hence tinerans, Riverfolk, Orcans, highlanders, et cetera. I suspect they're more influential, sociologically, than the city dwellers or rural gentry care to believe.'

Jowett halted and poured himself a cup of the tea which Desai had ordered brought in. He looked as if he would have preferred whiskey.

'Your account does interest me, as making clear how

32

an intelligent Aenean analyzes the history of his world,' Desai said. 'But what has it to do with my immediate problem?'

'A number of things, Commissioner, if I'm not mistaken,' Jowett answered. 'To begin, it emphasizes how essentially cut off persons like me are from … well, if not mainstream, then several mainstreams of this planet's life.

'Oh, yes, we have our representatives in tricameral legislature. But we – I mean our new, Imperium-oriented class of businessmen and their employees – we're minor part of Townfolk. Rest belong to age-old guilds and similar corporate bodies, which most times feel closer to Landfolk and University than to us. Subcultures might perhaps ally with us, but aren't represented; property qualification for franchise, you know. And … prior to this occupation, Firstman of Ilion was, automatically, Speaker of all three Houses. In effect, global President. His second was, and is, Chancellor of University, his third elected by Townfolk delegates. Since you have – wisely, I think – not dissolved Parliament, merely declared yourself supreme authority – this same configuration works on.

'I? I'm nothin' but delegate from Townfolk, from one single faction among them at that. I am not privy to councils of Frederiksens and their friends.'

'Just the same, you can inform me, correct me where I'm wrong,' Desai insisted. 'Now let me recite the obvious for a while. My impression may turn out to be false.

'The Firstman of Ilion is *primus inter pares* because Ilion is the most important region and Hesperia its richest area. True?'

'Originally,' Jowett said. 'Production and population have shifted. However, Aeneans are traditionalists.'

'What horrible bad luck in the inheritance of that title – for everybody,' Desai said. And, seated alone, he remembered his thoughts.

Hugh McCormac was a career Navy officer, who had risen to Fleet Admiral when his elder brother died childless in an accident and thus made him Firstman. That wouldn't have mattered, except for His Majesty (one dare not speculate why, aloud) appointing that creature

3

Snelund the Governor of Sector Alpha Crucis; and Snelund's excesses finally striking McCormac so hard that he raised a rebel banner and planet after planet hailed him Emperor.

Well, Snelund is dead, McCormac is fled, and we are trying to reclaim the ruin they left. But the seeds they sowed still sprout strange growths.

McCormac's wife was (is?) the sister of Edward Frederiksen, who for lack of closer kin has thereby succeeded to the Firstmanship of Ilion. Edward himself is a mild, professorial type. I could bless his presence – except for the damned traditions. His own wife is a cousin of McCormac. (Curse the way those high families intermarry! It may make for better stock, a thousand years hence; but what about us who must cope meanwhile?) The Frederiksens themselves are old-established University leaders. Why, the single human settlement on Dido is named after their main ancestor.

Everybody on this resentful globe discounts Edward Frederiksen: but not what he symbolizes. Soon everybody will know what Ivar Frederiksen has done.

Potentially, he is their exiled prince, their liberator, their Anointed. Siva, have mercy.

'As I understood it,' the image of Jowett said, 'the boy raised gang of hotheads without his parents' knowledge. He's only eleven and a half, after all – uh, that's twenty years Terran, right? Their idea was to take to wilderness and be guerrillas until . . . what? Terra gave up? Ythri intervened, and took Aeneas under its wing like Avalon? It strikes me as pathetically romantic.'

'Sometimes romantics do overcome realists,' Desai said. 'The consequences are always disastrous.'

'Well, in this case, attempt failed. His associates who got caught identified their leader under hypnoprobe. Don't bother denyin'; of course your interrogators used hypnoprobes. Ivar's disappeared, but shouldn't be impossible to track down. What do you need my advice about?'

'The wisdom of chasing him in the first place,' Desai said wearily.

'Oh. Positive. You dare not let him run loose. I do

34

know him slightly. He has chance of becomin' kind of prophet, to people who're waitin' for exactly that.'

'My impression too. But how should we go after him? How make the arrest? What kind of trial and penalty? How publicize? We can't create a martyr. Neither can we let a rebel, responsible for the deaths and injuries of Imperial personnel – and Aeneans, remember, Aeneans – we can't let him go scot-free. I don't know what to do,' Desai nearly groaned. 'Help me, Jowett. You don't want your planet ripped apart, do you?'

– He snapped off the playback. He had gotten nothing from it. Nor would he from the rest, which consisted of what-ifs and maybes. The only absolute was that Ivar Frederiksen must be hunted down fast.

Should I refer the problem of what to do after we catch him to Llynathawr, or directly to Terra? I have the right.
The legal right. No more. What do they know there?

Night had fallen. The room was altogether black, save for its glowboards and a shifty patch of moonlight which hurried Creusa cast through the still-active transparency. Desai got up, felt his way there, looked outward.

Beneath stars, moons, Milky Way, three sister planets, Nova Roma had gone elven. The houses were radiance and shadow, the streets dappled darkness, the river and canals mercury. Afar in the desert, a dust storm went like a ghost. Wind keened; Desai, in his warmed cubicle, shivered to think how its chill must cut.

His vision sought the brilliances overhead. Too many suns, too many.

He'd be sending a report Home by the next courier boat. (Home! He had visited Terra just once. When he stole a few hours from work to walk among relics, they proved curiously disappointing. Multisense tapes didn't include crowded airbuses, arrogant guides, tourist shops, or aching feet.) Such vessels traveled at close to the top hyperspeed: a pair of weeks between here and Sol. (But that was 200 light years, a radius which swept over four million suns.) He could include a request for policy guidelines.

But half a month could stretch out, when he faced possible turmoil or, worse, terrorism. And then his petition must be processed, discussed, annotated, supplemented, passed from committee to committee, referred through layers of executive officialdom for decision; and the return message would take its own days to arrive, and probably need to be disputed on many points when it did – No, those occasional directives from Llynathawr were bad enough.

He, Chunderban Desai, stood alone to act.

Of course, he was required to report everything significant: which certainly included the Frederiksen affair. If nothing else, Terra was *the* data bank, as complete as flesh and atomistics could achieve.

In which case . . . why not insert a query about that Aycharaych?

Well why?

I don't know, I don't know. He seems thoroughly legitimate; and he borrowed my Tagore . . . No, I will ask for a complete information scan at Terra. Though I'll have to invent a plausible reason for it, when Muratori's approved his proposal. We bureaucrats aren't supposed to have hunches. Especially not when, in fact, I like Aycharaych as much as any nonhuman I've ever met. Far more than many of my fellow men.

Dangerously more?

IV

The Hedin freehold lay well east of Windhome, though close enough to the edge of Ilion that westerlies brought moisture off the canals, marshes, and salt lakes of the Antonine Seabed – actual rain two or three times a year. While not passing through the property, the Wildfoss helped maintain a water table that supplied a few wells. Thus the family carried on agriculture, besides ranching a larger area.

Generation by generation, their staff had become more like kinfolk than hirelings: kinfolk who looked to them for leadership but spoke their own minds and often saw a child married to a son or daughter of the house. In short, they stood in a relationship to their employers quite similar to that in which the Hedins, and other Hesperian yeomen, stood to Windhome.

The steading was considerable. A dozen cottages flanked the manse. Behind, barns, sheds, and workshops surrounded three sides of a paved courtyard. Except for size, at first glance the buildings seemed much alike, white-washed rammed earth, their blockiness softened by erosion. Then one looked closer at the stone or glass mosaics which decorated them. Trees made a windbreak about the settlement: native delphi and rahab, Terran oak and acacia, Llynathawrian rasmin, Ythrian hammerbranch. Flower-beds held only exotic species, painstakingly cultivated, eked out with rocks and gravel. True blossoms had never evolved on Aeneas, though a few kinds of leaf or stalk had bright hues.

It generally bustled here, overseers, housekeepers, smiths, masons, mechanics, hands come in from fields or

37

range, children, dogs, horses, stathas, hawks, farm machinery, ground and air vehicles, talk, shouting, laughter, anger, tears, song, a clatter of feet and a whiff of beasts or smoke. Ivar ached to join in. His wait in the storeloft became an entombment.

Through a crack in the shutters he could look down at the daytime surging. His first night coincided with a birth-day party for the oldest tenant. Not only the main house was full of glow, but floodlights illuminated the yard for the leaping, stamping dances of Ilion, to music whooped forth by a sonor, while flagons went from mouth to mouth. The next night had been moonlight and a pair of young sweethearts. Ivar did not watch them after he realized what they were; he had been taught to consider privacy among the rights no decent person would violate. Instead, he threshed about in his sleeping bag, desert-thirsty with memories of Tatiana Thane and — still more, he discovered in shame — certain others.

On the third night, as erstwhile, he roused to the cautious unlocking of the door. Sam Hedin brought him his food and water and when nobody else was awake. He sat up. A pad protected him from the floor, but as his torso emerged from the sack, chill smote through his garments. He hardly noticed. The body of an Aenean perforce learned how to make efficient use of the shivering reflex. The dark oppressed him, however, and the smell of dust.

A flashbeam picked forth glimpses of seldom-used gear, boxes and loaded shelves. 'Hs-s-s,' went a whisper. 'Get ready to travel. Fast.'

'What?'

'Fast, I said. I'll explain when we're a-road.'

Ivar scrambled to his feet, out of his nightsuit and into the clothes he wore when he arrived. The latter were begrimed and blood-spotted, but the parched air had sucked away stinks as it did for the slop jar. The other garment he tucked into a bedroll he slung on his back, together with his rifle. Hedin gave him a packet of sandwiches to stuff in his pouchbelt, a filled canteen to hang opposite his knife — well insulated against freezing — and guidance down-stairs.

38

Though the man's manner was grim, eagerness leaped in Ivar. Regardless of the cause, his imprisonment was at an end.

Outside lay windless quiet, so deep that it was if he could hear the planet creak from the cold. Both moons were up to whiten stone and sand, make treetops into glaciers above caverns, strike sparkles from rime. Larger but remoter Lavinia, rising over eastern hills, showed about half her ever-familiar face. Creusa, hurtling toward her, seemed bigger because of being near the full, and glittered as her spin threw light off crystal raggedness. The Milky Way was a frozen cascade from horizon to horizon. Of fellow planets, Anchises remained aloft, lambent yellow. Among the uncountable stars, Alpha and Beta Crucis burned bright enough to join the moons in casting shadows.

A pair of stathas stood tethered, long necks and snouted heads silhouetted athwart the house. *We must have some ways to go,* Ivar thought, *sacrificin' horse-speed in pinch for endurance over long dry stretch. But then why not car?* He mounted. Despite the frigidity, he caught a scent of his beast, not unlike new-mown hay, before he adjusted hood and nightmask.

Sam Hedin led him onto the inland road, shortly afterward to a dirt track which angled off southerly through broken ground where starkwood bush and sword trava grew sparse. Dust puffed from the *plop-plop* of triple pads. Six legs gave a lulling rhythm. Before long the steading was lost to sight, the men rode by themselves under heaven. Afar, a catavale yowled.

Ivar cleared his throat. 'Ah-um! Where're we bound, Yeoman Hedin?'

Vapor smoked from breath slot. 'Best hidin' place for you I could think of quick, Firstlin'. Maybe none too good.' Fear jabbed. 'What's happened?'

'Vid word went around this day, garth to garth,' Hedin said. He was a stout man in his later middle years. 'Impies out everywhere in Hesperia, ransackin' after you. Reward offered; and anybody who looks as if he or she might know somethin' gets quick narcoquiz. At rate they're workin', they'll reach my place before noon.' He paused. 'That's why I kept you tucked away, so nobody except me *would* know you were there. But not much use against biodetectors. I invented business which'll keep me from home several days, rode off with remount – plausible, considerin' power shortage – and slipped back after dark to fetch you.' Another pause. 'They have aircars aprowl, too. Motor vehicle could easily get spotted and overtaken. That's reason why we use stathas, and no heatin' units for our clothes.'

Ivar glanced aloft, as if to see a metal teardrop pounce. An ula flapped by. Pride struggled with panic: 'They want me mighty badly, huh?'

'Well, you're Firstlin' of Ilion.'

Honesty awoke. Ivar bit his lip. 'I . . . I'm no serious menace. I bungled my leadership. No doubt I was idiot to try.'

'I don't know enough to gauge,' Hedin replied judiciously. 'Just that Feo Astaff asked if I could coalsack you from Terrans, because you and friends had had fight with marines. Since, you and I've gotten no proper chance to talk. I could just sneak you your rations at night, not dare linger. Nor have newscasts said more than there was unsuccessful assault on patrol. Never mentioned your name, though I suppose after this search they'll have to.'

The mask muffled his features, but not the eyes he turned to his companion. 'Want to tell me now?' he asked.

'W-well, I –'

'No secrets, mind. I'm pretty sure I've covered our spoor and won't be suspected, interrogated. Still, what can we reply on altogether?'

Ivar slumped. 'I've nothin' important to hide, except foolishness. Yes, I'd like to tell you, Yeoman.'

The story stumbled forth, for Hedin to join to what he already knew about his companion.

Edward Frederiksen had long been engaged in zoological research on Dido when he married Lisbet Borglund. She was of old University stock like him; they met when he came back to deliver a series of lectures. She followed him to the neighbor world. But even in Port Frederiksen, the

40

heat and wetness of the thick air were too much for her.

She recovered when they returned to Aeneas, and bore her husband Ivar and Gerda. They lived in a modest home outside Nova Roma; both taught, and he found adequate if unspectacular subjects for original study. His son often came along on field trips. The boy's ambitions presently focused on planetology. Belike the austere comeliness of desert, steppe, hills, and dry ocean floors brought that about – besides the hope of exploring among those stars which glittered through their nights.

Hugh McCormac being their uncle by his second marriage, the children spent frequent vacations at Windhome. When the Fleet Admiral was on hand, it became like visiting a hero of the early days, an affable one, say Brian McCormac who cast out the nonhuman invaders and whose statue stood ever afterward on a high pillar near the main campus of the University.

Aeneas had circled Virgil eight times since Ivar's birth, when Aaron Snelund became Governor of Sector Alpha Crucis. It circled twice more – three and a half Terran years – before the eruption. At first the developed worlds felt nothing worse than heightened taxes, for which they got semi-plausible explanations. (Given the size of the Empire, its ministers must necessarily have broad powers.) Then they got the venal appointees. Then they began to hear what had been going on among societies less able to resist and complain. Then they realized that their own petitions were being shunted aside. Then the arrests and confiscations for 'treason' started. Then the secret police were everywhere, while mercenaries and officials freely committed outrages upon individuals. Then it became plain that Snelund was not an ordinary corrupt administrator, skimming off some cream for himself, but a favorite of the Emperor, laying grandiose political foundations.

All this came piecemeal, and folk were slow to believe. For most of them, life proceeded about as usual. If times were a bit hard, well, they would outlast it, and meanwhile they had work to do, households and communities to maintain, interests to pursue, pleasures to seek, love to make, errands to run, friends to invite, unfriends to snub,

41

plans to consider, details, details, details like sand in an hourglass. Ivar did not enroll at the University, since it educated its hereditary members from infancy, but he began to specialize in his studies and to have off-planet classmates. Intellectual excitement outshouted indignation.

Then Kathryn McCormac, his father's sister, was taken away to Snelund's palace; and her husband was arrested, was rescued, and led the mutiny.

Ivar caught fire, like most Aenean youth. His military training, hitherto incidental, became nearly the whole. But he never got off the planet, and his drills ended when Imperial warcraft hove into the skies.

The insurrection was over. Hugh McCormac and his family had led the remnants of his fleet into the deeps outside of known space. Because the Jihannath crisis was resolved, the Navy available to guard the whole Empire, the rebels would not return unless they wanted immolation.

Sector Alpha Crucis in general, Aeneas in particular, was to be occupied and reconstructed.

Chaos, despair, shortages which in several areas approached famine, had grown throughout the latter half of the conflict. The University was closed. Ivar and Gerda went to live with their parents in poverty-stricken grandeur at Windhome, since Edward Frederiksen was now Firstman of Ilion. The boy spent most of the time improving his desertcraft. And he gained identification with the Landfolk. *He* would be their next leader.

After a while conditions improved, the University reopened — under close observation — and he returned to Nova Roma. He was soon involved in underground activity. At first this amounted to no more than clandestine bitching sessions. However, he felt he should not embarrass his family or himself by staying at the suburban house, and moved into a cheap room in the least desirable part of the Web. That also led to formative experience. Aeneas had never had a significant criminal class, but a petty one burgeoned during the war and its aftermath. Suddenly he met men who did not hold the laws sacred. (When McCormac rebelled, he did it in the name of rights and statutes violated. When Commissioner Desai arrived, he promised to restore the torn fabric.)

Given a conciliatory rule, complaints soon became demands. The favorite place for speeches, rallies, and demonstrations was beneath the memorial to Brian McCormac. The authorities conceded numerous points, reasonable in themselves – for example, resumption of regular mail service to and from the rest of the Empire. This led to further demands – for example, *no* government examination of mail, and a citizens' committee to assure this – which were refused. Riots broke out. Some property went up in smoke, some persons down in death.

The decrees came: No more assemblies. The monument to be razed. The Landfolk, who since the Troubles had served as police and military cadre, to disband all units and surrender all firearms, from a squire's ancestral cannon-equipped skyrover to a child's target pistol given last Founder's Day.

'We decided, our bunch, we'd better act before 'twas too late,' Ivar said. 'We'd smuggle out what weapons we could, ahead of seizure date, and use them to grab off heavier stuff. I had as much knowledge of back country as any, more than most; and, of course, I am Firstlin'. So they picked me to command our beginnin' operation, which'd be in this area. I joined my mother and sister at Windhome, pretendin' I needed break from study. Others had different cover stories, like charterin' an airbus to leave them in Avernus Canyon for several days' campout. We rendezvoused at Helmet Butte and laid our ambush accordin' to what I knew about regular Impy patrol routes.'

'What'd you have done next, if you'd succeeded?' Hedin asked.

'Oh, we had that planned. I know couple of oases off in Ironland that could support us, with trees, caves, ravines to hide us from air search. There aren't that many occupation troops to cover this entire world.'

'You'd spend your lives as outlaws? I should think you'd soon become bandits.'

'No, no. We'd carry on more raids, get more recruits

43

and popular support, gather strength enemy must reckon with. Meanwhile we'd hope for sympathy elsewhere in Empire bringin' pressure on our behalf, or maybe fear of Ythri movin' in.'

'Maybe,' Hedin grunted. After a moment: 'I've heard rumors. Great bein' with gold-bronze wings, a-flit in these parts. Ythrian agent? They don't necessarily want what we do, Firstlin'.'

Ivar's shoulders slumped. 'No matter. We failed anyhow. I did.'

Hedin reached across to clap him on the back. 'Don't take that attitude. First, military leaders are bound to lose men and suffer occasional disasters. Second, you never were one, really. You just happened to get thrown to top of cards that God was shufflin'.' His tone briskened. 'Firstlin', you've got no *right* to go off on conscience spin. You and your fellows together made bad mistake. Leave it at that, and carry on. Aeneas does need you.'

'Me?' Ivar exclaimed. His self-importance had crumbled while he talked, until he could not admit he had ever seen himself as a Maccabee. 'What in cosmos can I—'

Hedin lifted a gauntleted hand to quiet him. 'Hoy. Follow me.'

They brought their staths off the trail, and did not rejoin it for ten kilometers. What they avoided was a herd belonging to Hedin: Terran-descended cattle, gene-modified and then adapted through centuries – like most introduced organisms – until they were a genus of their own. Watchfires glimmered around their mass. Hedin didn't doubt his men were loyal to him; but what they hadn't noticed, they couldn't reveal.

On the way, the riders passed a fragment of wall. Glass-black, seamless, it sheened above moonlight brush and sand. Near the top of what remained, four meters up, holes made an intricate pattern, its original purpose hard to guess. Now stars gleamed through.

Hedin reined in, drew a cross, and muttered before he went on.

Ivar had seen the ruin in the past, and rangehands paying

it their respects. He had never thought he would see the yeoman – well-educated, well-traveled, hard-headed master and councilor – do likewise.

After a cold and silent while, Hedin said half defensively, 'Kind of symbol back yonder.'

'Well . . . yes,' Ivar responded.

'Somebody was here before us, millions of years ago. And not extinct natives, either. Where did they come from? Why did they leave? Traces have been found on other planets too, remember. Unreasonable to suppose they died off, no? Lot of people wonder if they didn't go onward instead – out there.'

Hedin waved at the stars. Of that knife-bright horde, some belonged to the Empire but most did not. For those the bare eye could see were mainly giants, shining across the light-years which engulfed vision of a Virgil or a Sol. Between Ivar and red Betelgeuse reached all the dominion of Terra, and more. Further on, Rigel flashed and the Pleiades veiled themselves in regions to which the Roidhunate of Merseia gave its name for a blink of time. Beyond these were Polaris, once man's lodestar, and the Orion Nebula, where new suns and worlds were being born even as he watched, and in billions of years life would look forth and wonder . . .

Hedin's mask swung toward Ivar again. His voice was low but eerily intense. 'That's why we need you, Firstlin'. You may be rash boy, yes, but four hundred years of man on Aeneas stand behind you. We'll need every root we've got when Elders return.'

Startled, Ivar said, 'You don't believe that, do you? I've heard talk; but you?'

'Well, I don't know.' Hedin's words came dwindled through the darkness. 'I don't know. Before war, I never thought about it. I'd go to church, and that was that.

'But since – Can so many people be entirely wrong? They are many, I'll tell you. Off in town, at school, you probably haven't any idea how wide hope is spreadin' that Elders will come back soon, bearin' Word of God. It's not crank, Ivar. Nigh everybody admits this is hope, no proof. But could Admiral McCormac have headed their way?

45

And surely we hear rumors about new prophet in barrens –

'I don't know. I do think, and I tell you I'm not alone in it, all this grief here and all those stars there can't be for nothin'. If God is makin' ready His next revelation, why not through chosen race, more wise and good than we can now imagine? And if that's true, shouldn't prophet come first, who prepares us to be saved?'

He shook himself, as if the freeze had pierced his unheated garb. 'You're our Firstlin',' he said. 'We must keep you free. Four hundred years can't be for nothin' either.'

Quite matter-of-factly, he continued: 'Tinarans are passin' through, reported near Arroyo. I figure you can hide among them.'

V

Each nomad Train, a clan as well as a caravan, wandered a huge but strictly defined territory. Windhome belonged in that of the Brotherband. Ivar had occasionally seen its camps, witnessed raffish performances, and noticed odd jobs being done for local folk before it moved on, afterward heard the usual half-amused, half-indignant accusations of minor thefts and clever swindles, gossip about seductions, whispers about occult talents exercised. When he dipped into the literature, he found mostly anecdotes, picturesque descriptions, romantic fiction, nothing in depth. The Aenean intellectual community took little serious interest in the undercultures on its own planet. Despite the centuries, Dido still posed too many enigmas which were more fascinating and professionally rewarding.

Ivar did know that Trains varied in their laws and customs. Hedin led him across a frontier which had no guards nor any existence in the registries at Nova Roma, identified solely by landmarks. Thereafter they were in Waybreak country, and he was still less sure of what to expect than he would have been at home. The yeoman took a room in the single inn which Arroyo boasted. 'I'll stay till you're gone, in case of trouble,' he said. 'But mainly, you're on your own from here.' Roughly: 'I wish 'twere otherwise. Fare always well, lad.'

Ivar walked through the village to the camp. Its people were packing for departure. Fifty or so brilliantly painted carriages, and gaudy garb on the owners, made their bustle and clamor into a kind of rainbowed storm in an otherwise drab landscape. Arroyo stood on the eastern slope of the hills, where scrub grew sparse on dusty ground

47

to feed some livestock. The soil became more dry and bare for every kilometer that it hunched on downward, until at the horizon began the Ironland desert.

Scuttling about in what looked like utter confusion, men, women, and children alike threw him glances and shouted remarks in their own language that he guessed were derisive. He felt awkward and wholly alone among them – this medium-sized, whip-slim race of the red-brown skins and straight blue-black hair. Their very vehicles hemmed him in alienness. Some were battered old trucks of city make; but fantastic designs swirled across them, pennons blew, amulets dangled, wind chimes rang. Most were wagons, drawn by four to eight stathas, and these were the living quarters. Stovepipes projected from their arched roofs and grimy curtains hung in their windows. Beneath paint, banners, and other accessories, their panels were elaborately carved; demon shapes leered, hex signs radiated, animals real and imaginary cavorted, male and female figures danced, hunted, worked, gambled, engendered, and performed acts more esoteric.

A man came by, carrying a bundle of knives and swords wrapped in a cloak. He bounded up into the stairless doorway of one wagon, gave his load to a person inside, sprang down again to confront Ivar. 'Hey-ah, varsiteer,' he said amicably enough. 'What'd you like? The show's over.'

'I . . . I'm lookin' for berth,' Ivar faltered. He wet his lips, which felt caked with dust. It was a hot day, 25 degrees Celsius or so. Virgil glared in a sky which seemed to lack its usual depth, and instead was burnished.

'No dung? What can a townsitter do worth his keep? We're bound east, straight across the Dreary. Not exactly a Romeburg patio. We'd have to sweep you up after you crumbled.' The other rubbed his pointed chin. 'Of course,' he added thoughtfully, 'you might make pretty good nose powder for some girl.'

Yet his mockery was not unkind. Ivar gave him closer regard. He was young, probably little older than the First-ling. Caught by a beaded fillet, his hair fell to his shoulders in the common style, brass earrings showing through. Like most tineran men, he kept shaved off what would have been a puny growth of beard. Bones and luminous gray eyes stood forth in a narrow face. He was nearly always grinning, and whether or not he stood still, there was a sense of quivering mobility about him. His clothes – fringed and varicolored shirt, scarlet sash, skin-tight leather trousers and buskins – were worn-out finery demoted to working dress. A golden torque encircled his neck, tawdry-jeweled rings his fingers, a spiral of herpetoid skin the left arm. A knife sat on either hip, one a tool, one a weapon, both delicate-looking compared to those miniature machetes the Landfolk carried.

'I'm not – well, yes, I am from Nova Roma, University family,' Ivar admitted. 'But, uh, how'd you know before I spoke?'

'O-ah, your walk, your whole way. Being geared like a granger, not a cityman, won't cover that.' The Anglic was rapid-fire, a language coequal in the Trains with Haisun and its argots. But this was a special dialect, archaic from the nord viewpoint, one which, for instance, made excessive use of articles while harshly clipping the syllables. 'That's a rifle to envy, yours, and relieve you of if you're uncareful. A ten-millimeter Valdemar convertible, right?'

'And I can use it,' Ivar said in a rush. 'I've spent plenty of time in outlands. You'll find me good pot hunter, if nothin' else. But I'm handy with apparatus too, especially electric. And strong, when you need plain muscle.'

'Well-ah, let's go see King Samlo. By the way, I'm Mikkal of Redtop.' The tineran nodded at his wagon, whose roof justified its name. A woman of about his age, doubtless his wife, poised in the doorway. She was as exotically pretty as girls of her type were supposed to be in the folklore of the sedentary people. A red-and-yellow-zig-zagged gown clung to a sumptuous figure, though Ivar thought it a shame how she had loaded herself with junk ornaments. Catching his eye, she smiled, winked, and swung a hip at him. Her man didn't mind; it was a standard sort of greeting.

'You'll take me?' Ivar blurted.

Mikkal shrugged. Infinitely more expressive than a nord's, the gesture used his entire body. Sunlight went

4

49

iridescent over the scales coiled around his left arm. 'Sure-ah. An excuse not to work.' To the woman: 'You, Dulcy, go fetch the rest of my gear.' She made a moue at him before she scampered off into the turmoil.

'Thanks ever so much,' Ivar said. 'I – I'm Rolf Mariner.' He had given the alias considerable thought, and was proud of the result. It fitted the ethnic background he could not hope to disguise, while free of silly giveaways like his proper initials.

'If that's who you want to be, fine,' Mikkal gibed, and led the way.

The racket grew as animals were brought in from pasture, stathas, mules, goats, neomoas. The dogs which herded them, efficiently at work in response to whistles and signals from children, kept silence. They were tall, ebon, and skeletally built except for the huge rib cages and water-storing humps on the shoulders.

Goldwheels was the largest wagon, the single motorized one. A small companion stood alongside, black save for a few symbols in red and silver, windowless. Above its roof, a purple banner bore two crescents. Mikkal sensed Ivar's curiosity and explained, 'That's the shrine.'

'Oh . . . yes.' Ivar remembered what he had read. The king of a band was also its high priest, who besides presid-ing over public religious ceremonies, conducted secret rites with a few fellow initiates. He was required to be of a certain family (evidently Goldwheels in the Waybreak Train) but need not be an eldest son. Most of a king's women were chosen with a view to breeding desired traits, and the likeliest boy became heir apparent, to serve appren-ticeship in another Train. Thus the wanderers forged alliances between their often quarrelsome groups, more potent than the periodic assemblies known as Fairs.

The men who were hitching white mules to the shrine seemed no more awed than Mikkal. They hailed him loudly. He gave them an answer which made laughter erupt. Youngsters milling nearby shrilled. A couple of girls tittered, and one made a statement which was doubtless bawdy. *At my expense,* Ivar knew.

50

It didn't matter. He smiled back, waved at her, saw her preen waist-long tresses and flutter her eyelids. *After all, to them – if I prove I'm no dumb clod, and I will, I will – to them I'm excitin' outsider.* He harked back to his half-desperate mood of minutes ago, and marveled. A buoyant confidence swelled in him, and actual merriment bubbled beneath. The whole carefree atmosphere had entered him, as it seemed to enter everybody who visited an encampment.

King Samlo returned from overseeing a job. Folk lifted hands in casual salute. When he cared to exercise it, his power was divine and total; but mostly he ruled by consensus.

He was a contrast to his people, large, blocky-boned, hooknosed. His mahogany features carried a fully developed beard and mustache. He limped. His garb was white, more clean than one would have thought possible here. Save for tooled-leather boots, crimson-plumed turban, and necklace of antique coins, it had little decoration.

His pale gaze fell on Ivar and remained as he lowered himself into an ornate armchair outside his wagon. 'Hey-ah, stranger,' he said. 'What's your lay?'

Ivar bowed, not knowing what else to do. Mikkal took the word: 'He tags himself Rolf Mariner, claims he's a hunter and jack-o'-hands as well as a varsiteer, and wants to come along.'

The king didn't smile. His gravity marked him off yet more than did his appearance. Nonetheless, Ivar felt unafraid. Whether dreamy runaways, failed adults, or fugitives from justice, occasionally nords asked to join a Train. If they made a plausible case for themselves, or if a whim blew in their favor, they were accepted. They remained aliens, and probably none had lasted as much as a year before being dismissed. The usual reason given was that they lacked the ability to pull their freight in a hard and tricky life.

Surely that was true. Ivar expected that a journey with these people would stretch him to his limits. He did not

51

expect he would snap. Who could await that, in this blithe tumult?

There passed through him: *In spite of everything they suffered, I've heard, I've read a little, about how those guests always hated to leave, always afterward mourned for lost high days – how those who'd lasted longest would try to get into different troop, or kill themselves – But let him not fret when all his blood sang.*

'Um-m-hm,' Samlo said. 'Why do you ask this?'

'I've tired of these parts, and have no readier way to leave them,' Ivar replied.

Mikkal barked laughter. 'He knows the formula, anyhow! Invoke the upper-class privacy fetish, plus a hint that if we don't know why he's running, we can't be blamed if the tentacles find him amongst us.'

'Impie agents aren't city police or gentry housecarls,' the king said. 'They got special tricks. And . . . a few days back, a clutch of seethe-heads affrayed a marine patrol on the Wildfoss, remember? Several escaped. If you're on the flit, Mariner, why should we risk trouble to help you across Ironland?'

'I didn't say I was, sir,' Ivar responded. 'I told Mikkal, here, I can be useful to you. But supposin' I am in sabota with Terrans, is that bad? I heard tinerans cheer Emperor Hugh's men as they left for battle.'

'Tinerans'll cheer anybody who's on hand with spending money,' Mikkal said. 'However, I'll 'fess most of us don't like the notion of the stars beswarmed by townsitters. It makes us feel like the universe is closing in.' He turned to Samlo. 'King, why not give this felly-oh a toss?'

'Will you be his keeper?' the seated man asked. Aside to Ivar: 'We don't abandon people in the desert, no matter what. Your keeper has got to see you through.'

'Sure-ah,' Mikkal said. 'He has a look of new songs and jokes in him.'

'Your keeper won't have much to spare,' Samlo warned. 'If you use up supplies and give no return – well, maybe after we're back in the green and you dismissed, he'll track you down.'

'He won't want to, sir . . . King,' Ivar promised.

'Better make sure of that,' Samlo said. 'Mikkal, the shooting gallery's still assembled. Go see how many light-sweeps he can hit with that rifle of his. Find some broken-down equipment for him to repair; the gods know we have enough. Run him, and if he's breathing hard after half a dozen clicks, trade him back, because he'd never get across the Dreary alive.' He rose, while telling Ivar: 'If you pass, you'll have to leave that slugthrower with me. Only hunting parties carry firearms in a Train, and just one to a party. We'd lose too many people otherwise. Now I have to go see the animal acts get properly bedded down. You be off too.'

VI

In a long irregular line, herd strung out behind, the caravan departed. A few persons rode in the saddle, a few more in or on the vehicles; most walked. The long Aenean stride readily matched wagons bumping and groaning over road-less wrinkled hills. However, the going was stiff, and nobody talked without need. Perched on rooftops, musicians gave them plangent marches out of primitive instruments, drums, horns, gongs, bagpipes, many-stringed guitars. A number of these players were handicapped, Ivar saw: crippled, blind, deformed. He would have been shocked by so much curable or preventable woe had they not seemed as exhilarated as he was.

Near sundown, Waybreak was out on the undulant plain of Ironland. Coarse red soil reached between clumps of gray-green starkwood or sword trava, dried too hard for there to be a great deal of dust. Samlo cried halt by an eroded lava flow from which thrust a fluted volcanic plug. 'The Devil's Tallywhacker,' Mikkal told his protégé. 'Tradi-tional first-night stopping place out of Arroyo, said to be protection against hostile gods. *I* think the practice goes back to the Troubles, when wild gangs went around, star-veling humans or stranded remnants of invader forces, and you might need a defensible site. Of course, nowadays we just laager the wagons in case a zoosny wind should blow up or something like that. But it's as well to maintain cautionary customs. The rebellion proved the Troubles can come again, and no doubt will . . . as if that'd ever needed proof.'

'Uh, excuse me,' Ivar said, 'but you sound, uh, sur-prisin'ly sophisticated – ' His voice trailed off.

Mikkal chuckled. 'For an illiterate semi-savage? Well, matter o' fact, I'm not. Not illiterate, anyhow. A part of us have to read and write if we're to handle the outside world, let alone operate swittles like the Treasure Map. Besides, I like reading, when I can beg or steal a book.'

'I can't understand why you – I mean, you're cut off from things like library banks, not to mention medical and genetic services, everything you could have –'

'At what price?' Mikkal made a spitting noise, though he did not waste the water. 'We'd either had to take steady work to gain the jingle, or become welfare clients, which'd mean settling down as even meeker law-lickers. The end of the Trains, therefore the end of us. Didn't you know? A tineran can't quit. Stuff him into a town or nail him down on a farm, it's a mercy when death sets his corpse free to rot.'

'I'd heard that,' Ivar said slowly.

'But thought the tale must be an extravaganza, hey? No, it's true. It's happened. Tinerans jailed for any length of time sicken and die, if they don't suicide first. Even if for some reason like exile from the Train, they have to turn sitter, "free workers"' – the tone spoke the quotation marks – 'they can't breed and they don't live long . . . That's why we have no death penalty. Twice I've seen the king order a really bad offender cast out, and word sent to the rest of the Trains so none would take him in. Both times, the felly begged for a hundred and one lashes instead.' Mikkal shook himself. 'C'mon, we've work to do. You unhitch the team, hobble them, and bring them to where the rest of the critters are. Dulcy'll answer your questions. Since I've got you for extra hands, I'll get my tools resharpened early, this trek.' He performed as juggler and caster of edged weapons and, he added blandly, card sharp and dice artist.

Men erected a collapsible trough, filled it from a water truck, added the vitamin solution necessary to supplement grazing upon purely native vegetation. Boys would spend the night watching over the small, communally owned herd and the draught animals. Besides spider wolves or a possible catavale, hazards included crevices, sand hells, a storm howling down with the suddenness and ferocity common anywhere on Aeneas. If the weather stayed mild, night chill would not be dangerous until the route entered the true barrens. These creatures were the product of long breeding, the quadrupeds and hexapods heavily haired, the big neomoas similarly well feathered.

Of course, all Ironland was not that bleak, or it would have been uncrossable. The Train would touch at oases where the tanks could be refilled with brackish water and the bins with forage.

Inside the wagon circle, women and girls prepared the evening meal. In this nearly fuelless land they cooked on glowers. Capacitors had lately been recharged at a power station. To have this done, and earn the wherewithal to pay, was a major reason why the migration passed through civilized parts.

Virgil went down. Night came almost immediately after. A few lamps glowed on wagonsides, but mainly the troop saw by stars, moons, auroral flickers to northward. A gelid breeze flowed off the desert. As if to shelter each other, folk crowded around the kettles. Voices racketed, chatter, laughter, snatches of song.

Except for being ferociously spiced, the fare was simple, a thick stew scooped up on rounds of bread, a tarry-tasting tea for drink. Tinerans rarely used alcohol, never carried it along. Ivar supposed that was because of its dehydrating effect.

Who needed it, anyway? He had not been this happy in the most joyous beer hall of Nova Roma, and his mind stayed clear into the bargain.

He got his first helping and hunkered down, less easily than they, beside Mikkal and Dulcy. At once others joined them, more and more till he was in a ring of noise, faces, unwashed but crisp-smelling bodies. Questions, remarks, japes roiled over him. 'Hey-ah, townboy, why've you gone walkabout? . . . Hoping for girls? Well, I hope you won't be too tired to oblige 'em, after a day's hike . . . Give us a song, a story, a chunk o' gossip, how 'bout that? . . . Ay-uh, Banji, don't ride him hard, not yet. Be welcome, lad . . . You got coin on you? Listen, come aside and I'll explain

56

how you can double your money ... Here, don't move, I'll fetch you your seconds ...'

Ivar responded as best he dared, in view of his incognito. He would be among these people for quite a while, and had better make himself popular. Besides, he liked them.

At length King Samlo boomed through the shadows: 'Cleanup and curfew!' His followers bounced to obey the first part of the command. Ivar decided that the chaos earlier in the day, and now, was only apparent. Everyone knew his or her job. They simply didn't bother about military snap and polish.

Musicians gathered around the throne. 'I thought we were ordered to bed,' Ivar let fall.

'Not right away,' Dulcy told him. 'Whenever we can, we have a little fun first, songfest or dance or – '. She squeezed his hand. 'You think what you can do, like tell us news from your home. He'll call on you. Tonight, though, he wants – Yes. Fraina. Fraina of Jubilee. Mikkal's sister ... half-sister, you'd say; their father can afford two wives. She's good. Watch.'

The wanderers formed a ring before their wagons. Ivar had found he could neither sit indefinitely on his hams like them, nor crosslegged on the ground; after dark, his bottom would soon have been frozen. There was no energy to lavish on heated garments. He stood leaned against Redtop, hidden in darkness.

The center of the camp was bright silver, for Lavinia was high and Creusa hurrying toward the full. A young woman trod forth, genuflected to the king, stood erect and drew off her cloak. Beneath she wore a pectoral, a broad brass girdle upholding filmy strips fore and aft, and incidental jewelry.

Ivar recognized her. Those delicate features and big gray eyes had caught his attention several times during the day. Virtually unclad, her figure seemed boy-slim save in the bosom. No, he decided, that wasn't right; her femaleness was just more subtle and supple than he had known among his own heavy folk.

The music wailed. She stamped her bare feet, once, twice, thrice, and broke into dance.

The wind gusted from Ivar. He had seen tineran girls perform before, and some were a wild equal of any ballerina – but none like this. *They save the best for their own,* he guessed; then thought vanished in the swirl of her.

She leaped, human muscles against Aenean gravity, rose flying, returned swimming. She flowed across ground, fountained upward again, landed to pirouette on a toe, a top that gyrated on and on, while it swung in ever wider precessions until she was a wheel, which abruptly became an arrow and at once the catavale which dodged the shaft and rent the hunter. She snapped her cloak, made wings of it, made a lover of it, danced with it and her floating hair and the plume of her breath. She banished cold; moonlight sheened on sweat, and she made the radiance ripple across her. She was the moonlight herself, the wind, the sound of pipes and drums and the rhythmic handclaps of the whole Train and of Ivar; and when she soared away into the night and the music ended, men roared.

Inside, Mikkal's wagon was well laid out but had scant room because of the things that crowded it. At the forward end stood a potbellied stove, for use when fuel was available. Two double-width bunks, one above the other, occupied the left wall, a locker beneath and extensible table between. The right wall was shelves, cupboard, racks, to hold an unholy number of items: the stores and equipment of everyday life, the costumes and paraphernalia of shows, a kaleidoscope of odd souvenirs and junk. From the ceiling dangled an oil lantern, several amulets, and bunches of dry food, sausages, onions, dragon apples, maufry, and more, which turned the air pungent.

Attached to the door was a cage. An animal within sat up on its hind legs as Mikkal, Dulcy, and Ivar entered. The Firstling wondered why anybody would keep so unprepossessing a creature. It was about 15 centimeters in length, quadrupedal though the forepaws came near resembling skinny hands. Coarse gray fur covered it beneath a leathery flap of skin which sprang from the shoulders and reached the hindquarters, a kind of natural mantle.

The head was wedge-shaped, ears pointed and curved like horns, mouth needle-fanged. That it could not be a native Aenean organism was proved by the glittery little red eyes, three of them in a triangle.

'What's that?' Ivar asked.

'Why, our luck,' Dulcy said. 'Name of Larzo.' She reached into the cage, which had no provision for closing. 'C'mon out and say hey-ah, Larzo, sweet.'

'Your, uh, mascot?'

'Our what?' Mikkal responded. 'Oh, I grab you. A ju, like those?' He jerked his thumb at the hanging grotesques. 'No. It's true, lucks're believed to help us, but mainly they're pets. I never heard of a wagon, not in any Train, that didn't keep one.

A vague memory of it came to Ivar from his reading. No author had done more than mention in passing a custom which was of no obvious attractiveness or significance.

Dulcy had brought the animal forth. She cuddled it on her lap when the three humans settled side by side onto the lower bunk, crooned and offered it bits of cheese. It accepted that, but gave no return of her affection.

'Where're they from originally?' Ivar inquired.

Mikkal spread his hands. 'Who knows? Some immigrant brought a pair or two along, I s'pose, 'way back in the early days. They never went off on their own, but tinerans got in the habit of keeping them and – ' He yawned. 'Let's doss. The trouble with morning is, it comes too damn early in the day.'

Dulcy returned the luck to its cage. She leaned across Ivar's lap to do so. When her hand was free, she stroked him there, while her other fingers rumpled his hair. Mikkal blinked, then smiled. 'Why not?' he said. 'You'll be our companyo a spell, Rolf, and I think we'll both like you. Might as well start right off.'

Unsure of himself, though immensely aware of the woman snuggled against him, the newcomer stammered, 'Wh-what? I, don't follow – '

'You take her first tonight,' Mikkal invited.

'*Huh?* But, but, but – '

'You left your motor running,' Mikkal said, while

Dulcy giggled. After a pause: 'Shy? You nords aften are, till you get drunk. No need among friends.'

Ivar's face felt ablaze.

'Aw, now,' Dulcy said. 'Poor boy, he's too unready.' She kissed him lightly on the lips. 'Never mind. We've time. Later, if you want. Only if you want.'

'Sure, don't be afraid of us,' Mikkal added. 'I don't bite, and she doesn't very hard. Go on to your rest if you'd rather.'

Their casualness was like a benediction. Ivar hadn't imagined himself getting over such an embarrassment, immediately at that. 'No offense meant,' he said. 'I'm, well, engaged to be married, at home.'

'If you change your mind, let me know,' Dulcy murmured. 'But if you don't, I'll not doubt you're a man. Different tribes have different ways, that's all.' She kissed him again, more vigorously. 'Good-night, dear.'

He scrambled into the upper bunk, where he undressed and crawled into his sleeping bag that she had laid out for him. Mikkal snuffed the lantern, and soon he heard the sounds and felt the quiverings below him, and thereafter were darkness, stillness, and the wind.

He was long about getting to sleep. The invitation given him had been too arousing. Or was it that simple? He'd known three of four sleazy women, on leaves from his military station. His friends had known them too. For a while he swaggered. Then he met star-clean Tatiana and was ashamed.

I'm no prig, he insisted to himself. Let them make what they would of their lives on distant corrupted Terra, or in a near and not necessarily corrupted tineran wagon. A child of Firstmen and scholars had another destiny to follow. Man on Aeneas had survived because the leaders were dedicated to that survival: disciplined, constant men and women who ever demanded more of themselves than they did of their underlings. And self-command began in the inmost privacies of the soul.

A person stumbled, of course. He didn't think he had fallen too hard, upon those camp followers, in the weird atmosphere of wartime. But a . . . an orgy was something else again. Especially when he had no flimsiest excuse. Then why did he lie there, trying not to toss and turn, and regret so *very* greatly that he should stay faithful to his Tanya? Why, when he summoned her image to help him, did Fraina come instead?

VII

Covering a hill in the middle of Nova Roma, the University of Virgil was a town within the city, and most of it older than most of the latter. The massive, crenelated wall around it still bore scars from the Troubles. *Older in truth than the Empire*, Desai thought. His glance passed over man-hewn red and gray stones to an incorporated section of glassy iridescence. A chill touched his spine. *That part is older than humanity.*

Beyond the main gateway, he entered a maze of courts, lanes, stairs, unexpected little gardens or trees, memorial plaques or statues, between the buildings. Architecture was different here from elsewhere. Even the newer structures – long, porticoed, ogive-windowed, until they rose in towers – preserved a tradition going back to the earliest settlers. *Or do they?* wondered Desai. *If these designs are from ancient Terra, they are crossbreeds that mutated. Gothic arches but Russko spires, except that in low gravity those vaultings soar while those domes bulge . . . and yet it isn't mismatched, it's strong and graceful in its own way, it belongs on Aeneas as . . . I do not.*

Chimes toned from a belfry which stood stark athwart darkling blue and a rusty streak of high-borne dustcloud. No doubt the melody was often heard. But it didn't sound academic to him; it rang almost martial.

Campus had not regained the crowded liveliness he had seen in holos taken before the revolt. In particular, there were few nonhumans, and perhaps still fewer humans from other colonies. But he passed among hundreds of Aeneans. Hardly a one failed to wear identification: the hooded, color-coded cloaks of teaching faculty, which might or might not overlay the smock of researcher; student jackets bearing emblems of their colleges and, if they were Landfolk, their Firstmen. (Beneath were the tunics, trousers, and half-boots worn by both sexes – among nords, anyhow – except on full-dress occasions when women revived antique skirts.) Desai noticed, as well, the shoulder patches on many, remembrance of military or naval units now dissolved. *Should I make those illegal? . . . And what if my decree was generally disobeyed?*

He felt anger about him like a physical force. Oh, here a couple of young fellows laughed at a joke, there several were flying huge kites, yonder came a boy and girl hand in hand, near two older persons learnedly conversing; but the smiles were too few, the feet on flagstones rang too loud.

He had visited the area officially, first taking pains to learn about it. That hadn't thawed his hosts, but today it saved his asking for directions and thus risking recognition. Not that he feared violence; and he trusted he had the maturity to tolerate insult; however – His way took him past Rybnikov Laboratories, behind Pickens Library, across Adzel Square to Borglund Hall, which was residential.'

The south tower, she had said. Desai paused to see where Virgil stood. After two years – more than one, Aenean – he had not developed an automatic sense of how he faced. The compass on a planet was always defined to make its sun rise in the east; and a 25-degree axial tilt wasn't excessive, shouldn't be confusing; and he ought to be used to alien constellations by now. *Getting old. Not very adaptable any longer.* Nor had he developed a reflex to keep him from ever looking straight at that small, savage disc. Blind for a minute, he worried about retinal burn. Probably none. Blue-eyed Aeneans kept their sight, didn't they? *Let's get on with business. Too much else is waiting back at the office as is, and more piling up every second.*

The circular stairway in the tower was gloomy enough to make him stumble, steep enough to make him pant and his heart flutter. Low gravity didn't really compensate for thin air, at his age. He rested for a time on the fourth-floor landing before he approached an oaken door and used a knocker which centuries of hands had worn shapeless.

Tatiana Thane let him in. 'Good day,' she said tonelessly.

Desai bowed. 'Good day, my lady. You are kind to give me this interview.'

'Do I have choice?'

'Certainly.'

'I didn't when your Intelligence Corps hauled me in for questionin'.' Her speech remained flat. A note of bitterness would at least have expressed some human relationship.

'That is why I wished to see you in your own apartment, Prosser Thane. To emphasize the voluntariness. Not that I believe you were arrested, were you? The officers merely assumed you would cooperate, as a law-abiding — citizen.' Desai had barely checked himself from saying 'subject of His Majesty.'

'Well, I won't assault you, Commissioner. Have you truly come here unescorted as you claimed you would?'

'Oh, yes. Who'd pay attention to a chubby chocolate-colored man in a particularly thick mantle? Apropos which, where may I leave it?'

Tatiana indicated a peg in the entry. This layout was incredibly archaic. No doubt the original colonists hadn't had the economic surplus to automate residences, and there'd been sufficient pinch ever afterward to keep alive a scorn of 'effete gadgetry.' The place was chilly, too, though the young woman was rather lightly if plainly clad.

Desai's glance recorded her appearance for later study. She was tall and slim. The oval face bore a curved nose, arched brows above brown eyes, broad full mouth, ivory complexion, between shoulder-length wings of straight dark hair. *Old University family*, he recalled, *steeped in its lore, early destined for a scholarly career. Somewhat shy and bookish, but no indoor plant; she takes long walks or longer animalback rides, spends time in the desert, not to mention the jungles of Dido. Brilliant linguist, already responsible for advances in understanding certain languages* on that planet. Her enthusiasm for the Terran classics doubtless kindled Ivar Frederiksen's interest in them and in history . . . though in his case, perhaps one might better say the vision of former freedom fighters inflamed him. She appears to have more sense than that: a serious girl, short on humor, but on the whole, as good a fiancée as any man could hope for.

That was the approximate extent of the report on her. There were too many more conspicuous Aeneans to investigate. The Frederiksen boy hadn't seemed like anyone to worry about either, until he ran amok.

Tatiana led Desai into the main room of her small suite. Its stone was relieved by faded tapestries and scuffed rug, where bookshelves, a fine eidophonic player, and assorted apparatus for logico-semantic analysis did not occupy the walls. Furniture was equally shabby-comfortable, leather and battered wood. Upon a desk stood pictures he supposed were of her kin, and Ivar's defiant in the middle of them. Above hung two excellent views, one of a Didonian, one of Aeneas seen from space, tawny-red, green- and blue-mottled, north polar cap as white as the streamers of ice-cloud. Her work, her home.

A trill sounded. She walked to a perch whereon, tiny and fluffy, a native tadmouse sat. 'Oh,' she said. 'I forgot it's his lunchtime.' She gave the animal seeds and a caress. A sweet song responded.

'What is his name, if I may ask?' Desai inquired.

She was obviously surprised. 'Why . . . Frumious Bandersnatch.'

'What?'

Desai sketched another bow. 'Pardon me, my lady. I was given a wrong impression of you.'

'No matter. When I was a boy on Ramanujan, I had a local pet I called Mock Turtle . . . Tell me, please, would a tadmouse be suitable for a household which includes young children?'

'Well, that depends on them. They mustn't get rough.'

'They wouldn't. Our cat's tail went unpulled until, lately, the poor beast died. It couldn't adjust to this planet.'

She stiffened. 'Aeneas doesn't make every newcomer

welcome, Commissioner. Sit down and describe what you want of me.'

The chair he found was too high for his comfort. She lowered herself opposite him, easily because she topped him by centimeters. He wished he could smoke, but to ask if he might would be foolish.

'As for Ivar Frederiksen,' Tatiana said, 'I tell you what I told your Corpsmen: I was not involved in his alleged action and I've no idea where he may be.'

'I have seen the record of that interview, Prosser Thane.' Desai chose his words with care. 'I believe you. The agents did too. None recommended a narcoquiz, let alone a hypnoprobing.'

'No Aenean constable has right to so much as propose that.'

'But Aeneas rebelled and is under occupation,' Desai said in his mildest voice. 'Let it re-establish its loyalty, and it will get back what autonomy it had before.' Seeing how resentment congealed her eyes, he added low: 'The loyalty I speak of does not involve more than a few outward tokens of respect for the throne, as mere essential symbols. It is loyalty to the Empire – above all, to its Pax, in an age when spacefleets can incinerate whole worlds and when the mutiny in fact took thousands of lives – it is that I mean, my lady. It is that I am here about, not Ivar Frederiksen.'

Startled, she swallowed before retorting, 'What do you imagine I can do?'

'Probably nothing, I fear. Yet the chance of a hint, a clue, any spark of enlightenment no matter how faint, led me to call you and request a confidential talk. I emphasize "request." You cannot help unless you do so freely.'

'What do you want?' she whispered. 'I repeat, I'm not in any revolutionary group – never was, unless you count me clerkin' in militia durin' independence fight – and I don't know zero about what may be goin' on.' Pride returned. 'If I did, I'd kill myself rather than betray him. Or his cause.'

'Do you mind talking about them, though? Him and his cause.'

'How – ?' Her answer faded out.

'My lady,' Desai said to her, 'I am a stranger to your people. I have met hundreds by now, myself, while my subordinates have met thousands. It has been of little use in gaining empathy. Your history, literature, arts are a bit more helpful, but the time I can devote to them is very limited, and summaries prepared by underlings assigned to the task are nearly valueless. One basic obstacle to understanding you is your pride, your ideal of disciplined self-reliance, your sense of privacy which makes you reluctant to bare the souls of even fictional characters. I know you have normal human emotions; but how, on Aeneas, do they normally work? How does it *feel* to be you?'

'The only persons here with whom I can reach some approximation of common ground are certain upper-class Townfolk, entrepreneurs, executives, innovators – cosmopolites who have had a good deal to do with the most developed parts of the Empire.'

'Squatters in Web,' she sneered. 'Yes, they're easy to fathom. Anything for profit.'

'Now you are the one whose imagination fails,' Desai reproved her. 'True, no doubt a number of them are despicable opportunists. Are there absolutely none among Landfolk and University? Can you not conceive that an industrialist or financier may honestly believe cooperation with the Imperium is the best hope of his world? Can you not entertain the hypothesis that he may be right?'

He sighed. 'At least recognize that the better we Impies understand you, the more to your advantage it is. In fact, our empathy could be vital. Had – Well, to be frank, had I known for sure what I dimly suspected, the significance in your culture of the McCormac Memorial and the armed households, I might have been able to persuade the sector government to rescind its orders for dismantling them. Then we might not have provoked the kind of thing which has made your betrothed an outlaw.'

Pain crossed her face. 'Maybe,' she said.

'My duty here,' he told her, 'is first to keep the Pax, including civil law and order; in the longer run, to assure

67

that these will stay kept, when the Terran troops finally go home. But what must be done? How? Should we, for example, should we revise the basic structure altogether? Take power from the landed gentry especially, whose militarism may have been the root cause of the rebellion, and establish a parliament based on strict manhood suffrage?' Desai observed her expressions; she was becoming more open to him. 'You are shocked? Indignant? Denying to yourself that so drastic a change is permanently possible?'

He leaned forward. 'My lady,' he said, 'among the horrors with which I live is this knowledge, based on all the history I have studied and all the direct experience I have had. It is terrifyingly easy to swing a defeated and occupied nation in *any* direction. It has occurred over and over. Sometimes, two victors with different ideologies divided such a loser among them, for purposes of "reform." Afterward the loser stayed divided, its halves perhaps more fanatical than either original conqueror.'

Dizziness assailed him. He must breathe deeply before he could go on: 'Of course, an occupation may end too soon, or it may not carry out its reconstruction thoroughly enough. Then a version of the former society will revive, though probably a distorted version. Now how soon is too soon, how thoroughly is enough? And to what end?

'My lady, there are those in power who claim Sector Alpha Crucis will never be safe until Aeneas has been utterly transformed: into an imitation Terra, say most. I feel that that is not only wrong – you have something unique here, something basically good – but it is mortally dangerous. In spite of the pretensions of the psychodynamicists, I don't believe the consequences of radical surgery, on a proud and energetic people, are foreseeable.

'I want to make minimal, not maximal changes. They may amount to nothing more than strengthening trade relations with the heart stars of the Empire, to give you a larger stake in the Pax. Or whatever seems necessary. At present, however, I don't know. I flounder about in a sea of reports and statistics, and as I go down for the third time, I remember the old saying, "Let me write a nation's songs, and I care not who may write its laws."

'Won't you help me understand your songs?'

Silence fell and lasted, save for a wind whittering outside, until the tadmouse offered a timid arpeggio. That seemed to draw Tatiana from her brown study. She shook herself and said, 'What you're askin' for is closer acquaintance, Commissioner. Friendship.'

His laugh was nervous. 'I'll settle for an agreement to disagree. Of course, I haven't time for anywhere near as much frank discussion as I'd like – as I really need. But if, oh, if you young Aeneans would fraternize with the young marines, technicians, spacehands – you'd find them quite decent, you might actually take a little pity on their loneliness, and they do have experiences to relate from worlds you've never heard of –'

'I don't know if it's possible,' Tatiana said. 'Certainly not on my sole recommendation. Not that I'd give any, when your dogs are after my man.'

'I thought that was another thing we might discuss,' Desai said. 'Not where he may be or what his plans, no, no. But how to get him out of the trap he's closed on himself. Nothing would make me happier than to give him a free pardon. Can we figure out a method?'

She cast him an astonished look before saying slowly, 'I do believe you mean that.'

'Beyond question I do. I'll tell you why. We Impies have our agents and informers, after all, not to mention assorted spy devices. We are not totally blind and deaf to events and to the currents beneath them. The fact could not be kept secret from the people that Ivar Frederiksen, the heir to the Firstmanship of Ilion, has led the first open, calculated renewal of insurgency. His confederates who were killed, hurt, imprisoned are being looked on as martyrs. He, at large, is being whispered of as the rightful champion of freedom – the rightful king, if you will – who shall return.' Desai's smile would have been grim were his plump features capable of it. 'You note the absence of public statements by his relatives, aside from nominal expressions of regret at an "unfortunate incident." We authorities have been careful not to lean on them. Oh, but we have been careful!'

69

The tenuous atmosphere was like a perpetual muffler on his unaccustomed ears. He could barely hear her: 'What might you do . . . for him?'

'If he, unmistakably of his own free will, should announce he's changed his mind – not toadying to the Imperium, no, merely admitting that through most of its history Aeneas didn't fare badly under it and this could be made true again – why, I think he could not only be pardoned, along with his associates, but the occupation government could yield on a number of points.'

Wariness brought Tatiana upright. 'If you intend this offer to lure him out of hidin' –'

'No!' Desai said, a touch impatiently. 'It's not the kind of message that can be broadcast. Arrangements would have to be made beforehand in secret, or it would indeed look like a sellout. Anyhow, I repeat that I don't think you know how to find him, or that he'll try contacting you in the near future.'

He sighed. 'But perhaps – Well, as I told you, what I mainly want to learn, in my clumsy and tentative fashion, is what drives him. What drives all of you? What are the possibilities for compromise? How can Aeneas and the Imperium best struggle out of this mess they have created for each other?'

She regarded him for a second period of quiet, until she asked, 'Would you care to have lunch?'

The sandwiches and coffee had been good; and seated in her kitchenette bay, which was vitryl supported on the backs of stone dragons, one had an unparalleled view across quads, halls, towers, battlements, down and on to Nova Roma, the River Flone and its belt of green, the ochreous wilderness beyond.

Desai inhaled fragrance from his cup, in lieu of the cigarette he had not yet ventured to mention. 'Then Ivar is paradoxical,' he remarked. 'By your account, he is a skeptic on his way to becoming the charismatic lord of a deeply religious people.'

'What?' He'd lost count of how often today he had taken the girl aback. 'Oh, no. We've never been such. We began as scientific base, remember, and in no age of piety.' She ran fingers through her hair and said after a moment, 'Well, true, there always were some believers, especially among Landfolk . . . m-m, I suppose tendency does go back beyond Snelund administration, maybe several lifetimes . . . reaction to general decadence of Empire? – but our woes in last several years have certainly accelerated it – more and more, people are turnin' to churches.' She frowned. 'They're not findin' what they seek, though. That's Ivar's problem. He underwent conversion in early adolescence, he tells me, then later found creed unbelievable in light of science – unless, he says, they dilute it to cluck of soothin' noises, which is not what he wants.'

'Since I came here for information, I have no business telling you what you are,' Desai said. 'Nevertheless, I do have a rather varied background and – Well, how would this interpretation strike you? Aenean society has always had a strong *faith*. A faith in the value of knowledge, to plant this colony in the first place; a faith in, oh, in the sheer right and duty of survival, to carry it through the particularly severe impact of the Troubles which it suffered; a faith in service, honor, tradition, demonstrated by the fact that what is essentially paternalism continued to be viable in easier times. Now hard times have come back. Some Aeneans, like Ivar, react by making a still greater emotional commitment to the social system. Others look to the supernatural. But however he does it, the average Aenean must serve something which is greater than himself.'

Tatiana frowned in thought. 'That may be. That may be. Still, I don't think "supernatural" is right word, except in highly special sense. "Transcendental" might be better. For instance, I'd call Cosmenosis philosophy rather than religion.' She smiled a trifle. 'I ought to know, bein' Cosmenosist myself.'

'I seem to recall – Isn't that an increasingly popular movement in the University community?'

'Which is large and ramified, don't forget. Yes. Commissioner, you're right. And I don't believe it's mere fad.'

'What are the tenets?'

71

'Nothing exact, really. It doesn't claim to be revealed truth, simply way of gropin' toward . . . insight, oneness. Work with Didonians inspired it, originally. You can guess why, can't you?'

Desai nodded. Through his mind passed the picture he had seen, and many more: in a red-brown rain forest, beneath an eternally clouded sky, stood a being which was triune. Upon the platformlike shoulders of a large monoceroid quadruped rested a feathered flyer and a furry brachiator with well-developed hands. Their faces ran out in tubes, which connected to the big animal to tap its bloodstream. It ate for all of them.

Yet they were not permanently linked. They belonged to their distinct genera, reproduced their separate kinds and carried out many functions independently.

That included a measure of thinking. But the Didonian was not truly intelligent until its – no, heesh's – three members were joined. Then not only did veins link; nervous systems did. The three brains together became more than the sum of the three apart.

How much more was not known, perhaps not definable in any language comprehensible to man. The next world sunward from Aeneas remained as wrapped in mystery as in mist. That Didonian societies were technologically primitive proved nothing; human ones were, until a geologically infinitesimal moment ago, and Terra was an easier globe on which to find lawfulness in nature. That communication with Didonians was extraordinarily difficult, limited after seven hundred years to a set of pidgin dialects, proved nothing either, beyond the truism that their minds were alien beyond ready imagining.

What is a mind, when it is the temporary creation of three beings, each with its own individuality and memories, each able to have any number of different partners? What is personality – the soul, even – when these shifting linkages perpetuate those recollections, in a ghostly diminuendo that lasts for generations after the experiencing bodies have died? How many varieties of race and culture and self are possible, throughout the ages of an entire infinite-faceted world? What may we learn from them, or they from us?

Without Dido for lure, probably men would never have possessed Aeneas. It was so far from Terra, so poor and harsh – more habitable for them than its sister, but by no great margin. By the time that humans who lacked such incentive had filled more promising planets, no doubt the Ythrians would have occupied this one. It would have suited them far better than it did *Homo sapiens.*

How well had it suited the Builders, uncertain megayears in the past, when there were no Didonians and Aeneas had oceans – ?

'Excuse me.' Desai realized he had gone off into a reverie. 'My mind wandered. Yes, I've meditated on the – the Neighbors, don't you call them? – quite a bit, in what odd moments fall to my lot. They must have influenced your society enormously, not just as an inexhaustible research object, but by their, well, example.'

'Especially of late, when we think we may be reachin' true communication in some few cases,' Tatiana replied. Ardor touched her tone. 'Think: such way of existence, on hand for us to witness and . . . and meditate on, you said. Maybe you're right, we do need transhumanness in our lives, here on this planet. But maybe, Commissioner, we're right in feelin' that need.' She swept her hand in an arc at the sky. 'What are we? Sparks, cast up from a burnin' universe whose creation was meanin'less accident? Or children of God? Or parts, masks of God? Or seed from which God will at last grow?' Quieter: 'Most of us Cosmenosists think – yes, Didonians have inspired it, their strange unity, such little as we've learned of their beliefs, dedications, poetry, dreams – we think reality is always growin' toward what is greater than itself, and first duty of those that stand highest is to help raise those lower –'

Her gaze went out the window, to the fragment of what had been . . . something, ages ago . . . and, in these latter centuries, had never really been lost in the wall which used it. 'Like Builders,' she finished. 'Or Elders, as Landfolk call them, or – oh, they've many names. Those who came before us.'

Desai stirred. 'I don't want to be irreverent,' he said uncomfortably, 'but, well, while apparently a starfaring civilization did exist in the distant past, leaving relics on a number of planets, I can't quite, um-m, swallow this notion I've heard on Aeneas, that it went onto a more exalted plane – rather than simply dying out.'

'What would destroy it?' she challenged. 'Don't you suppose we, puny mankind, are already too widespread for extinction, this side of cosmos itself endin' – or, if we perish on some worlds, we won't leave tools, carvin's, synthetics, fossilized bones, traces enough to identify us for millions of years to come? Why not Builders, then?'

'Well,' he argued, 'a brief period of expansion, perhaps scientific bases only, no true colonies, evacuated because of adverse developments at home –'

'You're guessin',' Tatiana said. 'In fact, you're whistlin' past graveyard that isn't there. I think, and I'm far from alone, Builders never needed to do more than they did. They were already beyond material gigantism, by time they reached here. I think they outgrew these last vestiges we see, and left them. And Didonian many-in-one gives us clue to what they became; yes, they may have started that very line of evolution themselves. And on their chosen day they will return, for all our sakes.'

'I have heard talk about these ideas, Prosser Thane, but –'

Her look burned at him. 'You assume it's crankery. Then consider this. Right on Aeneas are completest set of Builder ruins known: in Orcan region, on Mount Cronos. We've never investigated them as we should, at first because of other concerns, later because they'd become inhabited. But now . . . oh, rumors yet, nothin' but the kind of rumors that're forever driftin'' in on desert wind . . . still, they whisper of a forerunner –'

She saw she might have spoken too freely, broke off and snapped self-possession into place. 'Please don't label me fanatic,' she said. 'Call it hope, daydream, what you will. I agree we have no proof, let alone divine revelation.' He could not be sure how much or how little malice dwelt in her smile. 'Still, Commissioner, what if bein's five or ten million years ahead of us *should* decide Terran Empire is in need of reconstruction?'

Desai returned to his office so near the end of the posted working day that he planned to shove everything aside till tomorrow and get home early. It would be the first time in a couple of weeks he had seen his children before they were asleep.

But of course his phone told him he had an emergency call. Being a machine, it refrained from implying he ought to have left a number where he could be reached. The message had come from his chief of Intelligence.

Maybe it isn't crucial, went his tired thought. *Feinstein's a good man, but he's never quite learned how to delegate.*

He made the connection. The captain responded directly. After ritual salutations and apologies:

' – that Aycharaych of Jean-Baptiste, do you remember him? Well, sir, he's disappeared, under extremely suspicious circumstances.

' . . . No, as you yourself, and His Excellency, decided, we had no reasonable cause to doubt him. He actually arranged to travel with a patrol of ours, for his first look at the countryside.

' . . . As nearly as I can make out from bewildered reports, somehow he obtained the password. You know what precautions we've instituted since the Hesperian incident? The key guards don't know the passwords themselves, consciously. Those're implanted for posthypnotic recognition and quick re-forgetting. To prevent accidents, they're nonsense syllables, or phrases taken from obscure languages used at the far side of the Empire. If Aycharaych could read them in the minds of the men – remembering also his nonhuman brain structure – then he's more of a telepath, or knows more tricks, than is supposed to be possible.

'Anyhow, sir, with the passwords he commandeered a flyer, talked it past an aerial picket, and is flat-out gone.

' . . . Yes, sir, naturally I've had the file on him checked, cross-correlated, everything we can do with what we've got on this wretched dustball. No hint of motivation.

Could be simple piracy, I imagine, but dare we assume that?'

'My friend,' Desai answered, while exhaustion slumped his shoulders, 'I cannot conceive of one thing in the universe which we truly dare assume.'

VIII

'Hee-ah!' Mikkal lashed his statha into full wavelike gallop. The crag bull veered. Had it gone down the talus slope, the hunters could not have followed. Boots, or feet not evolved for this environment, would have been slashed open by the edges of the rocks. And the many cinnabar-colored needles which jutted along the canyon would have screened off a shot.

As was, the beast swung from the rim and clattered across the mountainside. Then, from behind an outcrop striped in mineral colors, Fraina appeared on her own mount.

The bull should have fled her too, uphill toward Ivar. Instead, it lowered its head and charged. The trident horns sheened like steel. Her statha reared in panic. The bull was almost as big as it, and stronger and faster.

Ivar had the only gun, his rifle; the others bore javelins. *'Ya-lawa!'* he commanded his steed: in Haisun, 'Freeze!' He swung stock to cheek and sighted. Bare rock, red dust, scattered gray-green bushes, and a single rahab tree stood sharp in the light of noontide. Virgil Shadows were purple but the sky seemed almost black above raw peaks. The air lay hot, suckingly dry, soundless except for hoof-drum and human cries.

If I don't hit that creature, Fraina may die, went through Ivar. *But no use hittin' him in the hump. And anywhere else is wicked to try for, at this angle and speed, and her in line of fire* – The knowledge flashed by as a part of taking aim. He had no time to be afraid.

The rifle hissed. The bullet trailed a whipcrack. The crag bull leaped, bellowed, and toppled.

77

'Rolf, Rolf, Rolf!' Fraina caroled. He rode down to her with glory in him. When they dismounted, she threw arms around him, lips against his.

For all its enthusiasm, it was a chaste kiss; yet it made him a trifle giddy. By the time he recovered, Mikkal had arrived and was examining the catch.

'Good act, Rolf.' His smile gleamed white in the thin face. 'We'll feast tonight.'

'We've earned it.' Fraina laughed. 'Not that folk always get paid what's owing them, or don't get it swittled from them afterward.'

'The trick is to be the swittler,' Mikkal said.

Fraina's gaze fell tenderly on Ivar. 'Or to be smart enough to keep what you've been strong enough to earn,' she murmured.

His heart knocked. She was more beautiful than she ought to be, now in this moment of victory, and in the trunks and haltar which clad her. Mikkal wore simply a loincloth and crossed shoulderbelts to support knives, pouch, canteen. Those coppery skins could stand a fair amount of exposure, and it was joy to feel warmth upon them again. Ivar struck to loose, full desert garb, blouse, trousers, sun-visored burnoose.

That plateau known as the Dreary of Ironland was behind them. There would be no more struggle over stonefields or around crevasses of a country where nothing stirred save them and the wind, nothing lived save them alone; no more thirst when water must be rationed till food went uncooked and utensils were cleaned with sand; no more nights so cold that tents must be erected to keep the animals alive.

As always, the passage had frayed nerves thin. Ivar appreciated the wisdom of the king in sequestering firearms. At that, a couple of knife fights had come near ending fatally. The travelers needed more than easier conditions, they needed something to cheer them. This first successful hunt on the eastern slope of the Ferric Mountains ought to help mightily.

And, though the country here was gaunt, they were

over the worst. The Waybreak Train was headed down toward the Flone Valley, to reach at last the river itself, its cool green banks and the merry little towns snuggled along it, south of Nova Roma. If now the hunters laughed overmuch and over-shrilly while they butchered the crag bull, Ivar thought it was not beneath a Firstling's dignity to join in.

Moreover, Fraina was with him, they were working together . . . Their acquaintance was not deep. Time and energy had been lacking for that. Besides, despite her dancing, she behaved shyly for a tineran girl. But for the rest of his stay in the troop – *I hope I've honor not to seduce her and leave her cryin' behind, when at last I go. (I begin to understand why, no matter hardships, sharpest pain may be to leave.) And Tanya, of course, mustn't forget Tanya.*

Let me, though, enjoy Fraind's nearness while I can. She's so vivid. Everything is. I never knew I could feel this fully and freely, till I joined wanderers.

He forced his attention to the task on hand. His heavy sheath knife went through hide, flesh, gristle, even the thinner bones, much more quickly and easily than did the slender blades of his comrades. He wondered why they didn't adopt the nord model, or at least add it to their tool kit; then, watching how cunningly they worked, he decided it wouldn't fit their style. *Hm, yes, I begin to see for my self, cultures are unities, often in subtle ways.*

Finished, meat loaded on stathas, the three of them went to rest by the spring which had attracted their quarry. It made a deliciously chilly bowlful in the hollow of a rock, the shadow of a bluff. Plume trava nodded white above mossy chromabryon; spearflies darted silver bright; the stream clinked away over stones till the desert swallowed it up. The humans drank deep, then leaned luxuriously back against the cliff, Fraina between the men.

'Ay-ah,' Mikkal sighed. 'No need for hurry. I make us barely ten clicks from the Train, if we set an intercept course. Let's relax before lunch.'

'Good idea,' Ivar said. He and Fraina exchanged smiles. Mikkal reached across her. In his hand were three

79

twists of paper enclosing brown shreds. 'Smoke?' he invited.

'What?' Ivar said. 'I thought you tinerans avoided tobacco. Dries mouth, doesn't it?'

'Oh, this's marwan.' At the puzzled look he got, Mikkal explained: 'Never heard of it? Well, I don't suppose your breed would use the stuff. It's a plant. You dry and smoke it. Has a similar effect to alcohol. Actually better, I'd say, though I admit the taste leaves a trifle to be desired alongside a fine whiskey.'

'*Narcotic?*' Ivar was shocked.

'Not that fierce, Rolf. Hell-near to a necessity, in fact, when you're away from the Train, like on a hunting or scouting trip.' Mikkal grimaced. 'These wilds are too inhuman. With a lot of friends around, you're screened. But by yourself, you need to take the edge off how alone and mortal you are.'

Never before had Ivar heard him confess to a weakness. Mikkal was normally cheerful. When his temper, too, flared in the Dreary, he had not gone for his steel but used an equally whetted tongue, as if he felt less pressure than most of his fellows to prove masculinity. Now – *Well, I reckon I can sympathize. It is oppressive, this size and silence. Unendin' memento mori. Never thought so before, out in back country, but I do now. If Fraina weren't here to keep me glad, I might be tempted to try his drug.*

'No, thank you,' Ivar said.

Mikkal shrugged. On the way back, his hand paused before the girl. She made a refusing gesture. He arched his brows, whether in surprise or sardonicism, till she gave him a tiny frown and headshake. Then he grinned, tucked away the extra cigarettes, put his between his lips and snapped a lighter to it. Ivar had scarcely noticed the byplay, and gave it no thought except to rejoice that in this, also, Fraina kept her innocence. Mostly he noticed the sweet odors of her, healthy flesh and sun-warmed hair and sweat that stood in beads on her half-covered breasts.

Mikkal drew smoke into his lungs, held it, let it out very slowly and drooped his lids. 'Aaah,' he said, 'and again aaah. I become able to think. Mainly about ways to treat these steaks and chops. The women'll make stew tonight, no doubt. I'll insist the rest of the meat be started in a proper marinade. Take the argument to the king if I must. I'm sure he'll support me. He may be a vinegar beak, our Samlo, but all kings are, and he's a sensible vinegar beak.'

'He certainly doesn't behave like average tineran,' Ivar said.

'Kings don't. That's why we have them. I can't deny we're a flighty race, indeed I boast of it. However, that means we must have somebody who'll tie us down to caution and foresight.'

'I, yes, I do know about special trainin' kings get. Must be real discipline, to last through lifetime in your society.'

Fraina giggled. Mikkal, who had taken another drag, kicked heels and whooped. 'What'd I say?' Ivar asked.

The girl dropped her glance. He believed he saw her blush, though that was hard to tell on her complexion. 'Please, Mikkal, don't be irrev'rant,' she said.

'Well, no more'n I have to,' her half-brother agreed. 'Still, Rolf might's well know. It's not a secret, just a matter we don't talk about. Not to disillusion youngsters too early, et cetera.' His eyes sparkled toward Ivar. 'Only the lodge that kings belong to is supposed to know what goes on in the shrines, and in the holy caves and booths where Fairs are held. But the royal wives and concubines take part, and girls will pass on details to their friends. You think we common tinerans hold lively parties. We don't know what liveliness is!'

'But it's our religion,' Fraina assured Ivar. 'Not the godlings and jus and spells of everyday. This is to honor the powers of life.'

Mikkal chuckled. 'Aye-ah, officially those're fertility rites. Well, I've read some anthropology, talked to a mixed bag of people, even taken thought once in a while when I'd nothing better to do. I figure the cult developed because the king has to have all-stops-out orgies fairly often, if he's to stay the kind of sobersides we need for a leader.'

Ivar stared before him, half in confusion, half in embarrassment. Wouldn't it make more sense for the tinerans as a whole to be more self-controlled? Why was this extreme emotionalism seemingly built into them? Or was that merely his own prejudices speaking? Hadn't he been becoming more and more like them, and savoring every minute of it?

Fraina laid a hand on his arm. Her breath touched his cheek. 'Mikkal has to poke fun,' she said. 'I believe it's both holy and unholy, what the king does. Holy because we must have young – too many die small, human and animal – and the powers of life are real. Unholy because, oh, he takes on himself the committing of . . . excesses, is that the word? On behalf of the Train, he releases our beast side, that otherwise would tear the Train apart.'

I don't understand, quite, Ivar thought. *But,* thrilled within him, *she's thoughtful, intelligent, grave, as well as sweet and blithe.*

'Yah, I should start Dulcy baby-popping,' Mikkal said. 'The wet stage isn't too ghastly a nuisance, I'm told.' When weaned, children moved into dormitory wagons. 'On the other hand,' he added, 'I've told a few whoppers myself, when I had me a mark with jingle in his pockets –'

A shape blotted out the sun. They bounded to their feet.

That which was descending passed the disc, and light blazed off the gold-bronze pinions of a six-meter wingspan. Air whistled and thundered. Fraina cried out. Mikkal poised his javelin. 'Don't!' Ivar shouted. '*Ya-lawa!* He's Ythrian!'

'O-o-oh, ye-e-es,' Mikkal said softly. He lowered the spear though he kept it ready. Fraina gripped Ivar's arm and leaned hard against him.

The being landed. Ivar had met Ythrians before, at the University and elsewhere. But his astonishment at this arrival was such that he gaped as if he were seeing one for the first time.

Grounded, the newcomer used those tremendous wings, folded downward, for legs, claws at the bend of them spreading out to serve as feet, the long rear-directed bones lending extra support when at rest. That brought his height to some 135 centimeters, mid-breast on Ivar, farther up on the tinerans; for his mass was a good 25 kilos. Beneath, a prowlike keelbone were lean yellow-skinned arms whose hands, evolved from talons, each bore three sharp-clawed fingers flanked by two thumbs, and a dewclaw on the inner wrist. Above were a strong neck and a large head proudly held. The skull bulged backward to contain the brain, for there was scant brow, the face curving down in a ridged muzzle to a mouth whose sensitive lips contrasted curiously with the carnivore fangs behind. A stiff feather-crest rose over head and neck, white edged with black like the fan-shaped tail. Otherwise, apart from feet, arms, and huge eyes which burned gold and never seemed to waver or blink, the body was covered with plumage of lustrous brown.

He wore an apron whose pockets, loops, and straps supported what little equipment he needed. Knife, canteen, and pistol were the only conspicuous items. He could live off the country better than any human.

Mikkal inhaled smoke, relaxed, smiled, lifted and dipped his weapon in salute. 'Hay-ah, wayfarer,' he said formally, 'be welcome among us in the Peace of Water, where none are enemies. We're Mikkal of Redtop and my sister Fraina of Jubilee, from the Waybreak Train; and our companyo is Rolf Mariner, varsiteer.'

The Anglic which replied was sufficiently fluent that one couldn't be sure how much of the humming accent and sibilant overtones were due to Ythrian vocal organs, how much simply to this being an offplanet dialect the speaker had learned. 'Thanks, greetings, and fair winds wished for you. I hight Erannath, of the Stormgate choth upon Avalon. Let me quench thirst and we can talk if you desire.'

As awkward on the ground as he was graceful aloft, he stumped to the pool. When he bent over to drink, Ivar glimpsed the gill-like antlibranchs, three on either side of his body. They were closed now, but in flight the muscles would work them like bellows, forcing extra oxygen into the bloodstream to power the lifting of the great weight. That meant high fuel consumption too, he remembered. No wonder Erannath traveled alone, if he had no vehicle. This land couldn't support two of him inside a practical radius of operations.

83

'He's gorgeous,' Fraina whispered to Ivar. 'What did you call him?'

'Ythrian,' the Firstling replied. 'You mean you don't know?'

'I guess I have heard, vaguely, but I'm an ignorant wanderfoot, Rolf. Will you tell me later?'

Ha! Won't I?

Mikkal settled himself back in the shade where he had been. 'Might I ask what brings you, stranger?'

'Circumstances,' Erannath replied. His race tended to be curt. A large part of their own communication lay in nuances indicated by the play of marvelously controllable quills.

Mikkal laughed. 'In other words, yes, I might ask, but no, I might not get an answer. Wouldn't you like to palaver a while anyhow? Yo, Fraina, Rolf, join the party.'

They did. Erannath's gaze lingered on the Firstling. 'I have not hitherto observed your breed fare thus,' he said.

'I – wanted a change – ' Ivar faltered.

'He hasn't told exactly why, and no need for you to, either,' Mikkal declared. 'But see here, Aeronaut, your remark implies you *have* been observing, and pretty extensively too. Unless you're given to reckless generalization, which I don't believe your kind is.'

Expressions they could not read rippled across the feathers. 'Yes,' the Ythrian said after a moment, 'I am interested in this planet. As an Avalonian, I am naturally familiar with humans, but of a rather special sort. Being on Aeneas, I am taking the opportunity to become acquainted, however superficially, with a few more.'

'U-u-uh-huh.' Mikkal lounged crosslegged, smoking, idly watching the sky, while he drawled. 'Somehow I doubt they've heard of you in Nova Roma. The occupation authorities have planted their heaviest buttocks on space traffic, in and out. Want to show me your official permit to flit around? As skittery as the guiders of our Terran destinies are nowadays, would they give a visitor from our esteemed rival empire the freedom of a key near-the-border world? I'm only fantasizing, but it goes in the direction of you being stranded here. You came in during the revolt, let's suppose, when that was easy to do unbeknownst, and you're biding your time till conditions ease up enough for you to get home.'

Ivar's fingers clenched on his gunstock. But Erannath sat imperturbable. 'Fantasize as you wish,' he said dryly, 'if you grant me the same right.' Again his eyes smote the Firstling.

'Well, our territory doesn't come near Nova Roma,' Mikkal continued. 'We'd make you welcome, if you care to roll with us as you've probably done already in two or three other Trains. Your songs and stories should be uncommon entertaining. And . . . maybe when we reach the green and start giving shows, we can work you into an act.'

Fraina gasped. Ivar smiled at her. 'Yes,' he whispered, 'without that weed in him – unless he was in camp – Mikkal wouldn't have nerve to proposition those claws and dignity, would he?' Her hair tickled his face. She squeezed his hand.

'My thanks,' Erannath said. 'I will be honored to guest you, for a few days at least. Thereafter we can discuss further.'

He went high above them, hovering, soaring, wheeling in splendor, while they rode back across the tilted land.
'What *is* he?' Fraina asked. Hoofbeats clopped beneath her voice. A breeze bore smoky orders of starkwood. They recalled the smell of the Ythrian, as if his forefathers once flew too near their sun.

'A sophont,' Mikkal said redundantly. He proceeded: 'More bright and tough than most. Maybe more than us. Could be we're stronger, we humans, simply because we outnumber them, and that simply because of having gotten the jump on them in space travel and, hm, needing less room per person to live in.'
'A bird?'
'No,' Ivar told her. 'They're feathered, yes, warm-blooded, two sexes. However, you noticed he doesn't have a beak, and females give live birth. No lactation – no milk, I mean; the lips're for getting the blood out of prey.'

'You bespoke an empire, Mikkal,' she said, 'and, ye-ih, I do remember mentions aforetime. Talk on, will you?'

'Let Rolf do that,' the man suggested. 'He's schooled. Besides, if he has to keep still much longer, he'll make an awful mess when he explodes.'

Ivar's ears burned. *True*, he thought. But Fraina gave him such eager attention that the plunged happily forward.

'Ythri's planet rather like Aeneas, except for havin' cooler sun,' he said. 'It's about a hundred light-years from here, roughly in direction of Beta Centauri.'

'That's the Angel's Eye,' Mikkal interpolated.

Don't itinerans use our constellations? Our sky is different. Ivar wondered. *Well, we don't use Terra's; our sky is different.* 'After humans made contact, Ythrians rapidly acquired modern technology,' he went on. 'Altogether variant civilization, of course, if you can call it civilization, they never havin' had cities. Noneless, it lent itself to spacefarin', same as Technic culture, and in time Ythrians began to trade and colonize, on smaller scale than humans. When League fell apart and Troubles followed, they suffered too. Men restored order at last by establishin' Terran Empire, Ythrians by their Domain. It isn't really an empire, Mikkal. Loose alliance of worlds.

'Still, it grew. So did Empire, Terra's, that is, till they met and clashed. Couple centuries ago, they fought. Ythri lost war and had to give up good deal of border territory. But it'd fought too stiffly for Imperium to think of annexin' entire Domain.

'Since, relations have been . . . variable, let's say. Some affrays, though never another real war; some treaties and joint undertakin's, though often skulduggery on both sides; plenty of trade, individuals and organizations visitin' back and forth. Terra's not happy about how Domain of Ythri is growin' in opposite direction from us, and in strength. But Merseia's kept Imperium too busy to do much in these parts – except stamp out freedom among its own subjects.'

'Nothing like that to make a person objective about his government,' Mikkal remarked aside.

'I see,' Fraina said. 'How clearly you explain . . . Didn't I hear him tell he was, m-m, from Avalon?'

'Yes,' Ivar replied. 'Planet in Domain, colonized by humans and Ythrians together. Unique society. It'd be reasonable to send Avalonian to spy out Aeneas. He'd have more rapport with us, more insight, than ordinary Ythrians.'

Her eyes widened. 'He's a spy?'

'Intelligence agent, if you prefer. Not skulkin' around burglarizin' Navy bases or any such nonsense. Gatherin' what bits of information he can, to become part of their picture of Terran Empire. I really can't think what else he'd be. They must've landed him here while space-traffic control was broken down because of independence war. As Mikkal says, eventually he'll leave – I'd guess when Ythrians again have consulate in Nova Roma, that can arrange to smuggle him out.'

'You don't care, Rolf?'

'Why should I? In fact –'

Ivar finished the thought in his head. *We got no Ythrian help in our struggle. I'm sure Hugh McCormac tried, and was refused. They wouldn't risk new war. But . . . if we could get clandestine aid – arms and equipment slipped to us, interstellar transport furnished, communications nets made available – we could build strength of freedom forces till – We failed because we weren't rightly prepared. McCormac raised standard almost on impulse. And he wasn't tryin' to split Empire, he wanted to rule it himself. What would Ythri gain by that? Whereas if our purpose was to break Sector Alpha Crucis loose, make it independent or even bring it under Ythri's easygoin' suzerainty – wouldn't that interest them? Perhaps be worth war, especially if we got Merseian help too –* He looked up at Erannath and dreamed of wings which stormed hitherward in the cause of liberty.

An exclamation drew him back to his body. They had topped a ridge. On the farther slope, mostly buried by a rockslide, were the remnants of great walls and of columns so slim and poised that it was as if they too were flying. Time had not dimmed their nacreous luster.

'Why . . . Builder relic,' Ivar said. 'Or do you call them Elders?'

'*La-Sarzen*,' Fraina told him, very low. 'The High Ones.'
Upon her countenance and, yes, Mikkal's, lay awe.

'We're off our usual route,' the man breathed. 'I'd forgotten that this is where some of them lived.'

He and his sister sprang from their saddles, knelt with uplifted arms, and chanted. Afterward they rose, crossed themselves, and spat: in this parched country, a deed of sacrifice. As they rode on, they gave the ruins a wide berth, and hailed them before dropping behind the next rise.

Erannath had not descended to watch. Given his vision, he need not. He cruised through slow circles like a sign in heaven.

After a kilometer, Ivar dared ask: 'Is that . . . back yonder . . . part of your religion? I wouldn't want to be profane.'

Mikkal nodded. 'I suppose you could call it sacred. Whatever the High Ones are, they're as near godhood as makes no difference.'

That doesn't follow, Ivar thought, keeping silence. *Why is it so nearly universal belief?*

'Some of their spirit must be left in what they made,' Fraina said raptly. 'We need its help. And, when they come back, they'll know we keep faith in them.'

'Will they?' Ivar couldn't help the question.

'Yes,' Mikkal said. In him, sober quiet was twice powerful. 'Quite likely during our own lifetimes, Rolf. Haven't you heard the tale that's abroad? Far south, where the dead men dwell, a prophet has arisen to prepare the way –'

He shivered in the warmth. 'I don't know if that's true, myself,' he finished in a matter-of-fact tone. 'But we can hope, can't we? C'mon, tingle up these lazy beasts and let's get back to the Train.'

IX

The mail from Terra was in. Chunderban Desai settled back with a box of cigarettes, a samovar of tea, and resignation to the fact that he would eat lunch and dinner and a midnight snack off his desk. This did not mean he, his staff, or his equipment were inefficient. He would have no need to personally scan two-thirds of what was addressed to his office. But he did bear ultimate responsibility for a globe upon which dwelt 400 million human beings.

Lord Advisor Petroff of the Policy Board was proposing a shakeup of organizational structure throughout the occupied zone, and needed reports and opinions from every commissioner. Lord Advisor Chardon passed on certain complaints from Sector Governor Muratori, about a seeming lack of zeal in the reconstruction of the Virgilian System, and asked for explanations. Naval Intelligence wanted various operations started which would attempt to learn how active Merseian agents were throughout the Alpha Crucis region. BuEc wanted a fresh survey made of mineral resources in the barren planets of each system in the sector, and studies of their exploitability as a method of industrial recovery. BuSci wanted increased support for research on Dido, adding that that should help win over the Aeneans. BuPsy wanted Dido evacuated, fearing that its cloud cover and vast wilderness made it potentially too useful to guerrillas. The Throne wanted immediate in-depth information on local results should His Majesty make a contemplated tour of the subjugated rebel worlds . . .

Night filled the wall transparency, and a chill tiny Creusa hurtled above a darkened city, when a thing Desai himself

89

had requested finally crossed the screen. He surged out of sleepiness with a gasp. *I'd better have that selector repro-grammed!* His fingers shook almost too badly for him to insert a fresh cigarette in his holder and inhale it to ignition. He never noticed how tongue, palate, throat, and lungs protested.

'—no planet named, nicknamed, or translated as Jean-Baptiste, assuredly not in any known language or dialect of the Empire, nor in any exterior space for which records are available. Saint John, Hagios Ioannes, and the conti-nent of San Juan on Nuevo México were all named after a co-author of the basic Christian canon, a person distinct from the one who figures as active in events described therein and is termed in Fransai Jean-Baptiste, in Anglic John the Baptist...

'The origin of the individual self-denominated. Aycha-raych (v. note 3 on transcription of the voice print) has been identified, from measurement upon holographic material supplied (ref. 2), with a probability deemed high albeit nonquantifiable due to paucity of data.

'When no good correlation was obtained with any species filed with the Imperial Xenological Register, application was made to Naval Intelligence. It was reported by this agency that as a result of a scan of special data banks, Aycharaych can be assumed to be from a planet subject to the Roidhun of Merseia. It was added that he should be considered an agent thereof, presumably dispatched on a mission inimical to the best interests of His Majesty.

'Unfortunately, very little is known about the planet in question. A full account is attached, but will be found scarcely more informative than the summary which fol-lows.

'According to a few casual mentions made in the pre-sence of Imperial personnel and duly reported by them, the planet is referred to as Chereion (v. note 3). It is recorded as having been called variously "cold, creepy", "a mummy dwarf", and "a silent ancient", albeit some favorable notice was taken of art and architecture. These remarks were made in conversation by Merseians (or, in one in-stance, a non-Merseian of the Roidhunate) by whom the planet had been visited briefly in the course of voyages directed elsewhere. From this it may perhaps be inferred that Chereion is terrestroid verging on subterrestroid, of low mean temperature, sufficiently small and/or old that a substantial loss of atmosphere and hydrosphere has been suffered. In short, it may be considered possibly not too dissimilar to Aeneas as the latter is described in the files. Nothing has been scanned which would make it possible for the sun to be located or spectrally classified. It must be emphasized that Chereion is obscure, seldom touched at, and never heard of by the average Merseian.

'Some indications were noted, which owing to lack of planet. Identification of subject Aycharaych as of this Chereion may be more highly regarded than this by the top levels of the Roidhunate hierarchy, and that indeed the dearth of it interest in it may have been deliberately instigated rather than straightforwardly caused by primitiveness, poverty, or other more usual factors. If so, presumably its entire populace has, effectively, been induced to cooperate, suggesting that some uniqueness may be found in their psychology.

'The Chereionites are not absolutely confined to their planet. Identification of subject Aycharaych as of this race was made from pictures taken with microcameras upon two different occasions, one a reception at the Terran Embassy on Merseia, one more recently during negotiations in re Jihannath. In either case, a large and mixed group being present, no more than brief queries were made, eliciting replies such as those listed above. But it should be pointed out that if a Chereionite was present at any affair of such importance (and presumably at others for which no data are on hand) then he must have been considered useful to the Roidhunate.

'As an additional fragment, the following last-minute and essentially anecdotal material is here inserted. Naval Intelligence, upon receipt of the request from this office, was moved to instigate inquiries among such of its own personnel as happened to be readily available. In response, this declaration, here paraphrased, was made by one Cmdr. Dominic Flandry.

'He had been on temporary assignment to Talwin, since he was originally concerned in events leading to the joint Terran-Merseian research effort upon that planet (v. note 27) and his special knowledge might conceivably help in gathering militarily useful data. While there, he cultivated the friendship of a young Merseian officer. The intimation is that he introduced the latter to various debaucheries; whatever the method was, he got him talking fairly freely. Having noticed a member of a species new to him in the Merseian group, Flandry asked what manner of sophont this might be. The officer, intoxicated at the time, gave the name of the planet, Chereion, then went on to mumble of a race of incredible antiquity, possessing powers his government keeps secret: a race which seemingly had once nurtured a high civilization, and which said officer suspected might now cherish ambitions wherein his own people are a mere means to an end. Flandry thinks the officer might well have said more; but abruptly the ranking Merseians present ended the occasion and left with all their personnel. Flandry would have pursued the matter further, but never saw his informant or the Chereionite again. He filed this story as part of his report, but Regional Data Processing did not evaluate it as more than a rumor, and thus did not forward it to the central banks.

'The foregoing is presented only in the interest of completeness. Sensationalism is to be discouraged. It is recommended that a maximum feasible effort be instigated for the apprehension of the being Aycharaych, while every due allowance is made for other programs which have rightfully been given a higher priority than the possible presence of a lone foreign operative. Should such effort be rewarded with success, the subject is to be detained while HQNI is notified . . . .'

Desai stared into darkness. *But there is mention of Jean-Baptiste in the files on Llynathawr,* he thought. *Easy enough for an employee in Merseia's pay to insert false data . . . probably during the chaos of the civil war . . . Uldwyr, you green devil, what have you or yours in mind for my planet?*

92

The Flone Valley is for the most part a gentler land than the edge of Ilion. Rolling on roads toward the great stream, Waybreak had no further need for the discipline of the desert. Exuberance kindled as spent energies returned.

On a mild night, the Train camped in a pasture belonging to a yeoman family with which it had made an agreement generations ago. There was no curfew; wood for a bonfire was plentiful; celebration lasted late. But early on, when Fraina had danced for them, she went to where Ivar sat and murmured, 'Want to take a walk? I'll be back soon's I've swapped clothes' – before she skipped off to Jubilee.

His blood roared. It drowned the talk to which he had been listening while he watched a succession of performances. When he could hear again, the words felt dwindled and purposeless, like the hum of a midgeling swarm.

'Yes, I was briefly with two other nomad groups,' Erannath was saying, 'the Dark Stars north of Nova Roma, near the Julia River, and the Gurdy Men in the Fort Lunacy area. The differences in custom are interesting but, I judge mere eddies in a single wind.'

King Samlo, seated on his chair, the only one put out, tugged his beard. 'You ought to visit the Magic Fathers, then, who I was apprenticed to,' he said. 'And the Glorious make women the heads of their wagons. But they're over in Tiberia, across the Antonine Seabed, so I don't know them myself.'

'Perhaps I will go see,' Erannath answered, 'though I feel certain of finding the same basic pattern.'

'Funny,' said the yeoman. 'You, xeno – no offense meant; I had some damn fine nonhuman shipmates durin' war of independence – you get around more on our planet than I ever have, or these professional travelers here.'

He had come with his grown sons to join the fun. Minors and womenfolk stayed behind. Not only was the party sure to become licentious; brawls might explode. Fascinated by Erannath, he joined the king, Padro of Roadlord, the widow Mara of Tramper, and a few more in conversation on the fringes of the circle. They were older folk, their bodies dimmed; the feverish atmosphere touched them less.

What am I doin' here? Ivar wondered. Exultation: *Waitin' for Fraina, that's what . . . Earlier, I thought I'd better not get too involved in things. Well, chaos take caution!*

The bonfire flared and rumbled at the center of the wagons. Whenever a stick went *crack*, sparks geysered out of yellow and red flames. The light flew across those who were seated on the ground, snatched eyes, teeth, earrings, bracelets, bits of gaudy cloth out of shadow, cast them back and brought forth instead a dice game, a boy and girl embraced, a playful wrestling match, a boy and girl already stealing off into the farther meadow. Around the blaze, couples had begun a stamping ring-dance, to the music of a lame guitarist, a hunchbacked drummer, and a blind man who sang in plangent Haisun. It smelled of smoke and humanity.

The flicker sheened off Erannath's plumage, turned his eyes to molten gold and his crest to a crown. In its skyey accent his speech did not sound pedantic: 'Outsiders often do explore more widely than dwellers, Yeoman Vasiliev, and see more, too. People tend to take themselves for granted.'

'I dunno,' Samlo argued. 'To you, don't the big differences shadow out the little ones that matter to us? You have wings, we don't; we have proper legs, you don't. Doesn't that make us seem pretty much alike to you? How can you say the Trains are all the same?'

'I did not say that, King,' Erannath replied. 'I said I have observed deep-going common factors. Perhaps you are blinkered by what you call the little differences that matter. Perhaps they matter more to you than they should.'

Ivar laughed and tossed in: 'Question is, whether we can't see forest for trees, or can't see trees for forest.'

Then Fraina was back, and he sprang up. She had changed to a shimmerlyn gown, ragged from years but cut so as to be hardly less revealing than her dancer's costume. Upon her shoulder, alongside a blueblack cataract of hair, sat the luck of Jubilee, muffled in its mantle apart from the imp head.

'Coming?' she chirruped.

'N-n-need you ask?' Ivar gave the king a nord-style bow. 'Will you excuse me, sir?'

Samlo nodded. A saturnine smile crossed his mouth.

As he straightened, Ivar grew aware of the intentness of Erannath. One did not have to be Ythrian to read hatred in erected quills and hunched stance. His gaze followed that of the golden orbs, and met the red triplet of the luck's. The animal crouched, bristled, and chittered.

'What's wrong, sweet?' Fraina reached to soothe her pet.

Ivar recalled how Erannath had declined the hospitality of any wagon and spent his whole time outdoors, even the bitterest night, when he must slowly pump his wings while he slept to keep his metabolism high enough that he wouldn't freeze to death. In sudden realization, the First-ling asked him, 'Don't you like lucks?'

'No,' said the Ythrian.

After a moment: 'I have encountered them elsewhere. In Planha we call them *liayalre*. Slinkers.'

Fraina pouted. 'Oh, foof! I took poor Tais along for a gulp of fresh air. C'mon, Rolf.'

She tucked her arm beneath Ivar's. He forgot that he had never cared for lucks either.

Erannath stared after him till he was gone from sight.

Beyond the ring of vehicles, the meadow rolled wide, its dawn trava turf springy and sweet underfoot, silver-gray beneath heaven. Trees stood roundabout, intricacies of pine, massivenesses of hammerbranch, cupolas of delphi. Both moons tinged their boughs white; and of the shadows, those cast by Creusa stirred as the half-disc sped eastward. Stars crowded velvet blackness. The Milky Way was an icefall.

Music faded behind him and her, until they were alone with a tadmouse's trill. He *was* speechless, content to marvel at the fact that she existed.

She said at last, quietly, looking before her: 'Rolf there's got to be High Ones. This much joy can't just've happened.'

'High Ones? Or God? Well – ' *Non sequitur, my dear. To us this is beautiful because certain apes were adapted to same kind of weather, long ago on Terra. Though we may feel subtle enchantment in deserts, can we feel it as wholly as Eramrath must? . . . But doesn't that mean that Creator made every kind of beauty? It's bleak, believin' in nothin' except accident.*

'Never mind philosophy,' he said Recklessly: 'Waste of time I could spend by your side,'

She slipped an arm around his waist. He felt it like fire. *I'm in love, he knew through the thunders. Never before like this, Tanya –*

She sighed, 'Aye-ah. How much've we left?'

'Forever?'

'No. You can't stay in the Train. It's never happened.'

'Why can't it?'

'Because you sitters – wait, Rolf, I'm sorry, you're too good for that word, you're a strider – you people who have rooted homes, you're – not weak – but you haven't got our kind of toughness.'

Which centuries of deaths have bred.

'I'm afraid for you,' Fraina whispered.

'What? Me?' His pride surged in a wave of anger that he knew, far off at the back of his mind, was foolish. 'Hoy, listen, I survived Dreary crossin' as well as next man, didn't I? I'm bigger and stronger than anybody else; maybe no so wiry, not so quick, but by chaos, if we struck dryout, starveout, gritstorm, whatever, I'd stay alive!'

She leaned closer, 'And you're smart, too, Rolf, full of book stories – what's more, full of skills we're always short on. Yet you'll have to go. Maybe because you're too much for us. What could we give you, for the rest of your life?'

You, his pulse replied. *And freedom to be myself . . . Drop your damned duties, Ivar Frederiksen. You never asked to be born to them. Stop thinkin' how those lights overhead are political points, and let them again be stars.*

'I, I, I don't think I could ever get tired of travelin', if you were along,' he blurted. 'And, uh, well, I can haul myload, maybe give Waybreak somethin' really valuable –'

'Until you got swittled, or knifed. Rolf, darling, you're

96

innocent. You know in your bones that most people are honest and don't get violent without reason. It's not true. Not in the Trains, it isn't. How can you change your skeleton, Rolf?'

'Could you help me?'

'Oh, if I could!' The shifty moonlight caught a glimmer of tears.

Abruptly Fraina tossed her head and stated, 'Well, if nothing else, I can shield you from the first and worst, Rolf.'

'What do you mean?' By now used to mercurial changes of mood, he chiefly was conscious of her looks, touch, and fragrance. They were still walking. The luck on her shoulder, drawn into its mantle, had virtually seceded from visibility.

'You've a fair clutch of jingle along, haven't you?'

He nodded. Actually the money was in bills, Imperial credits as well as Aenean libras, most of it given him in a wad by Sergeant Astaff before he left Windhome. ('Withdrew my savin's, Firstlin'. No worry. You'll pay me back if you live, and if you don't live, what futterin' difference'll my account make?' How remote and unreal it seemed!) Tinerans had no particular concept of privacy. (*I've learned to accept that, haven't I? Privacy is in my brain. What matter if Dulcy casually goes through my pockets, if she and Mikkal and I casually dress and undress in their wagon, if they casually make love in bunk below mine?*) Thus it was general knowledge that Rolf Mariner was well-heeled. No one stole from a fellow in the Train. The guilt would have been impossible to hide, and meant exile. After pickpocket practice, the spoils were returned. He had declined invitations to gamble, that being considered a lawful way of picking a companion clean.

'We'll soon reach the river,' Fraina said. 'We'll move along, from town to town, as far as our territory stretches. Carnival at every stop. Hectic – well, you've been to tineran pitches, you told me. The thing is, those times we're on the grab. It's us against – is "against" the word? – *zans*. We don't wish harm on the sitters, but we're after everything we can hook. At a time like that, somebody

7

might forget you're not an ordinary sitter. We even fall out with our kind, too often.'

Why? passed across Ivar. *Granted this society hasn't same idea as mine of what constitutes property or contract. Still, if anything, shouldn't nomads be more alert than usual when among aliens, more united and coordinated? But no, I remember from Brotherhood visits to Windhome, excitement always affected them too, till they'd as likely riot among each other as with Landfolk.*

He lost the question. They had halted near an argent-roofed delphi. Stars gleamed, moons glowed, and she held both his hands.

'Let me keep your moneta for you, Rolf,' she offered.

'I know how to stash it. Afterward —',

'There will be an afterward?'

'There's got to be,' she wept, and came to him.

He let go all holds, save upon her. Soon they went into the moon-dappled grotto of the delphi. The luck stayed outside, waiting.

He who had been Jaan the Shoemaker, until Caruith returned after six million swings of the world around the sun, looked from the snag of a tower across the multitude which filled the market place. From around the Sea of Orcus, folk had swarmed hither for Radmas. More were on Mount Cronos this year than ever before in memory or chronicle. They knew the Deliverer was come and would preach unto them.

They made a blue-shadowy dimness beneath the wall whereon he stood: a face, a lancehead, a burnoose, a helmet, picked out of the dusk which still welled between surrounding houses and archways. Virgil had barely risen over the waters, and the Arena blocked off the sight of it, so that a phantom mother-of-pearl was only just beginning to awaken in the great ruin. Some stars remained yet in the sky. Breath indrawn felt razor keen. Released, it ghosted. Endless underneath silence went the noise of the falls.

— Go, Caruith said.

Their body lifted both arms. Amplified, their voice spoke forth into the hush.

'People, I bring you stern tidings.

'You await rescue, first from the grip of the tyrant, next and foremost from the grip of mortality – of being merely, emptily human. You wait for transcendence.

'Look up, then, to yonder stars. Remember what they are, not numbers in a catalog, not balls of burning gas, but reality itself, even as you and I are real. We are not eternal, nor are they; but they are closer to eternity than we. The light of the farthest that we can see has crossed an eon to come to us. And the word it bears is that first it shone upon those who have gone before.

'They shall return. I, in whom lives the mind of Caruith, pledge this, if we will make our world worthy to receive them.

'Yet that may not be done soon nor easily. The road before us is hard, steep, bestrewn with sharp shards. Blood will mark the footprints we leave, and at our backs will whiten the skulls of those who fell by the way. Like one who spoke upon Mother Terra, long after Caruith but long before Jaan, I bring you not peace but a sword.'

X

Boseville was typical of the small towns along the Flone between Nova Roma and the Cimmerian Mountains. A cluster of neatly laid out, blocky but gaily colored buildings upon the right bank, it looked across two kilometers' width of brown stream to a ferry terminal, pastures, and timberlots. At its back, canals threaded westward through croplands. Unlike the gaunt but spacious country along the Ilian Shelf, this was narrow enough, and at the same time rich enough, that many of its farmers could dwell in the community. Besides agriculture, Boseville lived off service industries and minor manufacturing. Most of its trade with the outside world went through the Riverfolk. An inscribed monolith in the plaza commemorated its defenders during the Troubles. Nothing since had greatly disturbed it, including rebellion and an occupation force which it never saw.

Of was that true any longer? More and more, Ivar wondered.

He had accompanied Erannath into town while the tinerans readied their pitches. The chance of his being recognized was negligible, unless the Terrans had issued bulletins on him. He was sure they had not. To judge by what broadcasts he'd seen when King Samlo ordered the Train's single receiver brought forth and tuned in – a fair sample, even though the nomads were not much given to passive watching – the Wildfoss affair had been softpedaled almost to the point of suppression. Evidently Commissioner Desai didn't wish to inspire imitations, nor make a hero figure out of the Firstling of Ilion.

Anyhow, whoever might identify him was most unlikely to call the nearest garrison.

Erannath wanted to explore this aspect of nord culture. It would be useful having a member of it for companion, albeit one from a different area. Since he was of scant help in preparing the shows, Ivar offered to come along. The Ythrian seemed worth cultivation, an interesting and, in his taciturn fashion, likeable sort. Besides, Ivar discovered with surprise that, after the frenetic caravan, he was a bit homesick for his own people.

Or so he thought. Then, when he walked on pavement between walls, he began to feel stifled. How seldom these folk really laughed aloud! How drably they dressed! And where were the male swagger, the female ardor? He wondered how these sitters had gotten any wish to beget the children he saw. Why, they needed to pour their merriment out of a tankard.

Not that the beer wasn't good. He gulped it down. Erannath sipped.

They sat in a waterfront tavern, wood-paneled, rough-raftered, dark and smoky. Windows opened on a view of the dock. A ship, which had unloaded cargo here and taken on consignments for farther downstream, was girding to depart.

'Don't yonder crew want to stay for our carnival?' Ivar asked.

A burly, bearded man, among the several whom Erannath's exotic presence had attracted to this table, puffed his pipe before answering slow: 'No, I don't recall as how Riverfolk ever go to those things. Seems like they, m-m-m, shun tinerans. Maybe not a bad idea.'

'Why?' Ivar challenged. *Are they nonhuman, not to care for Fraina's dancin' or Mikkal's blade arts or –*

'Always trouble. I notice, son, you said, 'Our carnival.' Have care. It brings grief, tryin' to be what you're not born to be.'

'I'll guide my private life, if you please.'

The villager shrugged. 'Sorry.'

'If the nomads are a disturbing force,' Erannath inquired, 'why do you allow them in your territory?'

'They've always been passin' through,' said the oldest man present. 'Tradition gives rights. Includin' right to

101

pick up part of their livin' ' – by entertainments, cheap merchandise, odd jobs, and, yes, teachin' prudence by fleecin' the foolish.'

'Besides,' added a young fellow, 'they do bring color, excitement, touch of danger now and then. We might not live this quietly if Waybreak didn't overnight twice in year.'

The jaws of the bearded man clamped hard on his pipe-stem before he growled, 'We're soon apt to get over-supplied with danger, Jim.'

Ivar stiffened. A tingle went through him. 'What do you mean ... may I ask?'

A folk saying answered him: 'Either much or little.' But another customer a trifle drunk, spoke forth. 'Rumors only. And yet, somethin's astir up and down river, talk of one far south who's promised Elders will return and deliver us from Empire. Could be wishful thinkin', of course. But damn, it feels right somehow. Aeneas is special. I never paid a lot of attention to Dido before; however, lately I've begun givin' more and more thought to everything our filosofs have learned there. I've gone out under Mornin' Star and tried to think myself toward Oneness, and you know, it's helped me. Should we let Impies crush us back into subjects, when we may be right at next stage of evolution?'

The bearded man frowned. 'That's heathenish talk, Bob. Me, I'll hold my trust in God.' To Ivar: 'God's will be done. I never thought Empire was too bad, nor do I now. But it has gone morally rotten, and maybe we are God's chosen instruments to give it cleansin' shock.' After a pause: 'If's true, we'll need powerful outside help. Maybe He's preparin' that for us too.' All their looks bent on Erannath. 'I'm plain valley dweller and don't know anything,' the speaker finished, 'except that unrest is waxin', and hope of deliverance.'

Hastily, the oldster changed the subject.

Night had toppled upon them when Firstling and Ythrian returned to camp. After they left town, stars gave winter-keen guidance to their feet. Otherwise the air was soft, moist, full of growth odors. Gravel scrunched beneath the tread of those bound the same way. Voices tended to break off when a talker noticed the nonhuman, but manners did not allow butting into a serious conversation. Ahead, lamps on poles glowed above wagons widespread among tents. The skirl of music loudened.

'What I seek to understand,' Erannath said, 'is this Aenean resentment of the Imperium. My race would resist such overlordship bitterly. But in human terms, it has on the whole been light, little more than a minor addition to taxes and the surrender of sovereignty over outside, not domestic, affairs. In exchange, you get protection, trade, abundant offplanet contacts. Correct?'

'Perhaps once,' Ivar answered. The beer buzzed in his head. 'But then they set that Snelund creature over us. And since, too many of us are dead in war, while Impies tell us to change ways of our forefathers.'

'Was the late governorship really that oppressive, at least where Aeneas was concerned? Besides, can you not interpret the situation as that the Imperium made a mistake, which is being corrected? True, it cost lives and treasure to force the correction. But you people showed such deathpride that the authorities are shy of pushing you very hard. Simple cooperativeness would enable you to keep virtually all your institutions, or have them restored.'

'How do you know?'

Erannath ignored the question. 'I could comprehend anger at the start of the occupation,' he said, 'if afterward it damped out when the Imperial viceroy proved himself mild. Instead . . . my impression is that at first you Aeneans accepted your defeat with a measure of resignation – but since, your rebellious emotions have swelled; and lacking hopes of independence in reality, you project them into fantasy. *Why?*'

'I reckon we were stunned, and're startin' to recover. And could be those hopes aren't altogether wild.' Ivar stared at the being who trotted along beside him so clumsily, almost painfully. Erannath's crest bobbed to the crutchlike swing of his wings; shadows along the ground dimmed luster of eyes and feathers. 'What're you doin',' anyway, tellin' me I should become meek Imperial subject? You're Ythrian – from free race of hunters, they claim – from rival power we once robbed of plenty real estate – What're you tryin' to preach at me?'

'Nothing. As I have explained before, I am a xenologist specializing in anthropology, here to gather data on your species. I travel unofficially, *hyai*, illegally, to avoid restrictions. More than this it would be unwise to say, even as you have not seen fit to detail your own circumstances. I ask questions in order to get responses which may help me map Aenean attitudes. Enough.'

When an Ythrian finished on that word, he was terminating a discussion. Ivar thought: *Well, why shouldn't he pretend he's harmless? It'll help his case, get him merely deported, if Impies happen to catch him . . . Yes, probably he is spyin', no more. But if I can convince him, make him tell them at home, how we really would fight year after year for our freedom, if they'd give us some aid – maybe they would!*

The blaze of it in him blent into the larger brilliance of being nearly back in camp, nearly back to Fraina.

And then –

They entered a crowd milling between faded rainbows of tentcloth. Lamps overhead glared out the stars. Above the center pitch, a cylinder of colored panes rotated around the brightest light: red, yellow, green, blue, purple flickered feverish across the bodies and faces below. A hawker chanted of his wares, a barker of games of chance, a cook of the spiceballs whose frying filled every nostril around him. Upon a platform three girls danced, and though their performance was free and small-town nords were supposed to be close with a libra, coins glittered in arcs toward their leaping feet. Beneath, the blind and crippled musicians sawed out a melody which had begun to make visitors jig. No alcohol or other drugs were in sight; yet sober riverside men mingled with tinerans in noisy camaraderie, marveled like children at a strolling magician or juggler, whooped, waved, and jostled. Perched here and there upon wagons, the lucks of Waybreak watched.

It surged in Ivar: *My folk! My joy!*

And Fraina came by, scarcely clad, nestled against a middle-aged local whose own garb bespoke wealth. He looked dazed with desire.

Ivar stopped. Beside him, abruptly, Erannath stood on hands to free his wings.

'What goes?' Ivar cried through the racket. Like a blow to the belly, he knew. More often than not, whenever they could, nomad women did this thing.

But not Fraina! We're in love!

She rippled as she walked. Light sheened off blue-black hair, red skin, tilted wide eyes, teeth between half-parted lips. A musk of femaleness surfed outward from her.

'Let go my girl!' Ivar screamed.

He knocked a man over in his plunge. Others voiced anger as he thrust by. His knife came forth. Driven by strength and skill, that heavy blade could take off a human hand at the wrist, or go through a rib to the heart.

The villager saw. A large person, used to command, he held firm. Though unarmed, he crouched in a stance remembered from his military training days.

'Get away, clinkerbrain,' Fraina ordered Ivar.

'No, you slut!' He struck her aside. She recovered too fast to fall. Whirling, he knew in bare time that he really shouldn't kill this yokel, that she'd enticed him and – Ivar's empty hand made a fist. He smote at the mouth. The river-dweller blocked the blow, a shock of flesh and bone, and bawled:

'Help! Peacemen!' That was the alarm word. Small towns kept no regular police; but volunteers drilled and patrolled together, and heeded each other's summons.

'You starting a riot?' she shrilled. A Haisun call followed.

Rivermen tried to push close. Men of the Train tried to deflect them, disperse them. Oaths and shouts lifted. Scuffles broke loose.

Mikkal of Redtop slithered through the mob, bounded

105

toward the fight. His belt was full of daggers. '*Il-krozry ya?*' he barked.

Fraina pointed at Ivar, who was backing her escort against a wagon. '*Vakhabo!*' And in loud Anglic: 'Kill me that dog! He hit me — your sister!'

Mikkal's arm moved. A blade glittered past Ivar's ear, to thunk into a panel and shiver. 'Stop where you're at,' the tineran said. 'Drop your slash. Or you're dead.'

Ivar turned from an enemy who no longer mattered. Grief ripped through him. 'But you're my friend,' he pleaded.

The villager struck him on the neck, kicked him when he had tumbled. Fraina warbled glee, leaped to take the fellow's elbow, crooned of his prowess. Mikkal tossed knife after knife aloft, made a wheel of them, belled when he had the crowd's attention: 'Peace! Peace! We don't want this stranger. We cast him out. You care to jail him? Fine, go ahead. Let's the rest of us get on with our fun.'

Ivar sat up. He barely noticed the aches where he had been hit. Fraina, Waybreak were lost to him. He could no more understand why than he could have understood it if he had suddenly had a heart attack.

But a wanderer's aliveness remained. He saw booted legs close in, and knew the watch was about to haul him off. It jagged across his awareness that then the Imperials might well see a report on him.

His weapon lay on the ground. He snatched it and sprang erect. A war-whoop tore his throat. 'Out of my way!' he yelled after, and started into the ring of men. If need be, he'd cut a road through.

Wings, cannonaded, made gusts of air, eclipsed the lamps. Erannath was aloft.

Six meters of span roofed the throng in quills and racket. What light came through shone burnished on those feathers, those talons. Unarmed though he was, humans ducked away from scything claws, lurched from buffeting wingbones. 'Hither!' Erannath whistled. 'To me, Rolf Mariner! *Raiharo!*'

Ivar sprang through the lane opened for him, out past tents and demon-covered wagons, into night. The aquiline shape glided low above, black athwart the Milky Way. 'Head south,' hissed in darkness. 'Keep near the river-bank.' The Ythrian swung by, returned for a second pass. 'I will fly elsewhere, in their view, draw off pursuit, soon shake it and join you.' On the third swoop: 'Later I will go to the ship which has left, and arrange passage for us. Fair winds follow you.' He banked and was gone.

Ivar's body settled into a lope over the fields. The rest of him knew only: *Fraina, Waybreak. Forever gone? Then what's to live for?*

Nevertheless he fled.

XI

After a boat, guided by Erannath, brought him aboard the *Jade Gate*, Ivar fell into a bunk and a twisting, nightmare-haunted sleep. He was almost glad when a gong-crash roused him a few hours later.

He was alone in a cabin meant for four, cramped but pleasant. Hardwood deck, white-painted overhead, bulkheads lacquered in red and black, were surgically clean. Light came dimly through a brass-framed window to pick out a dresser and washbowl. Foot-thuds and voices made a cheerful clamor beneath the toning of the bronze. He didn't know that rapid, musical language.

I suppose I ought to go see whatever this is, he thought, somewhere in the sorrow of what he had lost. It took his entire will to put clothes on and step out the door.

Crewfolk were bouncing everywhere around. A young man noticed him, beamed, and said, 'Ahoa to you, welcome passenger,' in the singsong River dialect of Anglic.

'What's happenin'?' Ivar asked mechanically.

'We say good morning to the sun. Watch, but please to stand quiet where you are.'

He obeyed. The pre-dawn chill lashed some alertness into him and he observed his surroundings with a faint growth of interest.

Heaven was still full of stars, but eastward turning wan. The shores, a kilometer from either side of the vessel, were low blue shadows, while the water gleamed as if burnished, except where mist went eddying. High overhead, the wings of a vulch at hover caught the first daylight. As gong and crew fell silent, an utter hush returned, not really broken by the faint pulse of engines.

The craft was more than 50 meters in length and 20 in the beam, her timber sides high even at the waist, then at the blunt bow rising sharply in two tiers, three at the rounded stern. Two sizable deckhouses bracketed the amidships section, their roofs fancifully curved at the ends. Fore and aft of them, kingposts supported cargo booms, as well as windmills to help charge the capacitors which powered the vessel. Between reared a mast which could be set with three square sails. Ivar glimpsed Erannath on the topmost yard. He must have spent the night there, for lack of the frame which would suit him better than a bunk.

An outsize red-and-gold flag drooped from an after staff. At the prow the gigantic image of a Fortune Guardian scowled at dangers ahead. In his left hand he bore a sword against them, in his right a lotus flower.

There posed an old man in robe and tasseled cap, beside him a woman similarly clad though bareheaded, near them a band who wielded gong, flutes, pipas, and drum. The crew, on their knees save for what small children were held by their mothers, occupied the decks beneath.

As light strengthened, the stillness seemed to deepen yet further, and frost on brightwork glittered like the stars.

Then Virgil stood out of the east. Radiance shivered across waters. The ancient raised his arms and cried a brief chant, the people responded, music rollicked, everybody cheered, the ship's business resumed.

Ivar stretched numbed hands toward the warmth that began to flow out of indigo air. Vapors steamed away and he saw the cultivated lands roll green, a flock of beasts, an early horseman or a roadborne vehicle, turned into toys by distance. Closer were the brood of *Jade Gate*. A stubby tug drew a freight-laden barge, two trawlers spread their nets, and in several kayaks, each accompanied by an osel, herders kept a pod of river pigs moving along.

For those not on watch, the first order of the day was evidently to get cleaned up. Some went below, some peeled off their clothes and dived overboard, to frisk about till they were ready to climb back on a Jacob's ladder. Merriment loudened. It was not like tineran glee. Such japes as he heard in Anglic were gentle rather than stinging, laughter was more a deep clucking than a shrill peal. Whoever passed near Ivar stopped to make a slight bow and bid him welcome aboard.

They're civilized without bein' rigid, strong without bein' cruel, happy without bein' foolish, shrewd without bein' crooked, respectful of learnin' and law, useful in their work, he knew dully; *but they are not wild red wanderers.*

Handsome enough, of course. They averaged a bit taller than tinerans, shorter than nords, the build stocky, skin tawny, hair deep black where age had not bleached it. Heads were round, faces broad and high of cheekbones, eyes brown and slightly oblique, lips full, noses tending to flatness though beaks did occur. Only old men let beards grow, and both sexes banged their hair across the brows and bobbed it off just under the ears. Alike too was working garb, blue tunics and bell-bottomed trousers. Already now, before the frost was off, many went barefoot; and the nudity of the swimmers showed a fondness for elaborate tattoos.

He knew more about them than he had about the nomads. It was still not much. This was his first time aboard a craft of theirs, aside from once when one which plied as far north as Nova Roma held open house. Otherwise his experience was confined to casual reading and a documentary program recorded almost a century ago.

Nevertheless the Kuang Shih had bonds to the ruling culture of Aeneas, in a way that the tinerans did not. They furnished the principal transportation for goods, and for humans who weren't in a hurry, along the entire lower Flone – as well as fish, flesh, and fiber taken from the river, and incidental handicrafts, exchanged for the products and energy recharges of industrial culture.

If they held themselves aloof when ashore, it was not due to hostility. They were amply courteous in business dealings, downright cordial to passengers. It was simply that their way of life satisfied them, and had little in common with that of rooted people. The most conservative Landfolk maintained less far-reaching and deep-going blood ties – every ship and its attendants an extended

110

family, strictly exogamous and, without making a fuss about it, moral – not to speak of faith, tradition, law, custom, arts, skills, hopes, fears altogether different.

I dreamed Waybreak might take me in, and instead it cast me out. Jade Gate – is that her name? – will no doubt treat me kindly till we part, but I'd never imagine bein' taken into her.

No matter. O Fraina!

'Sir –',

The girl who shyly addressed him brought back the dancer, hurtfully, by her very unlikeness. Besides her race, she was younger, he guessed eight or nine, demurely garbed so that he couldn't be sure how much her slight figure had begun to fill out. (Not that he cared.) Her features were more delicate than usual, and she bowed lower to him.

'Your pardon, please, welcome passenger,' she said in a thin voice. 'Do you care for breakfast?'

She offered him a bowl of cereals, greens, and bits of meat cooked together, a cup of tea, a napkin, and eating utensils such as he was used to. He grew aware that crewfolk were in line at the galley entrance. A signal must have called them without his noticing through the darkness that muffled him. Most found places on deck to hunker and eat in convivial groups.

'Why, why, thank you,' Ivar said. He wasn't hungry, but supposed he could get the food down. It smelled spicy.

'We have one dining saloon below, with table and benches, if you wish,' the girl told him.

'No!' The idea of being needlessly enclosed, after desert heavens and then nights outdoors in valley summer with Fraina sickened him.

'Pardon, pardon.' She drew back a step. He realized he had yelled.

'I'm sorry,' he said. 'I'm in bad way. Didn't mean to sound angry. Right here will be fine.' She smiled and set her burden down on the planks, near a bulwark against which he could rest, 'Uh, my name is Iv – Rolf Mariner.'

'This person is Jao, fourth daughter to Captain Riho Mea. She bade me to see to your comfort. Can I help you in any wise, Sir Mariner?' The child dipped her head above bridged fingertips.

'I . . . well, I don't know.' *Who can help me, ever again?*

'Perhaps if I stay near you one while, show you over our ship later? You may think of something then.'

Her cleanliness reminded him of his grime and sour sweat-smell, unkempt hair and stubbly chin. 'I, uh, I should have washed before breakfast.'

'Eat, and I will lead you to the bath, and bring what else you need to your cabin. You are our only guest this trip.' Her glance swept aloft and came aglow. 'Ai, the beautiful flyer from the stars. How could I forget? Can you summon him while I fetch his food?'

'He eats only meat, you know. Or, no, I reckon you wouldn't. Anyhow, I'll bet he's already caught piece of wild game. He sees us, and he'll come down when he wants to.'

'If you say it, sir. May I bring my bowl, or would you rather be undisturbed?'

'Whatever you want,' Ivar grunted. 'I'm afraid I'm poor company this mornin'.'

'Perhaps you should sleep further? My mother the captain will not press you. But she said that sometime this day she must see you and your friend, alone.'

Passengers had quarters to themselves if and when a vessel was operating below capacity in that regard. Crew did not. Children were raised communally from birth . . . physically speaking. The ties between them and their parents were strong, far stronger than among tinerans, although their ultimate family was the ship as a whole. Married couples were assigned cubicles, sufficient for sleeping and a few personal possessions. Certain soundproofed cabins were available for study, meditation, or similar purposes. Aside from this, privacy of the body did not exist, save for chaplain and captain.

The latter had two chambers near the bridge. The larger was living-room, office, and whatever else she deemed necessary.

Her husband greeted her visitors at the door, then

politely excused himself. He was her third, Jao had remarked to Ivar. Born on the *Celestial Peace*, when quite a young girl Mea had been wedded by the usual prearrangement to a man of the *Red Bird Banner*. He drowned when a skiff capsized; the Flone had many treacheries. She used her inheritance in shrewd trading, garnering wealth until the second officer of the *Jade Gate* met her at a fleet festival and persuaded her to move in with him. He was a widower, considerably older than she; it was a marriage of convenience. But most were, among the Kuang Shih. Theirs functioned well for a number of years, efficiently combining their talents and credit accounts, incidentally producing Jao's youngest sister. At last an artery in his brain betrayed him, and rather than linger useless he requested the Gentle Cup. Soon afterward, the captain died also, and the officers elected Riho Mea his successor. Lately she had invited Haleku Uan of the *Yellow Dragon* to marry her. He was about Ivar's age.

Jao must have read distaste on the Firstling's countenance, for she had said quietly: 'They are happy together. He is merely one carpenter, nor can she raise him higher, nor can he inherit from her except in *lung* – pro-por-tion to children of hers that are his too; and she is past child-bearing and he knew it.'

He thought at the time that she was defending her mother, or even her stepfather. As days passed, he came to believe she had spoken unspectacular truth. The Riverfolk had their own concept of individuality.

To start with, what did riches mean? Those who were not content to draw their regular wage, but drove personal bargains with the Ti Shih, the Shorefolk, could obtain no more than minor luxuries for themselves; a ship had room for nothing else. Beyond that, they could simply make contributions to the floating community. That won rewards of prestige. But anybody could get the same by outstanding service or, to a lesser extent, unusual prowess or talent.

Prestige might bring promotion. However, authority gave small chance for self-aggrandizement either, in a society which followed the same peaceful round through century after century.

Why, then, did the people of the land think of Riverfolk as hustlers, honest but clever, courteous but ambitious? Ivar decided that these were the personality types who dealt with the people of the land. The rest kept pretty much to themselves. And yet, that latter majority had abundant ways to express itself.

These ideas came to him later. They did have their genesis the evening he first entered the cabin of Captain Riho.

Sunbeams struck level, amber-hued, through the starboard windows of the main room. They sheened off a crystal on a shelf, glowed off a scroll of trees and calligraphy above. The chamber was so austerely furnished as to feel spacious. In one corner, half-hidden by a carved screen, stood a desk and a minimum of data and communications equipment. In another stood a well-filled bookcase. Near the middle of the reed matting which covered the deck was a padded, ring-shaped bench, with a low table at the center and a couple of detachable back rests for the benefit of visiting Ti'Shih.

The skipper came forward, and Ivar began changing his mind about her and her man. She was of medium height, plump yet extraordinarily light on her feet. Years had scarcely touched the snubnosed, dark-ivory face, apart from crinkles around the eyes and scattered white in the hair. Her mouth showed capacity for a huge grin. She wore the common blue tunic and trousers, zori on bare feet, fireburst tattoo on the arm which slid from its sleeve as she offered her hand. The palm was warm and callused.

'Ahoa, welcome passengers.' Her voice verged on hoarseness. 'Will you not honor my by taking seats and refreshment?' She bowed them toward the bench, and from the inner room fetched a trayful of tea, cakes, and slices of raw ichthyoid flesh. The ship lurched in a cross-current off a newly formed sandbar, and she came near dropping her load. She rapped out a phrase. Catching Erannath's alert look, she translated it for him. Ivar was a little shocked. He had thought soldiers knew how to curse.

She kicked off her sandals, placed herself crosslegged opposite her guests, and opened a box of cigars that stood

114

on the table. 'You want?' she offered. They both declined 'Mind if I do?' Ivar didn't – *What has creation got that's worth mindin'?* – and Erannath stayed mute though a ripple passed over his plumes. Captain Riho stuck a fat black cylinder between her teeth and got it ignited. Smoke smote the air.

'I hope you are comfortable?' she said. 'Sir . . . Erannath . . . if you will give my husband the specs for your kind of bed –'

'Later, thank you,' the flyer snapped. 'Shall we get to the point?'

'Fine. Always I was taught, Ythrians do not waste words. Here is my first pleasure to meet your breed. If you will please to pardon seeming rudeness – you *are* aboard curious-wise. I would not pry but must know certain things, like where you are bound.'

'We are not sure. How far do you go?'

'Clear to the Linn, this trip. Solstice comes near, our Season of Returnings,'

'Fortunate for us, if I happen to have cash enough on my person to buy that long a passage for two.' Erannath touched his pocketed apron.

I have none, Ivar thought. *Fraina switled me out of everything, surely knowin' I'd have to leave Train. Only, did she have to provoke my leavin' so soon?* He paid no attention to the dickering.

' – well,' Erannath finished. 'We can come along to the end of the river if we choose. We may debark earlier.'

Riho Mea frowned behind an acrid blue veil. 'Why might that be?' she demanded. 'You understand, sirs, I have one ship to worry about, and these are much too interesting times.'

'Did I not explain fully enough, last night when I arrived on board? I am a scientist studying your planet. I happened to join a nomad group shortly after Rolf Mariner did – for reasons about which he has the right not to get specific. As often before, violence lofted at the carnival. It would have led either to his death at nomad hands, or his arrest by the Bosevilleans. I helped him escape.'

'Yes, those were almost your exact words.'

115

'I intended no offense in repeating them, Captain. Do humans not prefer verbal redundancy?'

'You miss my course, Sir Erannath,' she said a touch coldly. 'You have *not* explained enough. We could take you on in emergency, for maybe that did save lives. However, today is not one such hurry. Please to take refreshment, you both, as I will, to show good faith. I accuse you of nothing, but you are intelligent and realize I must be sure we are not harboring criminals. Matters are very skittly, what with the occupation.'

She laid her cigar in an ashtray, crunched a cookie, slurped a mouthful of tea. Ivar bestirred himself to follow suit. Erannath laid claws on a strip of meat and ripped it with his fangs. 'Good,' said the woman. 'Will you tell your tale, Sir Mariner?'

Ivar had spent most of the day alone, stretched on his bunk. He didn't care what became of him, and his mind wasn't working especially well. But from a sense of duty, or whatever, he had rehearsed his story like a dog mumbling a bone. It plodded forth:

'I'm not guilty of anything except disgust, Captain, and I don't think that's punishable, unless Impies have made it illegal since I left. You know, besides bannin' free speech, they razed McCormac Memorial in Nova Roma. My parents . . . well, they don't condone Imperium, but they kept talkin' about compromise and how maybe we Aeneans were partly in wrong, till I couldn't stand it. I went off into wilderness to be by myself – common practice ashore, you probably know – and met tinerans. Train there. Why not join them for while? It'd be change for me, and I had skills they could use. Last night, as my friend told, senseless brawl happened. I think, now, it was helped along by tinerans I'd thought were my . . . friends, so they could keep money and valuable rif – article I'd left with them.'

'As a matter of fact,' Erannath said, 'he is technically guilty of assault upon a Boseville man. He did no harm, though. He merely suffered it. I doubt that any complaint has been filed. These incidents are frequent at those affairs, and everyone knows it.' He paused. 'They do not know why this is. I do.'

116

Startled from his apathy, Ivar regarded the Ythrian almost as sharply as Riho Mea did. He met their gazes in turn – theirs were the eyes which dropped – and let time go by before he said with no particular infection: 'Perhaps I should keep my discovery for the Intelligence service of the Domain. However, it is of marginal use to us, whereas Aeneans will find it a claw struck into their backs.'

The captain chewed her cigar before she answered: 'You mean you will tell me if I let you stay aboard.' Erannath didn't bother to speak his response. 'How do I know – ', She caught herself. 'Please to pardon this person. I wonder what evidence you have for whatever you will say.'

'None,' he admitted. 'Once given the clue, you humans can confirm the statement.'

'Say on.'

'If I do, you will convey us, and ask no further questions?'

'I will judge you by your story.'

Erannath studied her. At length he said: 'Very well, for I hear your deathpride.' He was still during a heartbeat. 'The breath of tineran life is that creature they call the luck, keeping at least one in every wagon. *We* call it the slinker.'

'Hoy,' broke from Ivar, 'how would you know – ?'

'Ythrians have found the three-eyed beasts on a number of planets.' Erannath did not keep the wish to kill out of his voice; and his feathers began to stand erect. 'Not on our home. God did not lay that particular snare for us. But on several worlds like it, which naturally we investigated more thoroughly than your race normally does – the lesser terrestroid globes. Always slinkers are associated with fragments of an earlier civilization, such as Aeneas has. We suspect they were spread by that civilization, whether deliberately, accidentally, or through their own design. Some of us theorize that they caused its downfall.'

'Wait a minute,' Ivar protested. 'Why have we humans never heard of them?'

'You have, on this world,' Erannath replied. 'Probably elsewhere too, but quite incidentally, notes buried in your data banks, because you are more interested in larger and moister planets. And for our part, we have had no special reason to tell you. We learned what slinkers are early in our starfaring, when first we had scant contact with Terrans, afterward hostile contact. We developed means to eradicate them. They long ago ceased to be a problem in the Domain, and no doubt few Ythrians, even, have heard of them nowadays.'

Too much information, too big a universe, passed through Ivar.

'Besides,' Erannath went on, 'it seems humans are more susceptible than Ythrians. Our two brain-types are rather differently organized, and the slinkers' resonate better with yours.'

'Resonate?' Captain Riho scowled.

'The slinker nervous system is an extraordinary well-developed telepathic transceiver,' Erannath said. 'Not of thoughts. We really don't know what level of reasoning ability the little abominations possess. Nor do we care, in the way that human scientists might. When we had established what they do, our overwhelming desire was merely to slay them.'

'What do they do, then?' Ivar asked around a lump of nausea.

'They violate the innermost self. In effect, they receive emotions and feed these back; they act as amplifiers,' It was terrifying to see Erannath where he crouched. His dry phrases ripped forth. 'Perhaps those intelligences you call the Builders developed them as pets, pleasure sources. The Builders may have had cooler spirits than you or we do. Or perhaps they degenerated from the effects, and died.

'I said that the resonance with us Ythrians is weak. Nonetheless we found explorers and colonists showing ugly behavior. It would start as bad dreams, go on to murder-ously short temper, to year-around ovulation, to – Enough. We tracked down the cause and destroyed it.

'You humans are more vulnerable, it appears. You are lucky that slinkers prefer the deserts. Otherwise all Aeneans might be addicted.

'Yes, addiction. They don't realize it themselves, they think they keep these pets merely because of custom, but the tinerans are a nation of addicts. Every emotion they begin to feel is fed back into them, amplified, radiated, reamplified, to the limit of what the organism can generate. Do you marvel that they act like constitutional psychopaths? That they touch no drugs in their caravans, but require drugs when away, and cannot survive being away very long?

'At that, they must have adapted; there must have been natural selection. Many can think craftily, like the female who reaved your holdings, Rolf Mariner. I wonder if her kind are not born dependent on the poison.

'You should thank her, though, that she got you cast out as early as she did!'

Ivar covered his face. 'O God, no.'

'I need clean sky and a beast to hunt,' Erannath grated. 'I will be back tomorrow.'

He left. Ivar wept on Riho Mea's breast. She held him close, stroked his hair and murmured.

'You'll get well, poor dear, we'll make you well. The river flows, flows, flows . . . Here is peace.'

Finally she left him on her husband's bunk, exhausted of tears and ready to sleep. The light through the windows was gold-red. She changed into her robe and went onto the foredeck, to join chaplain and crew in wishing the sun goodnight.

XII

South of Cold Landing the country began to grow steep and stony, and the peaks of the Cimmerian range hung ghostlike on its horizon. There the river would flow too swiftly for the herds. But first it broadened to fill a valley with what was practically a lake: the Green Bowl, where ships bound farther south left their animals in care of a few crewfolk, to fatten on water plants and molluscoids.

Approaching that place, Ivar paddled his kayak with an awkwardness which drew amiable laughter from his young companions. They darted spearfly-fast over the surface; or, leaping into the stream, they raced the long-bodied webfooted brown osels which served them for herd dogs, while he wallowed more clumsily than the fat, flippered, snouted chuho — water pigs — which were being herded.

He didn't mind. Nobody is good at everything, and he was improving at a respectable pace.

Wavelets blinked beneath violet heaven, chuckled, swirled, joined livingly with his muscles to drive the kayak onward. This was the reality which held him, not stiff crags and dusty-green brush on yonder hills. A coolness rose from it, to temper windless warmth of air. It smelled damp, rich. Ahead, *Jade Gate* was a gaudily painted castle; farther on moved a sister vessel; trawlers and barges already waited at Cold Landing. Closer at hand, the chuho browsed on wetcress. Now and then an osel heeded the command of a boy or girl and sped to turn back a straggler. Herding on the Flone was an ideal task, he thought. Exertion and alertness kept a person fully alive, while nevertheless letting him enter into that peace, beauty, majesty which was the river.

To be sure, he was a mere spectator, invited along because these youngsters liked him. That was all right.

Jao maneuvered her kayak near his. 'Goes it well?' she asked. 'You do fine, Rolf.' She flushed, dropped her glance, and added timidly: 'I think not I could do that fine in your wilderness. But sometimes I would wish to try.'

'Sometime . . . I'd like to take you,' he answered.

On this duty in summer, one customarily went nude, so as to be ready at any time for a swim. Ivar was too fair-skinned for that, and wore a light blouse and trousers elsewhere. The girl was far too young for the thoughts she was old enough to arouse – besides being foreign to him – no, never mind that, what mattered was that she was sweet and trusting and –

Oh, damnation, I will not be ashamed of thinkin' she's female. Thinkin' is all it'll ever amount to. And that I do, that I do, measures how far I've gone toward gainin' back my sanity.

The gaiety and the ceremoniousnesses aboard ship; the little towns where they stopped to load and unload, and the long green reaches between; the harsh wisdom of Eran-nath, serene wisdom of Iang Weii the chaplain, pragmatic wisdom of Riho Mea the captain, counseling him; the friendliness of her husband and other people his age; the, yes, the way this particular daughter of hers followed him everywhere around; always the river, mighty as time, days and nights, days and nights, feeling like a longer stretch than they had been, like a fortaste of eternity: these had healed him.

Fraina danced no more through his dreams. He could summon a memory for inspection, and understand how the reality had never come near being as gorgeous as it seemed, and pity the wanderers and vow to bring them aid when he became able.

When would that be? How? How? He was an outlaw. As he emerged from his hurt, he saw ever more clearly how pas-sive he had been. Erannath had rescued him and provided him with this berth – why? What reason, other than pleasure, had he to go to the river's end? And if he did,

121

what next?

He drew breath. *Time to start actin' again, instead of bein' acted on. First thing I need is allies.*

Jao's cry brought him back. She pointed to the nigh shore. Her paddle flew. He toiled after. Their companions saw, left one in charge of the herd, and converged on the same spot.

A floating object lay caught in reeds: a sealed wooden box, arch-lidded, about two meters in length. Upon its black enamel he identified golden symbols of Sun, Moons, and River.

'*Ai-ya, ai-ya, ai-ya*,' Jao chanted. Suddenly solemn, the rest chimed in. Though ignorant of the Kuang Shih's primary language, Ivar could recognize a hymn. He held himself aside.

The herders freed the box. Swimmers pushed it out into midstream. Osels under sharp command kept *chuhos* away. It drifted on south. They must have seen aboard *Jade Gate*, because the flag went to half-mast.

'What was that?' Ivar then ventured to ask.

Jao brushed the wet locks off her brow and answered, surprised, 'Did you not know? That was one coffin.'

'Huh? I – Wait, I beg your pardon, I do seem to remember –'

'All our dead go down the river, down the Yun Kow at last – the Linn – to the Tien Hu, what you call the Sea of Orcus. It is our duty to launch again any we find stranded.' In awe: 'I have heard about one seer who walks there now, who will call back the Old Shen from the stars. Will our dead then rise from the waters?'

Tatiana Thane had never supposed she could mind being by herself. She had always had a worldful of things to do, read, watch, listen to, think about.

Daytimes still weren't altogether bad. Her present work was inherently solitary: study, meditation, cut-and-dry, bit by bit the construction of a semantic model of the language spoken around Mount Hamilcar on Dido, which would enable humans to converse with the natives on a more basic level than pidgin allowed. Her dialogues were

122

with a computer, or occasionally by vid with the man under whom she had studied, who was retired to his estate in Heraclea and too old to care about politics.

Since she became a research fellow, students had treated her respectfully. Thus she took a while – when she missed Ivar so jaggedly, when she was so haunted by fear for him – to realize that this behavior had become an avoidance. Nor was she overtly snubbed at faculty rituals, meetings, dining commons, chance encounters in corridor or quad. These days, people didn't often talk animatedly. Thus likewise she took a while to realize that they never did with her any more, and, except for her parents, had let her drop from their social lives.

Slowly her spirit wore down.

The first real break in her isolation came about 1700 hours on a Marsday. She was thinking of going to bed, however poorly she would sleep. Outside was a darker night than ordinary, for a great dustcloud borne along the tropopause had veiled the stars. Lavinia was a blurred dim crescent above spires and domes. Wind piped. She sprawled in her largest chair and played with Frumious Bandersnatch. The tadmouse ran up and down her body, from shins to shoulders and back, trilling. The comfort was as minute as himself.

The knocker rapped. For a moment she thought she hadn't heard aright. Then her pulse stumbled, and she nearly threw her pet off in her haste to open the door. He clung to her sweater and whistled indignation.

A man stepped through, at once closing the door behind him. Though the outside air that came along was cold as well as ferric-harsh, no one would ordinarily have worn a nightmask. He doffed his and she saw the bony middle-aged features of Gabriel Stewart. They had last been together on Dido. His work was to know the Hamilcar region backwards and forwards, guide scientific parties and see to their well-being.

'Why . . . why . . . hello,' she said helplessly.

'Draw your blinds,' he ordered. 'I'd as soon not be glimpsed from beneath.'

She stared. Her backbone pringled. 'Are you in trouble, Gabe?'

'Not officially – yet.'

'I'd no idea you were on Aeneas. Why didn't you call?'

'Calls can be monitored. Now cover those windows, will you.'

She obeyed. Stewart removed his outer garments. 'It's good to see you again,' she ventured.

'You may not think that after I've spoken my piece.' He unbent a little. 'Though maybe you will. I recall you as bold lass, in your quiet way. And I don't suppose First-lin' of Ilion made you his girl for nothin'.'

'Do you have news of Ivar?' she cried.

'Fraid not. I was hopin' you would . . . Well, let's talk.'

He refused wine but let her brew a pot of tea. Meanwhile he sat, puffed his pipe, exchanged accounts of everything that had happened since the revolution erupted. He had gone outsystem, in McCormac's hastily assembled Intelligence corps, and admitted ruefully that meanwhile the war was lost in his own bailiwick. As far as he could discover, upon being returned after the defeat, some Terran agent had not only managed to rescue the Admiral's wife from Snelund – a priceless bargaining counter, no doubt – but while on Dido had hijacked a patriot vessel whose computer held the latest codes . . . 'I got wonderin' about possibility of organizin' Didonians to help fight on, as guerrillas or even as navy personnel. At last I hitched ride to Aeneas and looked up my friend – m-m, never mind his name; he's of University too, on a secondary campus. Through him, I soon got involved in resistance movement.'

'There is one?'

He regarded her somberly. 'You ask that, Ivar Frederiksen's bride to be?'

'I was never consulted.' She put teapot and cups on a table between them, sank to the edge of a chair opposite his, and stared at the fingers wrestling in her lap. 'He – It was crazy impulse, what he did. Wasn't it?'

'Maybe then. Not any longer. Of course, your dear Commissioner Desai would prefer you believe that.'

Tatiana braced herself and met his look. 'Granted,' she said, 'I've seen Desai several times. I've passed on his remarks to people I know – not endorsin' them, simply passin' them on. Is that why I'm ostracized? Surely University folk should agree we can't have too much data input.'

'I've queried around about you,' Stewart replied. 'It's curious kind of tension. Outsider like me can maybe identify it better than those who're bein' racked. On one hand, you are Ivar Frederiksen's girl. It could be dangerous gettin' near you, because he may return any day. That makes cowardly types ride clear of you. Then certain others – Well, you do have *mana*. I can't think of better word for it. They sense you're big medicine, because of bein' his chosen, and it makes them vaguely uncomfortable. They aren't used to that sort of thing in their neat, scientifically ordered lives. So they find excuses to themselves for postponin' any resumption of former close relations with you.

'On other hand' – he trailed a slow streamer of smoke – 'you are, to speak blunt, lettin' yourself be used by enemy. You may think you're relayin' Desai's words for whatever those're worth as information. But mere fact that you will receive him, will talk civilly with him, means you lack full commitment. And this gets you shunned by those who have it. Cut off, you don't know how many already do. Well, they *are* many. And number grows day by day.'

He leaned forward. 'When I'd figured how matters stand, I had to come see you, Tatiana. My guess is, Desai's half persuaded you to try wheedlin' Frederiksen into surrender, if and when you two get back in touch. Well, you mustn't. At very least, hold apart from Impies.' Starkly: 'Freedom movement's at point where we can start makin' examples of collaborators. I know you'd never be one, consciously. Don't let yon Desai bastard snare you.'

'But,' she stammered in her bewilderment, 'but what do you mean to do? What can you hope for? And Ivar – he's nothin' but young man who got carried away – fugitive, completely powerless, if, if, if he's still alive at all –'

'He is,' Stewart told her. 'I don't know where or how, or what he's doin', but he is. Word runs too widely to have no truth behind it.' His voice lifted. 'You've heard also. You must have. Signs, tokens, precognitions . . . Never mind his weaklin' father. Ivar is rightful leader of free Aeneas – when Builders return, which they will, which they will. And you are his bride who will bear his son that Builders will make more than human.'

Belief stood incandescent in his eyes.

XIII

South of the Green Bowl, hills climbed ever faster. Yet for a while the stream continued to flow peaceful. Ivar wished his blood could do likewise.

Seeking tranquillity, he climbed to the foredeck for a clear view across night. He stopped short when he spied others on hand than the lookout who added eyes to the radar.

Through a crowd of stars and a torrent of galaxy, Creusa sped past Lavinia. Light lay argent ashore, touching crests and crags, swallowed by shadows farther down. It shivered and sparked on the water, made ghostly the sails which had been set to use a fair wind. That air murmured cold through quietness and a rustle at the bows.

Fore and aft, separated by a few kilometers for safety, glowed the lights of three companion vessels. No few were bound this way, to celebrate the Season of Returnings.

Ivar saw the lookout on his knees under the figurehead, and a sheen off Erannath's plumage, and Riho Mea and Iang Weii in their robes. Captain and chaplain were completing a ritual, it seemed. Mute, now and then lifting hands or bowing heads, they had watched the moons draw near and again apart.

'Ah,' Mea gusted. The crewman rose.

'I beg pardon,' Erannath said. 'Had I known a religious practice was going on, I would not have descended here. I stayed because that was perhaps less distracting than my takeoff would have been.'

'No harm done,' Mea assured him. 'In fact, the sight of you coming down gave one extra glory.'

'Besides,' Iang said in his mild voice, 'though this is

127

something we always do at certain times, it is not strictly religious.' He stroked his thin white beard. 'Have we Kuang Shih religion, in the same sense as the Christians or Jews of the Ti Shih or the pagans of the tineran society? This is one matter of definition, not so? We preach nothing about gods. To most of us that whole subject is not important. Whether or not gods, or God, exist, is it not merely one scientific question – cosmological?'

'Then what do you hunt after?' the Ythrian asked.

'Allness,' the chaplain replied. 'Unity, harmony. Through rites and symbols. We know they are only rites and symbols. But they say to the opened mind what words cannot. The River is ongoingness, fate; the Sun is life; Moons and Stars are the transhuman.'

'We contemplate these things,' Riho Mea added. 'We try to merge with them, with everything that is.' Her glance fell on Ivar. 'Ahoa, Sir Mariner,' she called. 'Come, join our party.'

Iang, who could stay solemn longer than her, continued: 'Our race, or yours, has less gift for the *whole ch'an* – understanding – than the many-minded people of the Morning Star. However, when the Old Shen return, mankind will gain the same immortal singleness, and have moreover the strengths we were forced to make in ourselves, in order to endure being alone in our skulls.'

'You too?' Erannath snapped. 'Is everybody on Aeneas waiting for these mentors and saviors?'

'More and more, we are,' Mea said. 'Up the Yun Kow drifts word –'

'Ivar, who had approached, felt as if touched by lightnings. Her gave had locked on him. He knew: *These are not just easy-goin', practical sailors. I should've seen it earlier. That coffin – and fact they're bound on dangerous trip to honor both their ancestors and their descendants – and now this – no, they're as profoundly eschatological as any Bible-and-blaster yeoman.*

'Word about liberation?' he exclaimed.

'Aye, though that's the bare beginning,' she answered. Iang nodded, while the lookout laid hand on sheath knife. Abruptly she said, 'Would you like to talk about this . . .

128

Rolf Mariner? I'm ready for one drink and cigar in my cabin anyway.'

His pulses roared. 'You also, good friend and wise man,' he heard her propose to Iang.

'I bid you goodnight, then,' Erannath said.

The chaplain bowed to him. 'Forgive us our confidentiality.'

'Maybe we should invite you along,' Mea said. 'Look here, you are not one plain scientist like you claim. You are one Ythrian secret agent, collecting information on the key human planet Aeneas, no?' When he stayed silent, she laughed. 'Never mind. Point is, we and you have the same enemy, the Terran Empire. At least, Ythri shouldn't mind if the Empire loses territory.'

'Afterward, though,' Iang murmured, 'I cannot help but wonder how well the carnivore soul may adapt to the enlightenment the Old Shen will bring.'

Moonlight turned Erannath's feather to silver, his eyes to mercury. 'Do you look on your species as a chosen people?' he said, equally low. At once he must have regretted his impulse, for he went on: 'Your intrigues are no concern of mine. Nor do I care if you decide I am something more than an observer. If you are opposed to the occupation authorities, presumably you won't betray me to them. I wish to go on a night hunt. May fortune blow your way.'

His wings spread, from rail to rail. The wind of his rising gusted and boomed. For a while he gleamed high aloft, before vision lost him among the stars.

Mea led Iang and Ivar to her quarters. Her husband greeted them, and this time he stayed: a bright and resolute young man, the dream of freedom kindled within him.

When the door had been shut, the captain said: 'Ahoa, Ivar Frederiksen, Firstling of Ilion.'

'How did you know?' he whispered.

She grinned, and went for the cigar she had bespoken. 'How obvious need it be? Surely that Ythrian has suspected. Why else should he care about one human waif? But to him, humans are so foreign – so alike-seeming – and besides, being a spy, he couldn't dare use data services – he

129

must have been holding back, trying to confirm his guess. I called up Nova Roma public files, asked for pictures and – O-ah, no fears. I am one merchant myself, I know how to disguise my real intents.'

'You, you will . . . help me?' he faltered.

They drew close around him, the young man, the old man, the captain. 'You will help *us*,' Iang said. 'You are the Firstling – our rightful leader that every Aenean can follow – to throw out those mind-stifling Terrans and make ready for the Advent that is promised – What can we do for you, lord?'

Chunderban Desai broke the connection and sat for a while staring before him. His wife, who had been out of the room, came back in and asked what was wrong.

'Peter Jowett is dead,' he told her.

'Oh, no.' The two families had become friendly in the isolation they shared.

'Murdered.'

'What?' The gentleness in her face gave way to horror.

'The separatists,' he sighed. 'It has to be. No melodramatic message left. He was killed by a rifle bullet as he left his office. But who else hated him?'

She groped for the comfort of his hand. He returned the pressure. 'A real underground?' she said. 'I didn't know.'

'Nor I, until now. Oh, I got reports from planted agents, from surveillance devices, all the usual means. Something was brewing, something being organized. Still, I didn't expect outright terrorism this soon, if ever.'

'The futility is nearly the worst part. What chance have they?'

He rose from his chair. Side by side, they went to a window. It gave on the garden of the little house they rented in the suburbs: alien plants spiky beneath alien stars and moons, whose light fell on the frosted helmet of a marine guard.

'I don't know,' he said. Despite the low gravity, his back slumped. 'They must have some. It isn't the hopeless who rebel, it's those who think they see the end of their particular tunnels, and grow impatient.'

'You have given them hope, dear.'

'Well . . . I came here thinking they'd accept their military defeat and work with me like sensible people, to get their planet reintegrated with the Empire. After all, except for the Snelund episode, Aeneas has benefited from the Imperium, on balance; and we're trying to set up precautions against another Snelund. Peter agreed. Therefore they killed him. Who's next?'

Her fingers tightened on his. 'Poor Olga. The poor children. Should I call her tonight or, or what?'

He stayed in the orbit of his own thoughts. 'Rumors of a deliverer – not merely a political liberator, but a savior – no, a whole race of saviors – that's what's driving the Aeneans,' he said. 'And not the dominant culture alone. The others too. In their different ways, they all wait for an apocalypse.'

'Who is preaching it?'

He chuckled saidly. 'If I knew that, I could order the party arrested. Or, better yet, try to suborn him. Or them. But my agents hear nothing except these vague rumors. Never forget how terribly few we are, and how marked, on an entire world . . . We did notice what appeared to be a centering of the rumors on the Orcan area. We investigated. We drew blank, at least as far as finding any proof of illegal activities. The society there, and its beliefs, always have been founded on colossal prehuman ruins, and evidently has often brought forth millennialist prophets. Our people had more urgent things to do than struggle with the language and ethos of some poverty-stricken dwellers on a dead sea floor.' His tone strengthened. 'Though if I had the personnel for it, I would probe further indeed. This wouldn't be the first time that a voice from the desert drove nations mad.'

The phone chimed again. He muttered a swear word before he returned to accept the call. It was on scramble code, which automatically heterodyned the audio output so that Desai's wife could not hear what came to him a couple of meters away. The screen was vacant, too.

She could see the blaze on his face; and she heard him shout after the conversation ended, as he surged from his chair: 'Brahma's mercy, yes! We'll catch him and end this thing!'

XIV

Jade Gate had nearly reached the Linn when the Terrans came.

The Cimmerian Mountains form the southern marge of Ilion. The further south the Flone goes through them, until its final incredible plunge off the continental rim, the steeper and deeper is the gorge it has cut for itself. In winter it runs quiet between those walls, under a sheath of ice. But by midsummer, swollen with melt off the polar cap, it is a race, and they must have skillful pilots who would venture along that violence.

At the port rail of the main deck, Ivar and Jao watched. Water brawled, foamed, spouted off rocks, filled air with an ongoing cannonade and made the vessel rock and shudder. Here the stream had narrowed to a bare 300 meters between heaped boulders and talus. Behind, cliffs rose for a pair of kilometers. The rock was gloomy-hued and there was only a strip of sky to see, from which Virgil had already sunk. The brighter stars gleamed in its duskiness. Down under the full weight of shadow, it was cold. Spray dashed into faces and across garments. Forward, the canyon dimmed out in mist. Nevertheless he spied three ships in that direction, and four aft. More than these were rendezvous-bound.

As the deck pitched beneath her, the girl caught his arm. 'What was that?' he shouted through the noise, and barely heard her reply:

'Swerve around one obstacle, I'm sure. Nothing here is ever twice the same.'

'Have you had any wrecks?'

'Some few per century. Most lives are saved.'

133

'God! You'll take such risk, year after year, for . . . ritual?'

'The danger is part of the ritual, Rolf. We are never so one with the world as when – Ai-ah!'

His gaze followed hers aloft, and his heart lurched. Downward came slanting the torpedo shape of a large flyer. Upon its armored flank shone the sunburst of Empire.

'Who is that?' she cried innocently.

'A marine troop. After me. Who else?' He didn't rasp it loud enough for her to hear. When he wrenched free and ran, she stared in hurt amazement.

He pounded up the ladder to the bridge, where he knew Mea stood by the pilot. She came out to meet him. Grimness bestrode her countenance. She had bitten her cigar across. 'Let's get you below,' she snapped, and shoved at him.

'They might know its name,' he replied. 'Whoever gave me away –'

'Aye. Here, this way . . . Hold.' Erannath had emerged from his cabin. 'You!' She pointed at the next deckhouse. 'Into that door!'

The Ythrian halted, lifted his talons. 'Move!' the captain bawled. 'Or I'll have you shot!'

For an instant his crest tood stiff. Then he obeyed. The three of them entered a narrow, throbbing corridor. Mea bowed to Erannath. 'I am sorry, honored passenger,' she said. Partly muffled by bulkheads, the air was less thunderous here. 'Time lacked for requesting your help courteously. You are most good that you obliged regardless. Please to come.'

She trotted on. Ivar and Erannath followed, the Ythrian rocking clumsily along on his wing-feet while he asked, 'What has happened?'

'Impies,' the young man groaned. "We had to get out of sight from above. If either of us got glimpsed, that'd've

He stumbled before her, among crewfolk who boiled with excitement. The aircraft whined toward the lead end of the line. *'Chao yu li!'* Mea exclaimed. 'We've that much luck, at least. They don't know which vessel is ours.'

ended this game. Not that I see how it can go on much longer.'

Erannath's eyes smoldered golden upon him. 'What game do you speak of?'

'I'm fugitive from Terrans.'

'And worth the captain's protection? A-a-a-ah . . .'

Mea stopped at an intercom unit, punched a number, spoke rapid-fire for a minute. When she turned back to her companions, she was the barest bit relaxed.

'I raised our radioman in time,' she said. 'Likely the enemy will call, asking which of us is *Jade Gate*. My man is alerting the others in our own language, which surely the Terrans don't understand. We Riverfolk stick together. Everybody will act stupid, claim they don't know, garble things as if they had one poor command of Anglic.' Her grin flashed. 'To act stupid is one skill of our people.'

'Were I the Terran commander,' Erannath said, 'I would thereupon beam to each ship individually, requiring its name. And were I the captain of any, I would not court punishment by lying, in a cause which has not been explained to me.'

Mea barked laughter. 'Right. But I suggested *Portal of Virtue* and *Way to Fortune* both answer they are *Jade Gate*, as well as this one. The real names could reasonably translate to the same as ours. They can safely give the Terrans that stab.'

She turned bleak again: 'At best, though, we buy short time to smuggle you off, Ivar Frederiksen, and you, Erannath, spy from Ythri. I dare not give you any firearms. That would prove our role, should you get caught.' The man felt the knife he had kept on his belt since he left Windhome. The nonhuman wasn't wearing his apron, thus had no weapons. The woman continued: 'When the marines flit down to us, we'll admit you were here, but claim we had no idea you were wanted. True enough, for everybody except three of us; and we can behave plenty innocent. We'll say you must have seen the airboat and fled, we know not where.'

Ivar thought of the starkness that walled them in and pleaded, 'Where, for real?'

Mea led them to a companionway and downward. As she hastened, she said across her shoulder: 'Some Orcans always climb the Shelf to trade with us after our ceremonies are done. You may meet them at the site, otherwise on their way to it. Or if not, you can probably reach the Tien Hu by yourselves, and get help. I feel sure they will help. Theirs is the seer they've told us of.'

'Won't Impies think of that?' Ivar protested.

'No doubt. Still, I bet it's one impossible country to ransack.' Mea stopped at a point in another corridor, glanced about, and rapped, 'Aye, you may be caught. But you *will* be caught if you stay aboard. You may drown crossing to shore, or break your neck off one cliff, or thousand other griefs. Well, are you our Firstling or not?'

She flung open a door and ushered them through. The room beyond was a storage space for kayaks, and also held a small crane for their launching. 'Get in,' she ordered Ivar. 'You should be able to reach the bank. Just work at not capsizing and not hitting anything, and make what shoreward way you can whenever you find one stretch not too rough. Once afoot, send the boat off again. No sense leaving any clue to where you landed. Afterward, rocks and mist should hide you from overhead, if you go carefully . . . Erannath, you fly across, right above the surface.'

Half terrified and half carried beyond himself, Ivar settled into the frail craft, secured the cover around his waist, gripped the paddle. Riho Mea leaned toward him. He had never before seen tears in her eyes. 'All luck sail with you, Firstling,' she said unsteadily, 'for all our hopes do.' Her lips touched his.

She opened a hatch in the hull and stood to the controls of the crane. Its motor whirred, its arm descended to lay hold with clamps to rings fore and aft, it lifted Ivar outward and lowered him alongside.

The river boomed and brawled. The world was a cold wet grayness of spray blown backward from the falls. Phantom cliffs showed through. Ivar and Erannath rested among house-sized boulders.

Despite his shoes, the stones along the bank had been cruel to the human. He ached from bruises where he had tripped and slashes where sharp edges had caught him. Weariness filled every bone like a lead casting. The Ythrian, who could flutter above obstacles, was in better shape, though prolonged land travel was always hard on his race.

By some trick of echo in their shelter, talk was possible at less than the top of a voice. 'No doubt a trail goes down the Shelf to the seabed,' Erannath said. 'We must presume the Terrans are not fools. When they don't find us aboard any ship, they will suppose us bound for Orcus, and call Nova Roma for a stat of the most detailed geodetic survey map available. They will then cruise above that trail. We must take a roundabout way.'

'That'll likely be dangerous to me,' Ivar said dully.

'I will help you as best I can,' Erannath promised. Perhaps the set of his feathers added: *If God the Hunter hurls you to your death, cry defiance as you fall.*

'Why are you interested in me, anyhow?' Ivar demanded.

The Ythrian trilled what corresponded to a chuckle. 'You and your fellows have taken for granted I'm a secret agent of the Domain. Let's say, first, that I wondered if you truly were plain Rolf Mariner, and accompanied you to try to find out. Second, I have no desire myself to be taken prisoner. Our interests in escape coincide.'

'Do they, now? You need only fly elsewhere.'

'But you are the Firstling of Ilion. Alone, you'd perish or be captured. Captain Riho doesn't understand how different this kind of country is from what you are used to. With my help, you have a fair chance.'

Ivar was too worn and sore to exult. Yet underneath, a low fire awoke. *He is interested in my success! So interested he'll gamble his whole mission, everything he might have brought home, to see me through. Maybe we really can get help from Ythri, when we break Sector Alpha Crucis free.*

This moment was premature to voice such things aloud. Presently the two of them resumed their crawling journey.

For a short stretch, the river again broadened until a fleet

137

could lie to, heavily anchored and with engineers standing by to supply power on a whistle's notice. The right bank widened also, in a few level hectares which had been cleared of detritus. There stood an altar flanked by stone guardians, eroded almost shapeless; but no Orcans had yet arrived. Here the rush of current was lost under the world-shivering steady roar of the Linn, only seven kilometers distant. Its edge was never visible through the spray flung aloft.

Tonight the wind had shifted, driving the perpetual fog south till it hung as a moon-whitened curtain between vast black walls. The water glistened. Darkling, upon it rested those vessels which had arrived. Somehow their riding lights and the colored lanterns strung throughout their rigging lacked cheeriness, when the Terran warcraft hung above on its negafield and watched. The air was cold; ice crackled in Ivar's clothes and Erannath's feathers.

Humans have beter night vision than Ythrians. Ivar was the first to see. 'Hssshh!' He drew his companion back, while sickness caught his throat. The Erannath identified those shimmers and shadows ahead. Three marines kept watch on the open ground.

No way existed to circle them unnoticed; the bank lay bare and moonlit to the bottom of an unscalable precipice. Ivar shrank behind a rock, thought wildly of swimming and knew that here he couldn't, of weeping and found that now he couldn't.

Unheard through the noise, Erannath lifted. Moon-glow tinged him. But sight was tricky for men who sat high in a hull. Otherwise they need not have placed sentries.

Ivar choked on a breath. He saw the great wings scythe back down. One man tumbled, a second, a third, in as many pulsebeats. Erannath landed among them where they sprawled and beckoned the Firstling.

Ivar ran. Strangely, what broke from him was, 'Are they dead?'

'No. Stunned. I hold a Third Echelon in *hyai-lu*. I used its triple blow, both alatan bones and a . . . do you say rabbit punch?' Erannath was busy. He stripped the two-ways off wrists, grav units off torsos, rifles off shoulders, gave one of each to Ivar and tossed the rest in the Flone. When they awoke, the marines would be unable to radio, rise, or fire signals, and must wait till their regular relief descended.

If they woke. The bodies looked ghastly limp to Ivar. He thrust that question aside, unsure why it should bother him when they were the enemy and when in joyous fact he and his ally had lucked out, had won a virtually certain means of getting to their goal.

They did not hazard immediate flight. On the further side of the meeting ground the Orcan trail began. Though narrow, twisting, and vague, often told only by cairns, it was better going than the shoreline had been. Anything would be. Ivar limped and Erannath hobbled as if unchained.

When they entered the concealing mists, they dared rise. And that was like becoming a freed spirit. Ivar wondered if the transcendence of humanness which the prophet promised could feel this miraculous. The twin cylinders he wore drove him through roaring wet smoke till he burst forth and beheld the side of a continent.

It toppled enormously, more steep and barren than anywhere in the west, four kilometers of palisades, headlands, ravines, raw slopes of old landslides, down and down to the dead ocean floor. Those were murky heights beneath stars and moons; but over them cascaded the Linn. It fell almost half the distance in a single straight leap, unhidden by spume, agleam like a drawn sword. The querning of it toned through heaven.

Below sheened the Orcan Sea, surrounded by hills which cultivation mottled. Beyond, desert glimmered death-white.

Erannath swept near. 'Quick!' he commanded. 'To ground before the Terrans come and spot us.'

Ivar nodded, took his bearings from the constellations, and aimed southwest, to where Mount Cronos raised its dim bulk. They might as well reduce the way they had left to go.

Air skirled frigid around him. His teeth clattered till he forced them together. This was not like the part of the

139

Antonine Seabed under Windhome. There it was often warm of summer nights, and never too hot by day. But there it was tempered by plenteous green life.

Yonder so-called Sea of Orcus was no more than a huge lake, dense and bitter with salts leached into it. Mists and lesser sreams off the Linn gave fresh water to the rim of its bowl. And that was all. Nothing ran far on southward. Winds bending up from the equator sucked every moisture into themselves and scattered it across immensities. That land lay bare because those same winds had long ago blown away the rich bottom soil which elsewhere was the heritage left Aeneas by its oceans.

Here was the sternest country where man dwelt upon this planet. Ivar knew it had shaped their tribe, their souls. He knew little more. No outsider did.

Aliens — He squinted at Erannath. The Ythrian descended as if upon prey, magnificent as the downward-rushing falls. *I thought for a moment you must've been one who betrayed me*, passed through Ivar. *Can't be, I reckon.*

Then: who did?

XV

Dawnlight shivered upon the sea and cast sharp blue shadows across dust. From the Grand Tower, a trumpet greeted the sun. Its voice blew colder than the windless air.

Jaan left his mother's house and walked a street which twisted between shuttered gray blocks of houses, down to the wharf. What few people were abroad crossed arms and bowed to him, some in awe, some in wary respect. In the wall-enclosed narrowness dusk still prevailed, making their robes look ghostly.

The wharf was Ancient work, a sudden dazzling contrast to the drabness and poverty of the human town. Its table iridescent, hard and cool beneath the feet, out of the mountainside. Millions of years had broken a corner off it but not eroded the substance. What they had done was steal the waves which once lapped its lower edge; now brush-grown slopes fell steeply to the water a kilometer beneath.

The town covered the mountain for a similar distance upward, its featureless adobe blocks finally huddling against the very flanks of the Arena which crowned the peak. That was also built by the Ancients, and even ruined stood in glory. It was of the same shining, enduring material as the wharf, elliptical in plan, the major axis almost a kilometer and the walls rearing more than 30 meters before their final upthrust in what had been seven towers and remained three. Those walls were not sheer; they fountained, in pillars, terraces, arches, galleries, setbacks, slim bridges, winglike balconies, so that light and shadow played endlessly and the building was like one eternal cool fire.

Banners rose, gold and scarlet, to the tops of flagstaffs on the parapets. The Companions were changing their guard.

Jaan's gaze turned away, to the northerly horizon where the continent reared above the Sea of Orcus. With Virgil barely over them, the heights appeared black, save for the Linn. It's dim thunder reverberated through air and earth.

— I do not see them flying, he said.

— No, they are not, replied Caruith. For fear of pursuit, they landed near Alsa and induced a villager to convey them in his truck. Look, there it comes.

Jaan was unsure whether his own mind or the Ancient's told his head to swing about, his eyes to focus on the dirt road snaking uphill from the shoreline. Were the two beginning to become one already? It had been promised. To be a part, no, a characteristic, a memory, of Caruith

... oh, wonder above wonders...

He saw the battered vehicle more by the dust it raised than anything else, for it was afar, would not reach the town for a while yet. It was not the only traffic at this early hour. Several groundcars moved along the highway that girdled the sea; a couple of tractors were at work in the hills behind, black dots upon brown and wan green, to coax a crop out of niggard soil; a boat slid across the thick waters, trawling for creatures which men could not eat but whose tissues concentrated minerals that men could use. And above the Arena there poised on its negafield an aircraft the Companions owned. Though unarmed by Imperial decree, it was on guard. These were uneasy times.

'Master.'

Jaan turned at the voice and saw Robhar, youngest of his disciples. The boy, a fisherman's son, was nearly lost in his ragged robe. His breath steamed around shoulder-length black eflocks. He made his bow doubly deep.

'Master,' he asked, 'can I serve you in aught?'

— He kept watch for hours till we emerged, and then did not venture to address us before we paused here, Caruith said. His devotion is superb.

— I do not believe the rest care less, Jaan replied out of his knowledge of humankind: which the mightiest nonhuman intellect could never totally sound. They are older, lack endurance to wait sleepless and freezing on the chance that we may want them; they have, moreover, their daily work, and most of them their wives and children.

– The time draws nigh when they must forsake those, and all others, to follow us.

– They know that. I am sure they accept it altogether. But then should they not savor the small joys of being human as much as they may, while still they may?

– You remain too human yourself, Jaan. You must become a lightning bolt.

Meanwhile the prophet said, 'Yes, Robhar. This is a day of destiny.' As the eyes before him flared: 'Nonetheless we have practical measures to take, no time for rejoicing. We remain only men, chained to the world. Two are bound hither, a human and an Ythrian. They could be vital to the liberation. The Terrans are after them, and will surely soon arrive in force to seek them out. Before then, they must be well hidden; and as few townsfolk as may be must know about them, lest the tale be spilled.

'Hurry. Go to the livery stable of Brother Boras and ask him to lend us a statha with a pannier large enough to hide an Ythrian – about your size, though we will also need a blanket to cover his wing-ends that will stick forth. Do not tell Boras why I desire this. He is loyal, but the tyrants have drugs and worse, should they come to suspect anyone knows something. Likewise, give no reasons to Brother Ezzara when you stop at his house to borrow a robe, sandals, and his red cloak with the hood. Order him to remain indoors until further word.

'Swiftly!'

Robhar clapped hands in sign of obedience and sped off, over the cobblestones and into the town.

Jaan waited. The truck would inevitably pass the wharf. Meanwhile, nobody was likely to have business here at this hour. Any who did chance by would see the prophet's lonely figure limned against space, and bow and not venture to linger.

– The driver comes sufficiently near for me to read his mind, whispered Caruith. I do not like what I see.

143

— What? asked Jaan, startled. Is he not true to us? Why else should he convey two outlaws?

— He is true, in the sense of wishing Aeneas free of the Empire and, indeed, Orcus free of Nova Roma. But he had not fully accepted our teaching, nor made an absolute commitment to our cause. For he is an impulsive and vacillating man. Ivar Frederiksen and Erannath of Avalon woke him up with a story about being scientists marooned by the failure of their aircraft, in need of transportation to Mount Cronos where they could get help. He knew the story must be false, but in his resentment of the Terrans agreed anyway. Now, more and more, he worries, he regrets his action. As soon as he is rid of them, he will drink to ease his fears, and the drink may well unlock his tongue.

— Is it not ample precaution that we transfer them out of his care? What else should we do? . . . No! Not murder!

— Many will die for the liberation. Would you hazard their sacrifice being in vain, for the sake of a single life today?

— Imprisonment, together with the Ythrian you warn me about —

— The disappearance of a person who has friends and neighbors is less easy to explain away than his death. Speak to Brother Velib. Recall that he was among the few Orcans who went off to serve with McCormac; he learned a good deal. It is not hard to create a believable 'accident'.

—No.

Jaan wrestled; but the mind which shared his brain was too powerful, too plausible. It is right that one man die for the people. Were not Jaan and Caruith themselves prepared to do so? By the time the truck arrived, the prophet had actually calmed.

By then, too, Robhar had returned with the statha and the disguise. Everybody knew Ezzara by the red cloak he affected. Its hood would conceal a nord's head; long sleeves, and dirt rubbed well into sandaled feet, would conceal fair skin. Folk would observe nothing save the prophet, accompanied by two of his disciples, going up to

144

the Arena and in through its gates, along with a beast whose burden might be, say, Ancient books that he had found in the catacombs.

The truck halted. Jaan accepted the salutation of the driver, while trying not to think of him as really real. The man opened the back door, and inside the body of the vehicle were the Ythrian and the Firstling of Ilion.

Jaan, who had never before seen an Ythrian in the flesh, found he was more taken by that arrogance of beauty (which must be destroyed, it mourned within him) than by the ordinary-looking blond youth who had so swiftly become a hinge of fate. He felt as if the blue eyes merely stared, while the golden ones searched.

They saw: a young man, more short and stocky than was common among Orcans, in an immaculate white robe, rope belt, sandals. The countenance was broad, curve-nosed, full-lipped, pale-brown, handsome in its fashion; long hair and short beard were mahogany, clean and well-groomed. His own eyes were his most striking feature, wide-set, gray, and enormous. Around his brows went a circlet of metal with a faceted complexity above the face, the sole outward token that he was an Ancient returned to life after six million years.

He said, in his voice that was as usual slow and soft: 'Welcome, Ivar Frederiksen, deliverer of your world.'

Night laired everywhere around Desai's house. Neighbor lights felt star-distant; and there went no whisper of traffic. It was almost with relief that he blanked the windows.

'Please sit down, Prosser Thane,' he said. 'What refreshment may I offer you?'

'None,' the tall young woman answered. After a moment she added, reluctantly and out of habit: 'Thank you.'

'Is it that you do not wish to eat the salt of an enemy?' His smile was wistful. 'I shouldn't imagine tradition requires you refuse his tea.'

'If you like, Commissioner.' Tatiana seated herself, stiff-limbed in her plain coverall. Desai spoke to his wife, who fetched a tray with a steaming pot, two cups, and a plate of

145

cookies. She set it down and excused herself. The door closed behind her.

To Desai, that felt like the room closing in on him. It was so comfortless, so . . . impoverished, in spite of being physically adequate. His desk and communications board filled one corner, a reference shelf stood nearby, and otherwise the place was walls, faded carpet, furniture not designed for a man of his race or culture: apart from a picture or two, everything rented, none of the dear clutter which makes a home.

Our family moves too much, too often, too far, like a bobbin shuttling to weave a fabric which tears because it is rotted. I was always taught on Ramanujan that we do best to travel light through life. But what does it do to the children, this flitting from place to place, though always into the same kind of Imperial-civil-servant enclave? He sighed. The thought was old in him.

'I appreciate your coming as I requested,' he began. 'I hope you, ah, took precautions.'

'Yes, I did. I slipped into alley, reversed my cloak, and put on my nightmask.'

'That's the reason I didn't visit you. It would be virtually impossible to conceal the fact. And surely the terrorists have you under a degree of surveillance.'

Tatiana withheld expression. Desai plodded on: 'I hate for you to take even this slight risk. The assassins of a dozen prominent citizens might well not stop at you, did they suspect you of, um, collaboration.'

'Unless I'm on their side, and came here to learn whatever I can for them,' Tatiana said in a metallic tone.

Desai ventured a smile. 'That's the risk *I* take. Not very large, I assume.' He lifted the teapot and raised his brows. She gave a faint nod. He poured for her and himself, lifted his cup and sipped. The heat comforted.

'How about gettin' to business?' she demanded.

'Indeed. I thought you would like to hear the latest news of Ivar Frederiksen.'

That caught her! She said nothing, but she sat bolt upright and the brown gaze widened.

'This is confidential, of course. From a source I shan't

146

describe, I have learned that he joined a nomad band, later got into trouble with it, and took passage on a south-bound ship of Riverfolk together with an Ythrian who may or may not have met him by chance but is almost certainly an Intelligence agent of the Domain. They were nearly at the outfall when I got word and sent a marine squad to bring him in. Thanks to confusion – obviously abetted by the sailors, though I don't plan to press charges – he and his companion escaped.'

Red and white ran across her visage. She breathed quickly and shallowly, caught up her cup and gulped deep.

'You know I don't want him punished if it can be avoided,' Desai said. 'I want a chance to reason with him.'

'I know that's what you claim,' Tatiana snapped.

'If only people would understand,' Desai pleaded. 'Yes, the Imperium wronged you. But we are trying to make it good. And others would make tools of you, for prying apart what unity, and safety in unity, this civilization has left.'

'What d'you mean? Ythrians? Merseians?' Her voice gibed.

Desai reached a decision. 'Merseians. Oh, they are far off. But if they can again preoccupy us on this frontier – They failed last time, because McCormac's revolt caught them, too, by surprise. A more carefully engineered sequel would be different. Terra might even lose this entire sector, while simultaneously Merseia grabbed away at the opposite frontier. The result would be a truncated, shaken, weakened Empire, a strengthened Roidhunate flushed with success . . . and the Long Night brought that much closer.'

He said into her unvoiced but unmistakable scorn: 'You disbelieve? You consider Merseia a mere bogeyman? Please listen. A special agent of theirs is loose on Aeneas. No common spy or troublemaker. A creature of unique abilities; so important that, for the sake of his mission, a whole nonexistent planet was smuggled into the data files at Catawrayannis; so able – including fantastic telepathic feats – that all by himself he easily, almost teasingly escaped our precautions and disappeared into the wilds. Prosser Thane, Merseia is risking more than this one

147

individual. It's giving away to us the fact that the Roid-hunate includes such a species, putting us on our guard against more like him. No competent Intelligence service would allow that for anything less than the highest stakes.

'Do you see what a net your betrothed could get tangled in?'

Have I registered? Her face has gone utterly blank.

After a minute, she said: 'I'll have to think on that, Commissioner. Your fears may be exaggerated. Let's stay with practicalities tonight. You were wonderin' about Ivar and this companion of his . . . who suggests Ythri may also be stickin' claws into our pot, right? Before I can suggest anything, you'd better tell me what else you know.'

Desai armored himself in dryness. 'Presumably they took refuge in the Orcan country,' he said. 'I've just had a report from a troop dispatched there to search for them. After several days of intensive effort, including depth quizzing of numerous people who might be suspected of knowledge, they have drawn blank. I can't leave them tied down, futile except for fueling hatred of us by their presence: not when sedition, sabotage, and violence are growing so fast across the whole planet. We need them to patrol the streets of, say, Nova Roma.'

'Maybe Ivar didn't make for Orcus,' Tatiana suggested.

'Maybe. But it would be logical, no?'

She uttered a third 'Maybe', and then surprised him: 'Did your men quiz that new prophet of theirs?'

'As a matter of fact, yes. No result. He gave off weird quasi-religious ideas that we already know a little about; they're anti-Imperial, but it seems better to let him vent pressure on behalf of his followers than to make a martyr of him. No, he revealed no knowledge of our Firstling. Nor did such as we could find among those persons who've constituted themselves an inner band of apostles.'

It was clear that Tatiana stayed impersonal only by an effort. Her whole self must be churning about her sweetheart. 'I'm astonished you got away with layin' hands on him or them. You could've touched off a full-dress revolt, from all I've heard.'

'I did issue instructions to handle cult leaders with micromanipulators. But after the search had gone on for a while, this . . . Jaan . . . voluntarily offered to undergo narco with his men, to end suspicion and, as he put it, leave the Terrans no further reason to remain. A shrewd move, if what he wanted was to get rid of them. After that big a concession from his side, they could scarcely do less than withdraw.'

'Well,' she challenged, 'has it occurred to you that Ivar man *not* be in yon area?'

'Certainly. Although . . . the lead technician of the quiz team reported Jaan showed an encephalogram not quite like any ever recorded before. As if his claim were true, that – what is it? – he is possessed by some kind of spirit. Oh, his body is normal-human. There's no reason to suppose the drug didn't suppress his capacity to lie, as it would for anyone else. But –'

'Mutation, I'd guess, would account for brain waves. They're odd and inbred folk, in environment our species never was evolved for.'

'Probably. I'd have liked to borrow a Ryellian telepath from the governor's staff – considered it seriously, but decided that the Merseian agent, with the powers and knowledge he must have, would know who to guard against that, if he were involved. If I had a million skilled investigators, to study every aspect of this planet and its different peoples for a hundred intensive years –'

Desai abandoned his daydream. 'We don't escape the possibility that Ivar and the Ythrian are in that region, unbeknownst to the prophet,' he said. 'A separate group could have smuggled them in. I understand Mount Cronos is riddled with tunnels and vaults, dug by the Elder race and never fully explored by men.'

'But 'twould be hopeless quest goin' through them, right?' Tatiana replied.

'Yes. Especially when the hiding place could as well be far out in the desert.' Desai paused. 'This is why I asked you to come here, Prosser Thane. You know your fiancé. And surely you have more knowledge of the Orcans than our researchers can dig out of books, data banks, and

149

superficial observation. Tell me, if you will, how likely would Ivar and they be to, m-m, get together?'

Tatiana fell silent. Desai loaded his cigarette holder and puffed and puffed. Finally she said, slowly:

'I don't think close cooperation's possible. Differences go too deep. And Ivar, at least, would have sense enough to realize it, and not try.'

Desai refrained from comment, merely saying, 'I wish you would describe that society for me.'

'You must've read reports.'

'Many. All from an outside, Terran viewpoint, including summaries my staff made of nord writings. They lack feel. You, however – your people and the Orcans have shared a world for centuries. If nothing else, I'm trying to grope toward an intuition of the relationship: not a bald socio-economic redaction, but a sense of the spirit, the tensions, the subtle and basic influences between cultures.'

Tatiana sat for another time, gathering her thoughts. At last she said: 'I really can't tell you much, Commissioner. Would you like capsule of history? You must know it already.'

'I do not know what you consider important. Please.'

'Well . . . those're by far our largest, best-preserved Builder relics, on Mount Cronos. But they were little studied, since Dido commanded most attention. Then Troubles came, raids, invasions, breakdown toward feudalism. Certain non-nords took refuge in Arena for lack of better shelter.'

'Arena?' Desai wondered.

'Giant amphitheater on top of mountain, if amphitheater is what it was.'

'Ah, that's not what "arena" means . . . No matter. I realize words change in local dialects. Do go on.'

'They lived in that fortresslike structure, under strict discipline. When they went out to farm, fish, herd, armed men guarded them. Gradually these developed into military order, Companions of Arena, who were also magistrates, technical decision-makers – land bein' held in common – and finally became leaders in religious rites, religion naturally comin' to center on those mysterious remains.

'When order was restored, at first Companions resisted planetary government, and had to be beaten down. That made them more of priesthood, though they keep soldierly traditions. Since, they've given Nova Roma no particular trouble; but they hold aloof, and see their highest purpose as findin' out what Builders were, and are, and will be.'

'Hm.' Desai stroked his chin. 'Are their people – these half million or so who inhabit the region – would you call them equally isolated from the rest of Aeneas?'

'Not quite. They trade, especially caravans across Antonine Seabed to its more fertile parts, bringin' minerals and bioproducts in exchange for food, manufactures, and whatnot. Number of their young men take service with nords for several years, to earn stake; they've high talent for water dowsin', which bears out what I said earlier about mutations among them. On whole, though, average continent dweller never sees an Orcan. And they do keep apart, forbid outside marriages on pain of exile, hold themselves to be special breed who will at last play special role related to Builders. Their history's full of prophets who had dreams about that. This Jaan's merely latest one.'

Desai frowned. 'Still, isn't his claim unique – that he is, at last, the incarnation, and the elder race will return in his lifetime – or whatever it is that he preaches?'

'I don't know.' Tatiana drew breath. 'One thing, however; and this's what you called me here for, right? In spite of callin' itself objective rather than supernatural, what Orcans have got behaves like religion. Well, Ivar's skeptic; in fact, he's committed unbeliever. I can't imagine him throwin' in with gang of visionaries. They'd soon conflict too much.'

Now Desai went quiet to ponder. *The point is well taken. That doesn't mean it's true.*

And yet what can I do but accept it . . . unless and until I hear from my spy, whatever has happened to him? (And that is something I may well never know.)

He shook himself. 'So whether or not Ivar received help from an individual Orcan or two, you doubt he's contacted anyone significant, or will have any reason to linger in so forbidding an area. Am I correct, Prosser Thane?'

She nodded.

'Could you give me an idea as to where he might turn, how we might reach him?' Desai pursued.

She did not deign to answer.

'As you will,' he said tiredly. 'Bear in mind, he's in deadly danger as long as he is on the run: danger of getting shot by a patrol, for instance, or of committing a treasonable act which it would be impossible to pardon him for.'

Tatiana bit her lip.

'I will not harass you about this,' he promised. 'But I beg you — you're a scientist, you should be used to entertaining radical new hypotheses and exploring their consequences — I beg you to consider the proposition that his real interests, and those of Aeneas, may lie with the Empire.'

'I'd better go pretty soon,' she said.

Later, to Gabriel Stewart, she exulted:

'He's got to be among Orcans. Nothin' else makes sense. He our rightful temporal leader, Jaan our mental one. Word'll go like fire in dry trava under a zoosny wind.'

'But if prophet didn't know where he was — ' fretted the scout.

Tatiana rapped forth a laugh. 'Prophet did know! Do you imagine Builder mind couldn't control human body reactions to miserable dose of narcotic? Why, simple schizophrenia can cause that.'

He considered her. 'You believe those rumors, girl? Rumors they are, you understand, nothin' more. Our outfit has no liaison with Arena.'

'We'd better develop one . . . Well, I admit we've no proof Builders are almost ready to return. But it makes sense.' She gestured as if at the stars which her blinded window concealed. 'Cosmenosis — What'd be truly fantastic is no purpose, no evolution, in all of that yonder.' Raptly: 'Desai spoke about Merseian agent operatin' on Aeneas. Not Merseian by race, though. Somebody strange enough to maybe, just maybe, be forerunner for Builders.'

'Huh?' he exclaimed.

'I'd rather not say more at this point, Gabe. However,

Desai also spoke about adoptin' workin' hypothesis. Until further notice, I think this ought to be ours, that there is at least *somethin'* to those stories. We've got to dig deeper, collect hard information. At worst, we'll find we're on our own. At best, who knows?'

'If nothin' else, it'd make good propaganda,' he remarked cynically. He had not been back on Aeneas sufficiently long to absorb its atmosphere of expectation. 'Uh, how do we keep enemy from reasonin' and investigatin' along same lines?'

'We've no guaranteed way,' Tatiana said. 'I've been thinkin', though, and – Look, suppose I call Desai tomorrow or next day, claim I've had change of heart, try wheedlin' more out of him concernin' yon agent. But mainly what I'll do is suggest he check on highlanders of Chalce. They're tough, independent-minded clansmen, you probably recall. It's quite plausible they'd rally 'round Ivar if he went to them, and that he'd do so on his own initiative. Well, it's big and rugged country, take many men and lots of time to search over. Meanwhile –'

XVI

The room within the mountain was spacious, and its lining of Ancient material added an illusion of dreamlike depths beyond. Men had installed heated carpeting, fluoropanels, furniture, and other basic necessities, including books and an eidophone to while away the time. Nevertheless, as hours stretched into days he did not see, Ivar grew half wild. Erannath surely suffered worse; from a human viewpoint, all Ythrians are born with a degree of claustrophobia. But he kept self-control grimly in his talons.

Conversation helped them both. Erannath even reminisced:

'— wing-free. As a youth I wandered the whole of Avalon . . . hai-ha, storm-dawns over seas and snowpeaks! Hunting a spathodont with spears! Wind across the plains, that smelled of sun and eternity! . . . Later I trained to become a tramp spacehand. You do not know what that is? An Ythrian institution. Such a crewman may leave his ship whenever he wishes to stay for a while on some planet, provided a replacement is available; and one usually is.' His gaze yearned beyond the shimmering walls. 'Khrrr, this is a universe of wonders. Treasure it, Ivar. What is outside our heads is so much more than what can nest inside them.'

'Are you still spaceman?' the human asked.

'No. I returned at length to Avalon with Hlirr, whom I had met and wedded on a world where rings flashed rainbow over oceans the color of old silver. That also is good, to ward a home and raise a brood. But they are grown now, and I, in search of a last long-faring before God stoops on me, am here' — he gave a harsh equivalent of a chuckle — 'in this cave.'

'You're spyin' for Domain, aren't you?'

'I have explained, I am a xenologist, specializing in anthropology. That was the subject I taught throughout the settled years on Avalon, and in which I am presently doing field work.'

'Your bein' scientist doesn't forbid your bein' spy. Look, I don't hold it against you. Terran Empire is my enemy same as yours, if not more. We're natural allies. Won't you carry that word back to Ythri for me?'

Ripplings went over Erannath's plumage. 'Is every opponent of the Empire your automatic friend? What of Merseia?'

'I've heard propaganda against Merseians till next claim about their bein' racist and territorially aggressive will throw me into anaphylactic shock. Has Terra *never* provoked, yes, menaced them? Besides, they're far off: Terra's problem, not ours. Why should Aeneas supply young men to pull Emperor's fat out of fire? What's he ever done for us? And, God, what hasn't he done to us?'

Erannath inquired slowly, 'Do you indeed hope to lead a second, successful revolution?'

'I don't know about leadin',' Ivar said, hot-faced. 'I hope to help.'

'For what end?'

'Freedom.'

'What is freedom? To do as you, an individual, choose? Then how can you be certain that a fragment of the Empire will not make still greater demands on you? I should think it would have to.'

'Well, uh, well, I'd be willin' to serve, as long as it was my own people.'

'How willing are your people themselves to be served – as individuals – in your fashion? You see no narrowing of your freedom in whatever the requirements may be for a politically independent Alpha Crucis region, any more than you see a narrowing of it in laws against murder or robbery. These imperatives accord with your desires. But others may feel otherwise. What is freedom, except having one's particular cage reach further than one cares to fly?'

Ivar scowled into the yellow eyes. 'You talk strange,

155

for Ythrian. For Avalonian, especially. Your planet sure resisted bein' swallowed up by Empire.'

'That would have wrought a fundamental change in our lives: for example, by allowing unrestricted immigration, till we were first crowded and then outvoted. You, however – In what basic way might an Alpha Crucian Republic, or an Alpha Crucian province of the Empire? You get but one brief flight through reality, Ivar Frederiksen. Would you truly rather pass among ideologies than among stars?'

'Uh, I'm afraid you don't understand. Your race doesn't have our idea of government.'

'It's irrelevant to us. My fellow Avalonians who are of human stock have come to think likewise. I must wonder why you are so intense, to the point of making it a death-pride matter, about the precise structure of a political organization. Why do you not, instead, concentrate your efforts toward arrangements whereby it will generally leave you and yours alone?'

'Well, if our motivation here is what puzzles you, then tell them on Ythri –' Ivar drew breath.

Time wore away; and all at once, it was a not a single man who came in a plain robe, bringing food and removing discards: it was a figure in uniform that trod through the door and announced, 'The High Commander!'

Ivar scrambled to his feet. The feather-crest stood stiff upon Erannath's head. For this they had abided.

A squad entered, forming a double line at taut attention. They were typical male Orcans: tall and lean, brown of skin, black and bushy of hair and closely cropped beard, their faces mostly oval and somewhat flat, their nostrils flared and lips full. But these were drilled and dressed like soldiers. They wore steel helmets which swept down over the neck and bore self-darkening vitryl visors now shoved up out of the way; blue tunics with insignia of rank and, upon the breast of each, an infinity sign; gray trousers tucked into soft boots. Besides knives and knuckledusters at their belts they carried, in defiance of Imperial decree, blasters and rifles which must have been kept hidden from confiscation.

Yakow Harolsson, High Commander of the Companions of the Arena, followed. He was clad the same as his men, except for adding a purple cloak. Though his beard was white and his features scored, the spare form remained erect. Ivar snapped him a salute.

Yakow returned it and in the nasal Anglic of the region said: 'Be greeted, Firstling of Ilion.'

'Have . . . Terrans gone . . . sir?' Ivar asked. His pulse banged, giddiness passed through him, the cool underground air felt thick in his throat.

'Yes. You may come forth.' Yakow frowned. 'In disguise, naturally, garb, hair and skin dyes, instruction about behavior. We dare not assume the enemy has left no spies or, what is likelier, hidden surveillance devices throughout the town – perhaps in the very Arena.' From beneath discipline there blazed: 'Yet forth shall you come, to prepare for the Deliverance.'

Erannath stirred. 'I could ill pass as an Orcan,' he said dryly.

Yakow's gaze grew troubled as it sought him. 'No. We have provided for you, after taking counsel.'

A vague fear made Ivar exclaim, 'Remember, sir, he's liaison with Ythri, which may become our ally.'

'Indeed,' Yakow said without tone. 'We could simply keep you here, Sir Erannath, but from what I know of your race, you would find that unendurable. So we have prepared a safe place elsewhere. Be patient for a few more hours. After dark you will be led away.'

To peak afar in wilderness, Ivar guessed, happy again, *where he can roam skies, hunt, think his thoughts, till we're ready for him to rejoin us – or we rejoin him – and afterward send him home.*

On impulse he seized the Ythrian's right hand. Talons closed sharp but gentle around his fingers. 'Thanks for everything, Erannath,' Ivar said. 'I'll miss you . . . till we meet once more.'

'That will be as God courses,' answered his friend.

The Arena took its name from the space it enclosed. Through a window in the Commander's lofty sanctum, Ivar looked across tier after tier, sweeping in an austere but subtly eye-compelling pattern of grand ellipses, down toward the central pavement. Those levels were broad enough to be terraces rather than seats, and the walls between them held arched openings which led to the halls and chambers of the interior. Nevertheless, the suggestion of an antique theater was strong.

A band of Companions was drilling; for though it had seldom fought in the last few centuries, the order remained military in character, and was police as well as quasi-priesthood. Distance and size dwindled the men to insects. Their calls and footfalls were lost in hot stillness, as were any noises from town; only the Linn resounded, endlessly grinding. Most life seemed to be in the building itself, its changeful iridescences and the energy of its curves.

'Why did Elders make it like this?' Ivar wondered aloud.

A scientific base, combining residences and workrooms? But the ramps which connected floors twisted so curiously; the floors themselves had their abrupt rises and drops, for no discernible reason; the vaulted corridors passed among apartments no two of which were alike. And what had gone on in the crater middle? Mere gardening, to provide desert-weary eyes with a park? (But these parts were fertile, six million years ago.) Experiments? Games? Rites? Something for which man, and every race known to man, had no concept?

'Jaan says the chief purpose was to provide a gathering place, where minds might conjoin and thus achieve transcendence,' Yakow answered. He turned to his escort. 'Dismissed,' he snapped. They saluted and left, closing behind them the human-installed door.

It had had to be specially shaped, to fit the portal of this suite. The outer office where the two men stood was like the inside of a multi-faceted jewel; colors did not sheen softly, as they did across the exterior of the Arena, but glanced and glinted, fire-fierce, wherever a sunbeam struck. Against such a backdrop, the few articles of furniture and equipment belonging to the present occupancy seemed twice austere: chairs fashioned of gnarly stark-wood, a similar table, a row of shelves holding books and a comset, a carpet woven from the mineral-harsh plants that grew in Orcan shallows.

'Be seated, if you will,' Yakow said, and folded his lankness down.

Won't he offer me anyhow a cup of tea? flickered in Ivar. Then, recollection from reading: *No, in this country, food or drink shared creates bonds of mutual obligation. Reckon he doesn't feel quite ready for that with me.*

Do I with him? Ivar took a seat confronting the stern old face.

Disconcertingly, Yakow waited for him to start conversation. After a hollow moment, Ivar attempted: 'Uh, that Jaan you speak of, sir. Your prophet, right?' I'd not demean your faith, please believe me. But may I ask some questions?'

Yakow nodded; the white beard brushed the infinity sign on his breast. 'Whatever you wish, Firstling. Truth can only be clarified by questionings.' He paused. 'Besides – let us be frank from our start – in many minds it is not yet certitude that Jaan has indeed been possessed by Caruith the Ancient. The Companions of the Arena have taken no official position on the mystery.'

Ivar started. 'But I thought – I mean, religion –'

Yakow lifted a hand. 'Pray hearken, Firstling. We serve no religion here.'

'What?' Sir, you believe, you've believed for, for hundreds of years, in Elders!'

'As we believe in Virgil or the moons.' A ghost-smile flickered. 'After all, we see them daily. Likewise do we see the Ancient relics.'

Yakow grew earnest. 'Of your patience, Firstling, let me explain a little. "Religion" means faith in the supernatural, does it not? Most Orcans, like most Aeneans everywhere, do have that kind of faith. They maintain a God exists, and observe different ceremonies and injunctions on that account. If they have any sophistication, however, they admit their belief is nonscientific. It is not subject to empirical confirmation or disconfirmation.

159

Miracles may have happened through divine intervention; but a miracle, by definition, involves a suspension of natural law, hence cannot be experimentally repeated. Aye, its historical truth or falsity can be indirectly investigated. But the confirmation of an event proves nothing, since it *could* be explained away scientifically. For example, if we could show that there was in fact a Jesus Christ who did in fact rise from his tomb, he may have been in a coma, not dead. Likewise, a disconfirmation proves nothing. For example, if it turns out that a given saint never lived, that merely shows people were naïve, not that the basic creed is wrong.'

Ivar stared. *This talk – and before we've even touched on any practicalities – from hierophant of impoverished isolated desert dwellers?*

He collected his wits. *Well, nobody with access to electronic communications is truly isolated. And I wouldn't be surprised if Yakow studied at University. I've met a few Orcans there myself.*

Just because person lives apart, in special style, it doesn't mean he's ignorant or stupid . . . M-m, do Terrans think this about us? The question aroused a mind-sharpening resentment.

'I repeat,' Yakow was saying, 'in my sense of the word, we have no shared religion here. We do have a doctrine.

'It is a fact, verifiable by standard stratigraphic and radioisotopic dating methods, a fact that a mighty civilization kept an outpost on Aeneas, six thousand thousand years ago. It is a reasonable inference that those beings did not perish, but rather went elsewhere, putting childish things away as they reached a new stage of evolution. And it may conceivably be wishful thinking, but it does seem more likely than otherwise, that the higher sentiences of the cosmos take a benign interest in the lower, and seek to aid them upward.

'This hope, if you wish to call it no more than that, is what has sustained us.'

The words were in themselves dispassionate; and though the voice strengthened, the tone was basically calm. Yet

Ivar looked into the countenance and decided to refrain from responding:

What proof have we of any further evolution? We've met many different races by now, and some are wildly different, not just in their bodies but in their ways of thinkin' and their capabilities. Still, we've found none we could call godlike. And why should intelligence progress indefinitely? Nothin' else in nature does. Beyond that point where technology becomes integral to species survival, what selection pressure is there to increase brains? If anything, we sophonts already have more than's good for us.

He realized: *That's orthodox modern attitude, of course. Maybe reflectin' sour grapes, or weariness of decadent society. No use denyin', what we've explored is one atom off outer skin of one dustmote galaxy. . . .*

Aloud, he breathed, 'Now Jaan claims Elders are about to return? And mind of theirs is already inside him?'

'Crudely put,' Yakow said. 'You must talk to him yourself, at length.' He paused. 'I told you, the Companions do not thus far officially accept his claims. Nor do we reject them. We do acknowledge that, overnight, somehow a humble shoemaker gained certain powers, certain knowledge. "Remarkable" is an altogether worthless word for whatever has happened.'

'Who is he?' Ivar dared ask. 'I've heard nothin' more than rumors, hints, guesses.'

Yakow spoke now as a pragmatic leader. 'When he first arose from obscurity, and ever more people began accepting his preachments: we officers of the Arena saw what explosive potential was here, and sought to hold the story quiet until we could at least evaluate it and its consequences. Jaan himself has been most cooperative with us. We could not altogether prevent word from spreading beyond our land. But thus far, the outside planet knows only vaguely of a new cult in this poor corner.'

It may not know any more than that, Ivar thought; *however, it's sure ready to believe more. Could be I've got news for you, Commander.* 'Who is he, really?'

'The scion of a common family, though once well-to-do as prosperity goes in Orcus. His father. Gileb, was a trader

11

who owned several land vehicles and claimed descent from the founder of the Companions. His mother, Nomi, has a genealogy still more venerable, back to the first humans on Aeneas.'

'What happened?'

'You may recall, some sixteen years ago this region suffered a period of turmoil. A prolonged sandstorm brought crop failure and the loss of caravans; then quarreling over what was left caused old family feuds to erupt anew. They shook the very Companions. For a time we were ineffective.'

Ivar nodded. He had been searching his memory for news stories, and come upon accounts of how this man had won to rule over the order, restored its discipline and morale, and gone on to rescue his entire society from chaos. But that had been the work of years.

'His possessions looted by enemies who sought his blood, Gileb fled with his wife and their infant son,' Yakow went on in a level tone. 'They trekked across the Antonine, barely surviving, to a small nord settlement in the fertile part of it. There they found poverty-stricken refuge.

'When Gileb died, Nomi returned home with her by then half-dozen children, to this by then pacified country. Jaan had learned the shoemaker's trade, and his mother was – is – a skillful weaver. Between them, they supported the family. There was never enough left over for Jaan to consider marrying.

'Finally he had his revelation . . . made his discovery . . . whatever it was.'

'Can you tell me?' Ivar asked low.

The gaze upon him hardened. 'That can be talked of later,' said Yakow. 'For now, methinks best we consider what part you might play. Firstling, in the liberation of Aeneas from the Empire – maybe of mankind from humanness.'

XVII

In headcloth, robe, and sandals, skin stained brown and hair black, Ivar would pass a casual glance. His features, build, and blue eyes were not typical; but though the Orcans had long been endogamous, not every gene of their originally mixed heritage was gone, and occasional throwbacks appeared; to a degree, the prophet himself was one. More serious anomalies included the dialect of Anglic, his ignorance of the native language, his imperfect imitation of manners, gait, a thousand subtleties.

Yet surely no Terran, boredly watching the playback from a spy device, would notice those differences. Many Orcans would likewise fail to do so, or would shrug off what they did see. After all, there were local and individual variations within the region; besides, this young man might well be back from several years' service among nords who had influenced him.

Those who looked closely and carefully were the least likely to mention a word of what they saw. For the stranger walked in company with the shoemaker.

It had happened erenow. Someone would hear Jaan preach, and afterward request a private audience. Customarily, the two of them went off alone upon the mountain.

Several jealous pairs of eyes followed Jaan and Ivar out of town. They spoke little until they were well away from people, into a great and aloof landscape.

Behind and above, rocks, bushes, stretches of bare gray dirt reached sharply blue-shadowed, up toward habitation and the crowning Arena. Overhead, the sky was empty save for the sun and one hovering vulch. Downward, land tumbled to the sullen flatness of the sea. Around were hills which bore thin green and scattered houses. Traffic trudged on dust-smoking roads. Ilion reared dark, the Linn blinding white, to north and northeast; elsewhere the horizon was rolling nakedness. A warm and pungent wind stroked faces, fluttered garments, mumbled above the mill-noise of the falls.

Jaan's staff swung and thumped in time with his feet as he picked a way steadily along a browser trail. Ivar used no aid but moved like a hunter. That was automatic; his entire consciousness was bent toward the slow words:

'We can talk now, Firstling. Ask or declare what you will. You cannot frighten or anger me, you who have come as a living destiny.'

'I'm no messenger of salvation,' Ivar said low. 'I'm just very fallible human bein', who doesn't even believe in God.'

Jaan smiled. 'No matter. I don't myself, in conventional terms. We use "destiny" in a most special sense. For the moment, let's put it that you were guided here, or aided to come here, in subtle ways' – his extraordinary eyes locked onto the other and he spoke gravely – 'because you have the potential of becoming a savior.'

'No, I, not me.'

Again Jaan relaxed, clapped him on the shoulder, and said, 'I don't mean that mystically. Think back to your discussions with High Commander Yakow. What Aeneas needs is twofold, a uniting faith and a uniting secular leader. The Firstman of Ilion, for so you will become in time, has the most legitimate claim, most widely accepted, to speak for this planet. Furthermore, memory of Hugh McCormac will cause the entire sector to rally around him, once he raises the liberation banner afresh.

'What Caruith proclaims will fire many people. But it is too tremendous, too new, for them to live with day-to-day. They must have a . . . a political structure they understand and accept, to guide them through the upheaval. You are the nucleus of that, Ivar Frederiksen.'

'I, I don't know – I'm no kind of general or politician, in fact I failed miserably before, and –'

'You will have skilled guidance. But never think we

164

want you for a figurehead. Remember, the struggle will take years. As you grow in experience and wisdom, you will find yourself taking the real lead.'

Ivar squinted through desert dazzlement at a far-off dust devil, and said with care:

'I hardly know anything so far . . . Jaan . . . except what Yakow and couple of his senior officers have told me. They kept insistin' that to explain – religious? – no, transcendental – to explain transcendental aspect of this, only you would do.'

'Your present picture is confused and incomplete, then,' Jaan said.

Ivar nodded. 'What I've learned – Let me try and summarize, may I? Correct me where I'm wrong.

'All Aeneas is primed to explode again. Touchoff spark would be hope, any hope. Given some initial success, more and more peoples elsewhere in Sector Alpha Crucis would join in. But how're we to start? We're broken, disarmed, occupied.

'Well, you preach that superhuman help is at hand. My part would be to furnish political continuity. Aeneans, especially nords, who couldn't go along with return of Elders, might well support Firstman of Ilion in throwin' off Terran yoke. And even true believers would welcome that kind of reinforcement, that human touch: especially since we men must do most of work, and most of dyin', ourselves.'

Jaan nodded. 'Aye,' he said. 'Deliverance which is not earned is of little worth in establishing freedom that will endure, of no worth in raising us toward the next level of evolution. The Ancients will *help* us. As we will afterward help them, in their millennial battle . . . I repeat, we must not expect an instant revolution. To prepare will take years, and after that will follow years more of cruel strife. For a long time to come, your chief part will be simply to stay alive and at large, to be a symbol that keeps the hope of eventual liberation alight.'

Ivar nerved himself to ask, 'And you, meanwhile, do what?'

'I bear the witness,' Jaan said; his tone was nearer

humble than proud. 'I plant the seeds of faith. As Caruith, I can give you, the Companions, the freedom leaders everywhere, some practical help: for instance, by reading minds under favorable circumstances. But in the ultimate, I am the embodiment of that past which is also the future.

'Surely at last I too must go hide in the wilds from the Terrans, after they realize my significance. Or perhaps they will kill me. No matter. That only destroys this body. And in so doing, it creates the martyr, it fulfills the cycle. For Caruith shall rise again.'

The wind seemed to blow cold along Ivar's bones. 'Who is Caruith? What is he?'

'The mind of an Ancient,' Jaan said serenely.

'Nobody was clear about it, talkin' to me—'

'They felt best I explain to you myself. For one thing, you are not a semi-literate artisan or herdsman. You are well educated; you reject supernaturalism; to you, Caruith must use a different language from my preachings to common Orcans.'

Ivar walked on, waiting. A jackrat scuttered from the bleached skull of a statha.

Jaan looked before him. He spoke in a monotone that, somehow, sang.

'I will begin with my return hither, after the exile years. I was merely a shoemaker, a trade I had learned in what spare time I found between the odd jobs which helped keep us alive. Yet I had also the public data screens, to read, watch, study, learn somewhat of this universe; and at night I would often go forth under the stars to think.

'Now we came back to Mount Cronos. I dreamed of enlisting in the Companions, but that could not be; their training must begin at a far earlier age than mine. However, a sergeant among them, counselor and magistrate to our district, took an interest in me. He helped me carry on my studies. And at last he arranged for me to assist, part time and for a small wage, in archaeological work.

'You realize that that is the driving force behind the Companions today. They began as a military band, and continue as civil authorities. Nova Roma could easily reorganize that for us, did we wish. But generations of prophets have convinced us the Ancients cannot be dead, must still dwell lordly in the cosmos. Then what better work is there than to seek what traces and clues are left among us? And who shall better carry it out than the Companions?'

Ivar nodded. This was a major reason why the University had stopped excavation in these parts: to avoid creating resentment among the inhabitants and their leaders. The paucity of reported results, ever since, was assumed to be due to lack of notable finds. Suddenly Ivar wondered how much had been kept secret.

The hypnotic voice went on: 'That work made me feel, in my depths, how vastly space-time overarches us and yet how we altogether belong in it. I likewise brooded upon the idea, an idea I first heard while in exile, that the Didonians have a quality of mind, of being, which is as far beyond ours as ours is beyond blind instinct. Could the Ancients have it too – not in the primitive dim unities of our Neighbors, but in perfection? Might *we* someday have it?

'So I wondered, and took ever more to wandering by myself, aye, into the tunnels beneath the mountain when no one else was there. And my heart would cry out for an answer that never came.

'Until –

'It was a night near midwinter. The revolution had not begun, but even here we knew how the oppression waxed, and the people seethed, and chaos grew. Even we were in scant supply of certain things, because offworld trade was becoming irregular, as taxation and confiscation caused merchantmen to move from this sector, and the spaceport personnel themselves grew demoralized till there was no proper traffic control. Yes, a few times out-and-out pirates from the barbarian stars slipped past a fragmented guard to raid and run. The woe of Aeneas was heavy on me.

'I looked at the blaze of the Crux twins, and at the darkness which cleaves the Milky Way where the nebulae hide from us the core of our galaxy: and walking along the mountainside, I asked if, in all that majesty, our lives alone could be senseless accidents, our pain and death for nothing.

'It was cruelly cold, though. I entered the mouth of a newly dug-out Ancient corridor, for shelter; or did something call me? I had a flashbeam, and almost like a sleep-walker found myself bound deeper and deeper down those halls.

'You must understand, the wonderful work itself had not collapsed, save at the entrance, after millions of years of earthquake and landslide. Once we dug past that, we found a labyrinth akin to others. With our scanty man-power and equipment, we might take a lifetime to map the entire complex.

'Drawn by I knew not what, I went where men have not yet been. With a piece of chalkstone picked from the rubble, I marked my path; but that was will-nigh the last glimmer of ordinary human sense in me, as I drew kilo-meter by kilometer near to my finality.

'I found it in a room where light shone cool from a tall thing off whose simplicity my eyes glided; I could only see that it must be an artifact, and think that most of it must be not matter but energy. Before it lay this which I now wear on my head. I donned it and —

' — there are no words, no thoughts for what came — 'After three nights and days I ascended; and in me dwelt Caruith the Ancient.'

XVIII

A bony sketch of a man, Colonel Mattu Luuksson had returned Chunderban Desai's greetings with a salute, declined refreshment and sat on the edge of his lounger as if he didn't want to submit his uniform to its self-adjusting embrace. Nevertheless the Companion of the Arena spoke courteously enough to the High Commissioner of Imperial Terra.

' – decision was reached yesterday. I appreciate your receiving me upon such short notice, busy as you must be.'

'I would be remiss in my duty, did I not make welcome the representative of an entire nation,' Desai answered. He passed smoke through his lungs before he added, 'It does seem like, um, rather quick action, in a matter of this importance.'

'The order to which I have the honor to belong does not condone hesitancy,' Mattu declared. 'Besides, you understand, sir, my mission is exploratory. Neither you nor we will care to make a commitment before we know the situation and each other more fully.'

Desai noticed he was tapping his cigarette holder on the edge of the ashtaker, and made himself stop. 'We could have discussed this by vid,' he pointed out with a mildness he didn't quite feel.

'No, sir, not very well. More is involved than words. An electronic image of you and your office and any number of your subordinates would tell us nothing about the total environment.'

'I see. Is that why you brought those several men along?'

'Yes. They will spend a few days wandering around the city, gathering experiences and impressions to report to our council, to help us estimate the desirability of more visits.'

Desai arched his brows. 'Do you fear they may be corrupted?' The thought of fleshpots in Nova Roma struck him as weirdly funny; he choked back a laugh.

Mattu frowned – in anger or in concentration? *How can I read so foreign a face?* 'I had best try to explain from the foundations, Commissioner,' he said, choosing each word. 'Apparently you have the impression that I am here to protest the recent ransacking of our community, and to work out mutually satisfactory guarantees against similar incidents in future. That is only a minor part of it.

'Your office appears to feel the Orcan country is full of rebellious spirits, in spite of the fact that almost no Orcans joined McCormac's forces. The suspicion is not unnatural. We dwell apart; our entire ethos is different from yours.'

From Terra's sensate pragmatism, you mean, Desai thought. *Or its decadence, do you imply?* 'As a keeper of law and order myself,' he said, 'I trust you sympathize with the occasional necessity of investigating every possibility, however remote.'

A Terran, in a position similar to Mattu's, would generally have grinned. The colonel stayed humorless: 'More contact should reduce distrust. But this would be insufficient reason to change long-standing customs and policies.

'The truth is, the Companions of the Arena and the society they serve are not as rigid, not as xenophobic, as popular belief elsewhere has it. Our isolation was never absolute; consider our trading caravans, or those young men who spend years outside, in work or in study. It is really only circumstance which has kept us on the fringe – and, no doubt, a certain amount of human inertia.

'Well, the times are mutating. If we Orcans are not to become worse off, we must adapt. In the course of adaptation, we can better our lot. Although we are not obsessed with material wealth, and indeed think it disastrous to acquire too much, yet we do not value poverty, Commissioner; nor are we afraid of new ideas. Rather, we feel our own ideas have strength to survive, and actually spread among people who may welcome them.'

Desai's cigarette was used up. He threw away the ill-smelling stub and inserted a fresh one. Anticipating, his palate winced. 'You are interested in enlarged trade relationships, then,' he said.

'Yes,' Mattu replied. 'We have more to offer than is commonly realized. I think not just of natural resources, but of hands and brains, if more of our youth can get adequate modern educations.'

'And, hm-m-m, tourism in your area?'

'Yes,' Mattu snapped. Obviously the thought was distasteful to him as an individual. 'To develop all this will take time, which we have, and capital, which we have not. The nords were never interested . . . albeit I confess the Companions never made any proposal to them. We have now conceived the hope that the Imperium may wish to help.'

'Subsidies?'

'They need not be great, nor continue long. In return, the Imperium gains not simply our friendship, but our influence, as Orcans travel further and oftener across Aeneas. You face a nord power structure which, on the whole, opposes you, and which you are unlikely to win over. Might not Orcan influence help transform it?'

'Perhaps. In what direction, though?'

'Scarcely predictable at this stage, is it? For that matter, we could still decide isolation is best. I repeat, my mission is no more than a preliminary exploration – for both our sides, Commissioner.'

Chunderban Desai, who had the legions of the Empire at his beck, looked into the eyes of the stranger; and it was Chunderban Desai who felt a tinge of fear.

The young lieutenant from Mount Cronos had openly called Tatiana Thane to ask if he might visit her 'in order to make the acquaintance of the person who best knows Ivar Frederiksen. Pray understand, respected lady, we do not lack esteem for him. However, indirectly he has been the cause of considerable trouble for us. It has occurred to me that you may advise us how we can convince the authorities we are not in league with him.'

'I doubt it,' she answered, half amused at his awkward earnestness. The other half of her twisted in re-aroused pain, and wanted to deny his request. But that would be cowardice.

When he entered her apartment, stiff in his uniform, he offered her a token of appreciation, a hand-carved pendant from his country. To study the design, she must hold it in her palm close to her face; and she read the engraved question, *Are we spied on?*

Her heart sprang. After an instant, she shook her head, and knew the gesture was too violent. No matter. Stewart sent a technician around from time to time, who verified that the Terrans had planted no bugs. Probably the underground itself had done so . . . The lieutenant extracted an envelope from his tunic and bowed as he handed it to her.

'Read at your leisure,' he said, 'but my orders are to watch you destroy this afterward.'

He seated himself. His look never left her. She, in her own chair, soon stopped noticing. After the third time through Ivar's letter, she mechanically heeded Frumious Bandersnatch's plaintive demand for attention.

Following endearments which were nobody else's business, and a brief account of his travels:

' — prophet, though he denies literal divine inspiration. I wonder what difference? His story is latter-day Apocalypse.

'I don't know whether I can believe it. His quiet certainty carries conviction; but I don't claim any profound knowledge of people. I could be fooled. What *is* undeniable is that under proper conditions he can read my mind, better than any human telepath I ever heard of, better than top-gifted humans are supposed to be able to. Or non-humans, even? I was always taught telepathy is not universal language; it's not enough to sense your subject's radiations, you have to learn what each pattern means to *him*; and of course patterns vary from individual to individual, still more from culture to culture, tremendously from species to species. And to this day, phenomenon's not too well understood. I'd better just give you Jaan's

172

own story, though my few words won't have anything of overwhelming *impression* he makes.

'He says, after finding this Elder artifact I mentioned, he put "crown" on his head. I suppose that would be natural thing to do. It's adjustable, and ornamental, and maybe he's right, maybe command was being broadcast. Anyhow, something indescribable happened, heaven and hell together, at first mostly hell because of fear and strangeness and uprooting of his whole mind, later mostly heaven – and now, Jaan says, neither word is any good, there are no words for what he experiences, what he is.

'In scientific terms, if they aren't pseudoscientific (where do you draw line, when dealing with unknown?), what he says happened is this. Long ago, Elders, or Ancients as they call them here, had base on Aeneas, same as on many similar planets. It was no mere research base. They were serving huge purpose I'll come to later. Suggestion is right that they actually caused Didonians to evolve, as one experiment among many, all aimed at creating more intelligence, more consciousness, throughout cosmos.

'At last they withdrew, but left one behind whom Jaan gives name of Caruith, though he says spoken name is purely for benefit of our limited selves. It wasn't original Caruith who stayed; and original wasn't individual like you or me anyway, but part – aspects? – attribute? – of glorious totality which Didonians only hint at. What Caruith did was let heeshself be scanned, neurone by neurone, so entire personality pattern could be recorded in some incredible fashion.

'Sorry, darling, I just decided pronoun like "heesh" is okay for Neighbors but too undignified for Ancients. I'll say "he," because I'm more used to that; could just as well, or just as badly, be "she", of course.

'When Jaan put on circlet, apparatus was activated, and stored pattern was imposed on his nervous system.

'You can guess difficulties. What shabby little word, "difficulties"! Jaan has human brain, human body; and in fact, Elders thought mainly in terms of Didonian finding their treasure. Jaan can't do anything his own organism hasn't got potential for. Original Caruith could maybe

173

solve a thousand simultaneous differential equations in his "head", in split second, if he wanted to; but Caruith using Jaan's primitive brain can't. You get idea?

'Noneless, Elders had realized Didonians might not be first in that room. They'd built flexibility into system. Furthermore, all organisms have potentials that aren't ordinarily used. Let me give you clumsy example. You play chess, paint pictures, hand-pilot aircraft, and analyze languages. I know. But suppose you'd been born into world where nobody had invented chess, paint aircraft, or semantic analysis. You see? Or think how sheer physical and mental training can bring out capabilities in almost anybody.

'So after three days of simply getting adjusted, to point where he could think and act at all, Jaan came back topside. Since then, he's been integrating more and more with this great mind that shares his brain. He says at last they'll become one, more Caruith than Jaan, and he rejoices at prospect.

'Well, what does he preach? What do Elders want? Why did they do what they have done?

'Again, it's impossible to put in few words. I'm going to try but I know I will fail. Maybe your imagination can fill in gaps. You've certainly got good mind, sweetheart.

'Ancients, Elders, Builders, High Ones, Old Shen, whatever we call them — and Jaan won't give them separate name, he says that would be worse misleading than "Caruith" already is — evolved billions of years ago, near galactic center where stars are older and closer together. We're way out on thin fringe of spiral arm, you remember. At that time, there had not been many generations of stars, elements heavier than helium were rare, planets with possibility of life were few. Elders went into space and found it lonelier than we can dream, we who have more inhabited worlds around than anybody has counted. They turned inward, they deliberately forced themselves to keep on evolving mind, lifetime after lifetime, because they had no one else to talk to — How I wish I could send you record of Jaan explaining!

'Something happened. He says he isn't yet quite able to

174

understand what. Split in race, in course of millions of years; not ideological difference as we think of ideology, but two different ways of perceiving, of evaluating reality, two different purposes to impose on universe. We dare not say one branch is good, one evil; we can only say they are irreconcilable. Cal them Yang and Yin, but don't try to say which is which.

'In crudest possible language, *our* Elders see goal of life as consciousness, transcendence of everything material, unification of mind not only in this galaxy but throughout cosmos, so its final collapse won't be end but will be beginning. While Others seek – mystic oneness with energy – supreme experience of Acceptance – No, I don't suppose you can fairly call them death-orientated.

'Jaan likes old Terran quotation I know, as describing Elders: "To strive, to seek, to find, and not to yield" (Do you know it?) And for Others, what? Not "Kismet", really; that at least implies doing God's will, and Others deny God altogether. Nor "nihilism", which I reckon implies desire for chaos, maybe as necessary for rebirth. What Others stand for is so alien that – Oh, I'll write, knowing I'm wrong, that they believe rise, fall, and infinite extinction are our sole realities, and sole fulfillment that life can ultimately have is harmony with this curve.

'In contrast, Jaan says life, if it follows Elders star, will at last *create* God, *become* God.

'To that end, Elders have been watching new races arise on new planets, and helping them, guiding them, sometimes even bringing them into being like Didonians. They can't watch always over everything; they haven't over us. For Others have been at work too, and must be opposed.

'It's not war as we understand war; not on that level. On our level, it is.

'Analogy again. You may be trying to arrive at some vital decision that will determine your entire future. You may be reasoning, you may be wrestling with your emotions, but it's all in your mind; nobody else need see a thing.

'Only it's *not* all in your mind. Unhealthy body means unhealthy thinking. Therefore, down on cellular level, your white blood corpuscles and antigens are waging relentless, violent war on invaders. And its outcome will have much to do with what happens in your head – maybe everything. Do you see?

'It's like that. What intelligent life (I mean sophonts as we know them; Elders and Others are trans-intelligent) does is crucial. And one tiny bit of one galaxy, like ours, can be turning point. Effects multiply, you see. Just as it took few starfaring races to start many more on same course, irreversible change, so it could take few new races who go over to wholly new way of evolution for rest to do likewise eventually.

'Will that level be of Elders or of Others? Will we break old walls and reach, however painfully, for what is infinite, or will we find most harmonious, beautiful, noble way to move toward experience of oblivion?

'You see what I was getting at, that words like "positive" and "negative", "active" and "passive", "evolutionism" and "nihilism", "good" and "evil" don't mean anything in this context? Beings unimaginably far beyond us have two opposing ways of comprehending reality. Which are we to choose?

'We have no escape from choosing. We can accept authority, limitations, instructions; we can compromise; we can live out our personal lives safely; and it's victory for Others throughout space we know, because right now *Homo sapiens* does happen to be leading species in these parts. Or we can take our risks, strike for our freedom, and if we win it, look for Elders to return and raise us, like children of theirs, toward being more than what we have ever been before.

'That's what Jaan says. Tanya, darling, I just don't know –'

She lifted eyes from the page. It flamed in her: *I do. Already.*

Nomi dwelt with her children in a two-room abode at the bottom end of Grizzle Alley. Poverty flapped and racketed everywhere around them. It did not stink, for even the poorest Orcans were of cleanly habits and while there was scant water to spare for washing, the air quickly parched out any maladors. Nor were there beggars; the Companions took in the desperately needy, and assigned them what work they were capable of doing. But ragged shapes crowded this quarter with turmoil: milling and yelling children, women overburdened with jugs and baskets, men plying their trades, day laborer, muledriver, carter, scavenger, artisan, butcher, tanner, priest, minstrel, vendor chanting of chaffering about his pitiful wares. Among battered brown walls, on tangled lanes of rutted iron-hard earth, Ivar felt more isolated than if he had been alone in the Dreary.

The mother of the prophet put him almost at ease. They had met briefly. Today he asked for Jaan, and heard the latter was absent, and was invited to come in and wait over a cup of tea. He felt a trifle guilty, for he had in fact made sure beforehand that Jaan was out, walking and earnestly talking with his disciples, less teaching them than using them for a sounding board while he groped his own way toward comprehension and integration of his double personality.

But I must learn more myself, before I make that terrible commitment he wants. And who can better give me some sense of what he really is, than this woman?

She was alone, the youngsters being at work or in school. The inside of the hut was therefore quiet, once its door had closed off street noise. Sunlight slanted dusty through the glass of narrow windows; few Orcans could afford vitryl. The room was cool, shadowy, crowded but, in its neatness, not cluttered. Nomi's loom filled one corner, a half-finished piece of cloth revealing a subtle pattern of subdued hues. Across from it was a set of primitive kitchen facilities. Shut-beds for her and her oldest son took most of the remaining space. In the middle of the room was a plank table surrounded by benches, whereat she seated her guest. Food on high shelves or hung from the rafters – a little preserved meat, more dried vegetables and hardtack – made the air fragrant. At the rear an open doorway showed a second room, occupied mostly by bunks.

Nomi moved soft-footed across the clay floor, poured

from the pot she had made ready, and sat down opposite Ivar in a rustle of skirts. She had been beautiful when young, and was still handsome in a haggard fashion. If anything, her gauntness enhanced a pair of wonderful gray eyes, such as Jaan had in heritage from her. The coarse blue garb, the hood which this patriarchal society laid over the heads of widows, on her were not demeaning; she had too much inner pride to need vanity.

They had made small talk while she prepared the bitter Orcan tea. She knew who he was. Jaan said he kept no secrets from her, because she could keep any he asked from the world. Now Ivar apologized: 'I didn't mean to interrupt your work, my lady.'

She smiled. 'A welcome interruption, Firstling.'

'But, uh, you depend on it for your livin'. If you'd rather go on with it –'

She chuckled. 'Pray take not away from me this excuse for idleness.'

'Oh. I see.' He hated to pry, it went against his entire training, and he knew he would not be good at it. But he had to start frank discussion somehow. 'It's only, well, it seemed to me you aren't exactly rich. I mean, Jaan hasn't been makin' shoes since – what happened to him.'

'No. He has won a higher purpose.' She seemed amused by the inadequacy of the phrase.

'Uh, he never asks for contributions, I'm told. Doesn't that make things hard for you?'

She shook her head. 'His next two brothers have reached an age where they can work part time. It could be whole time, save that I will not have it; they must get what learning they can. And . . . Jaan's followers help us. Few of them can afford any large donation, but a bit of food, a task done for us without charge, such gifts mount up.'

Her lightness had vanished. She frowned at her cup and went on with some difficulty: 'It was not quite simple for me to accept at first. Ever had we made our own way, as did Gileb's parents and mine ere we were wedded. But what Jaan does is so vital that – Ay-ah, acceptance is a tiny sacrifice.'

'You do believe in Caruith, then?'

178

She lifted her gaze to his, and his dropped as she answered, 'Shall I not believe my own good son and my husband's?'

'Oh, yes, certainly, my lady,' he floundered. 'I beg your pardon if I seemed to – Look, I am outsider here, I've only known him few days and – Do you see? You have knowledge of him to guide you in decidin' he's not, well, victim of delusion. I don't have that knowledge, not yet, anyway.'

Nomi relented, reached across the table and patted his hand. 'Indeed, Firstling. You do right to ask. I am gladdened that in you he has found the worthy comrade he needs.'

Has he?

Perhaps she read the struggle on his face, for she continued, low-voiced and looking beyond him:

'Why should I wonder that you wonder? I did likewise. When he vanished for three dreadful days, and came home utterly changed – Yes, I thought a blood vessel must have burst in his brain, and wept for my kind, hard-working first-born boy, who had gotten so little from life.

'Afterward I came to understand how he had been singled out as no man ever was before in all of space and time. But that wasn't a joy, Firstling, as we humans know joy. His glory is as great and as cruel as the sun. Most likely he shall have to die. Only the other night, I dreamed he was Shoemaker Jaan again, married to a girl I used to think about for him, and they had laid their first baby in my arms. I woke laughing . . . .' Her fingers closed hard on the cup. 'That cannot be, of course.'

Ivar never knew if he would have been able to probe further. An interruption saved him: Robhar, the youngest disciple, knocking at the door.

'I thought you might be here, sir,' the boy said breathlessly. Though the master had identified the newcomer only by a false name, his importance was obvious. 'Carruth will come as soon as he can.' He thrust forward an envelope. 'For you.'

'Huh?' Ivar stared.

'The mission to Nova Roma is back, sir,' Robhar said,

179

nigh bursting with excitement. 'It brought a letter for you. The messenger gave it to Caruith, but he told me to bring it straight to you.'

To Heraz Hyronsson stood on the outside. Ivar ripped the envelope open. At the end of several pages came the bold signature Tanya. His own account to her had warned her how to address a reply.

'Excuse me,' he mumbled, and sat down to gulp it.

Afterward he was very still for a while, his features locked. Then he made an excuse for leaving, promised to get in touch with Jaan soon, and hurried off. He had some tough thinking to do.

XIX

None but a few high-ranking officers among the Companions had been told who Ivar was. They addressed him as Heraz when in earshot of others. He showed himself as seldom as feasible, dining with Yakow in the Commander's suite, sleeping in a room nearby which had been lent him, using rear halls, ramps, and doorways for his excursions. In that vast structure, more than half of it unpopulated, he was never conspicuous. The corps knew their chief was keeping someone special, but were too disciplined to gossip about it.

Thus he and Yakow went almost unseen to the chamber used as a garage. Jaan was already present, in response to word from a runner. A guard saluted as the three men entered an aircar; and no doubt much went on in his head, but he would remain close-mouthed. The main door glided aside. Yakow's old hands walked skillfully across the console. The car lifted, purred forth into the central enclosure, rose a vertical kilometer, and started leisurely southward.

A wind had sprung up as day rolled toward evening. It whined around the hull, which shivered. The Sea of Orcus bore whitecaps on its steel-colored surface and flung waves against its shores; where spray struck and evaporated, salt was promptly hoar. The continental shelf glowed reddish from long rays filtered through a dust-veil which obscured the further desert; the top of that storm broke off in thin clouds and streamed yellow across blue-black heaven.

Yakow put controls on automatic, swiveled his seat around, and regarded the pair who sat aft of him. 'Very well, we have the meeting place you wanted, Firstling,' he said. 'Now will you tell us why?'

Ivar felt as if knives and needles searched him. He flicked his glance toward Jaan's mild countenance, remembered what lay beneath it, and recoiled to stare out the canopy at the waters which they were crossing. *I'm supposed to cope with these two?* he thought despairingly.

Well, there's nobody else for job. Nobody in whole wide universe. Against his loneliness, he hugged to him the thought that they might prove to be in truth his comrades in the cause of liberation.

'I, I'm scared of possible spies, bugs,' he said.

'Not in my part of the Arena,' Yakow snapped. 'You know how often and thoroughly we check.'

'But Terrans have resources of, of entire Empire to draw on. They could have stuff we don't suspect. Like telepathy.' Ivar forced himself to turn back to Jaan. 'You scan minds.'

'Within limits,' the prophet cautioned. 'I have explained.'

Yes. He took me down into mountains heart and showed me machine – device – whatever it is that he says held record of Caruith. He wouldn't let me touch anything, though I couldn't really blame him, and inside I was just as glad for excuse not to. And there he sensed my thoughts. I tested him every way I could imagine, and he told me exactly what I was thinkin', as well as some things I hadn't quite known I was thinkin'. Yes.

He probably wouldn't've needed telepathy to see my sense of privacy outraged. He smiled and told me –

'Fear not. I have only my human nervous system, and it isn't among the half-talented ones which occur rarely in our species. By myself, I cannot resonate any better than you, Firstling.' Bleakly: 'This is terrible for Caruith, like being deaf or blind; but he endures, that awareness may be helped to fill reality. And down here – .' Glory: 'Here his former vessel acts to amplify, to recode, like a living brain center. Within its range of operation, Caruith-Jaan is part of what he rightfully should be: of what he will be again, when his people return and make for us that body we will have deserved.'

I can believe anyway some fraction of what he claimed. Artificial amplification and relayin' of telepathy are beyond

182

Terran science; but I've read of experiments with it, in past eras when Terran science was more progressive than now. Such technology is not too far beyond our present capabilities: almost matter of engineerin' development rather than pure research.

Surely it's negligible advance over what we know, compared to recordin' of entire personality, and reimposition of pattern on member of utterly foreign species . . .

'Well,' Ivar said, 'if you, usin' artifact not really intended for your kind of organism, if you scan minds within radius of hundred meters or so – then naturally endowed bein's ought to do better.'

'There are no nonhumans in Orcan territory,' Yakow said.

'Except Erannath,' Ivar retorted.

Did the white-bearded features stiffen? Did Jaan wince? 'Ah, yes,' the Commander agreed. 'A temporary exception. No xenosophonts are in Arena or town.'

'Could be human mutants, maybe genetic-tailored, who've infiltrated.' Ivar shrugged. 'Or maybe no telepathy at all; maybe some gadget your detectors won't register. I repeat, you probably don't appreciate as well as I do what variety must exist on thousands of Imperial planets. Nobody can keep track. Imperium could well import surprise for us from far side of Empire.' He sighed. 'Or, okay, call me paranoid. Call this trip unnecessary. You're probably right. Fact is, however, I've got to decide what to do – question involvin' not simply me, but my whole society – and I feel happier discussin' it away from any imaginable surveillance.'

Such as may lair inside Mount Cronos.

If it does, I don't think it's happened to tap my thoughts these past several hours. Else my sudden suspicions that came from Tanya's letter could've gotten me arrested.

Jaan inquired shrewdly, 'Has the return of our Nova Roma mission triggered you?'

Ivar nodded with needless force.

'The message you received from your betrothed – '

'I destroyed it,' Ivar admitted, for the fact could not

183

be evaded were he asked to show the contents. 'Because of personal elements.' They weren't startled; most nords would have done the same. 'However, you can guess what's true, that she discussed her connection with freedom movement. My letter to her and talks with your emissary had convinced her our interests and yours are identical in throwin' off Imperial yoke.'

'And now you wish more details,' Yakow said.

Ivar nodded again. 'Sir, wouldn't you? Especially since it looks as if Commissioner Desai will go along with your plan. That'll mean Terrans comin' here, to discuss and implement economic growth of this region. What does that imply for our liberation?'

'I thought I had explained,' said Jaan patiently. 'The plan is Caruith's. Therefore it is long-range, as it must be; for what hope lies in mere weapons? Let us rise in force before the time is ready, and the Empire will crush us like a thumb crushing a sandmite.'

Caruith's plan – The aircar had passed across the sea and the agricultural lands which fringed its southern shore, to go out over the true desert. This country made the Dreary of Ironland seem lush. Worn pinnacles lifted above ashen dunes; dust scudded and whirled; Ivar glimpsed fossil bones of an ocean monster, briefly exposed for wind to scour away, the single token of life. Low in the west, Virgil glowered through a haze that whistled.

'Idea seems . . . chancy, over subtle . . . Can any non-human fathom our character that well?' he fretted.

'Remember, in me he is half human,' Jaan replied; 'and he has a multimillion-year history to draw on. Men are no more unique than any other sophonts. Caruith espies likenesses among races to which we are blind.'

'I too grow impatient,' Yakow sighed. 'I yearn to see us free, but can hardly live long enough. Yet Caruith is right. We must prepare all Aeneans, so when the day comes, all will rise together.'

'The trade expansion is a means to that end,' Jaan assured. 'It should cause Orcans to travel across the planet, meeting each sort of other Aenean, leavening with faith and fire. Oh, our agents will not be told to preach; they will not know anything except that they have practical bargains to drive and arrangements to make. But they will inevitably fall into conversations, and this will arouse interest, and nords or Riverfolk or tinerans or whoever will invite friends to come hear what the outlander has to say.'

'I've heard that several times,' Ivar replied, 'and I still have trouble understandin'. Look, sirs. You don't expect mass conversion to Orcan beliefs, do you? I tell you, that's impossible. Our different cultures are too strong in their particular reverences – traditional religions, paganism, Cosmenosis, ancestor service, whatever it may be.'

'Of course,' Jaan said softly. 'But can you not appreciate, Firstling, their very conviction is what counts? Orcans will by precept and example make every Aenean redouble his special fervor. And nothing in my message contradicts any basic tenet of yonder faiths. Rather, the return of the Ancients fulfills all hopes, no matter what form they have taken.'

'I know, I know. Sorry, I keep on bein' skeptical. But never mind. I don't suppose it can do any harm; and as you say, it might well keep spirit of resistance alive. What about me, though? What am I supposed to be doin' meanwhile?'

'At a time not far in the future,' Yakow said, 'you will raise the banner of independence. We need to make preparations first; mustn't risk you being seized at once by the enemy. Most likely, you'll have to spend years offplanet, waging guerrilla warfare on Dido, for example, or visiting foreign courts to negotiate for their support.'

Ivar collected his nerve and interrupted: 'Like Ythri?'

'Well . . . yes.' Yakow dismissed his own infinitesimal hesitation. 'Yes, we might get help from the Domain, not while yours is a small group of outlaws, but later, when our cause comes to look more promising.' He leaned forward. 'To begin with, frankly, your role will be a gadfly's. You will distract the Empire from noticing too much the effects of Orcans traveling across Aeneas. You cannot

185

hope to accomplish more, not for the first several years.'

'I don't know,' Ivar said with what stubbornness he could rally. 'We might get clandestine help from Ythri sooner, maybe quite soon. Some hints Erannath let drop –' He straightened in his seat. 'Why not go talk to him right away?'

Jaan looked aside. Yakow said, 'I fear that isn't practical at the moment, Firstling.'

'How come? Where is he?'

Yakow clamped down sternness. 'You yourself worry about what the enemy may eavesdrop on. What you don't know, you cannot let slip. I must request your patience in this matter.'

It shuddered in Ivar as if the wind outside blew between his ribs. He wondered how well he faked surrender and relaxation. 'Okay.'

'We had better start back,' Yakow said. 'Night draws nigh.'

He turned himself around and then the aircraft. A dusk was already in the cabin, for the storm had thickened. Ivar welcomed the concealment of his face. And did outside noise drown the thud-thud-thud of his pulse? He said most slowly, 'You know, Jaan, one thing I've never heard bespoken. What does Caruith's race look like?'

'It doesn't matter,' was the reply. 'They are more mind than body. Indeed, their oneness includes numerous different species. Think of Dido. In the end, all races will belong.'

'Uh-huh. However, I can't help bein' curious. Let's put it this way. What did the body look like that actually lay down under scanner?'

'Why . . . well – '

'Come on. Maybe your Orcans are so little used to pictures that they don't insist on description. I assure you, companyo, other Aeneans are different. They'll ask. Why not tell me?'

'Kah, hm, kah – ' Jaan yielded. He seemed a touch confused, as if the consciousness superimposed on his didn't work well at a large distance from the reinforcing radiations of the underground vessel. 'Yes. He . . . male, aye, in a bisexual warm-blooded species . . . not mammalian; descended from ornithoids . . . human-seeming in many ways, but beautiful, far more refined and sculptured than us. Thin features set at sharp angles; a speaking voice like music – No.' Jaan broke off. 'I will not say further. It has no significance.'

You've said plenty, tolled in Ivar.

Talk was sparse for the rest of the journey. As the car moved downward toward an Arena that had become a bulk of blackness studded with a few lights, the Firstling spoke. 'Please, I want to go off by myself and think. I'm used to space and solitude when I make important decisions. How about lendin' be this flitter? I'll fly to calm area, settle down, watch moons and stars – return before mornin' and let you know how things appear to me. May I?'

He had well composed and mentally rehearsed his speech. Yakow raised no objection; Jaan gave his shoulder a sympathetic squeeze. 'Surely,' said the prophet. 'Courage and wisdom abide with you, dear friend.'

When he had let the others out, Ivar lifted fast, and cut a thunderclap through the air in his haste to be gone. The dread of pursuit bayed at his heels.

Harsh through him went: *They aren't infallible. I took them by surprise. Jaan should've been prepared with any description but true one – one that matches what Tanya relayed to me from Commissioner Desai, about Merseian agent loose on Aeneas.*

Stiffening wind after sunset filled the air around the lower mountainside with fine sand. Lavinia showed a dim half-disc overhead, but cast no real light; and there were no stars. Nor did villages and farmsteads scattered across the hills reveal themselves. Vision ended within meters.

Landing on instruments. Ivar wondered if this was lucky for him. He could descend unseen, where otherwise he would have had to park behind some ridge or grove kilometers away and slink forward afoot. Indeed, he had scant choice. Walking any distance through a desert storm, without special guidance equipment he didn't have along, posed too much danger of losing his way. But coming so near town and Arena, he risked registering on the detectors of a guard post, and somebody dispatching a squad to investigate.

Well, the worst hazard lay in a meek return to his quarters. He found with a certain joy that fear had left him, as had the hunger and thirst of supperlessness, washed away by the excitement everyone now coursing through him. He donned the overgarment everyone took with him on every trip, slid back the door, and jumped to the ground.

The gate hooted and droned. It sheathed him in chill and a scent of iron. Grit stung. He secured his nightmask and groped forward.

For a minute he worried about going astray in spite of planning. Then he stubbed his toe on a rock which had fallen off a heap, spoil from the new excavation. The entrance was dead ahead uphill, to that tunnel down which Jaan had taken him.

He didn't turn on the flashbeam he had borrowed from the car's equipment, till he stood at the mouth. Thereafter he gripped it hard, as his free hand sought for the latch.

Protection from weather, the manmade door needed no lock against a folk whose piety was founded on relics. When he had closed it behind him, Ivar stood in abrupt silence, motionless cold, a dark whose thickness was broken only by the wan ray from the flash. His breath sounded too loud in his ears. Fingers sought comfort from the heavy sheath knife he had borne from Windhome; but it was his solitary weapon. To carry anything more, earlier, would have provoked instant suspicion.

What will I find?

Probably nothin'. I can take closer look at Caruith machine, but I haven't tools to open it and analyze. As for what might be elsewhere . . . these corridors twist on and on, in dozen different sets.

Noneless, newest discovery, plausibly barred to public while exploration proceeds, is most logical place to hide – whatever is to be hidden. And – his gaze went to the dust of megayears, tumbled and tracked like the dust of Luna when man first fared into space – I could find traces which'll lead me further, if any have gone before me.

He began to walk. His footfalls clopped hollowly back off the ageless vaulting.

Why am I doin' this? Because Merseians may have part in events? Is it bad if they do? Tanya feels happy about what she's heard. She thinks Roidhunate might really come to our aid, and hopes I can somehow contact that agent.

But Ythri might help too. In which case, why won't Orcan chiefs let me see Erannath? Their excuse rings thin.

And if Ancients are workin' through Merseians, as is imaginable, why have they deceived Jaan? Shouldn't he know?

(*Does he? It wouldn't be information to broadcast. Terran Imperium may well dismiss Jaan's claims as simply another piece of cultism, which it'd cause more trouble to suppress than it's worth . . . but never if Imperium suspected Merseia was behind it! So maybe he is withholdin' full story. Except that doesn't feel right. He's too sincere, too rapt, and, yes, too bewildered, to play double game. Isn't he?*)

'I've got to discover truth, or lose what right I ever had to lead my people.'

Ivar marched on into blindness.

XX

A kilometer deep within the mountain, he paused outside the chamber of Jaan's apotheosis. His flashbeam barely skimmed the metal enigma before seeking back to the tunnel floor.

Here enough visits had gone on of late years that the dust was scuffed confusion. Ivar proceeded down the passage. The thing in the room cast him a last reflection and was lost to sight. He had but the one bobbing blob of luminance to hollow out a place for himself in the dark. Now that he advanced slowly, carefully, the silence was well nigh total. *Bad-a-bad*, went his heart, *bad-a-bad, bad-a-bad.*

After several meters, the blurriness ended. He would not have wondered to see individual footprints. Besides Jaan, officers of the Companions whom the prophet brought hither had surely ventured somewhat further. What halted him was sudden orderliness. The floor had been swept smooth.

He stood for minutes while his thoughts grew fangs. When he continued, the knife was in his right fist.

Presently the tunnel branched three ways. That was a logical point for people to stop. Penetrating the maze beyond was a task for properly equipped scientists; and no scientists would be allowed here for a long while to come. Ivar saw that the broom, or whatever it was, had gone down all the mouths. *Quite reasonable,* trickled through him. *Visitors wouldn't likely notice sweepin' had been done, unless they came to place where change in dust layers was obvious. Or unless they half expected it, like me . . . expected strange traces would have to be wiped out . . .*

He went into each of the forks, and found that handi-work ended after a short distance in two of them. What reached onward was simply the downdrift of geological ages. The third had been swept for some ways farther, though not since the next-to-last set of prints had been made. Two sets of those were human, one Ythrian; only the humans had returned. Superimposed were other marks, which were therefore more recent.

They were the tracks of a being who walked on birdlike claws.

Again Ivar stood. Cold gnawed him.

Should I turn right around and run?

Where could I run to?

And Erannath – That decided him. What other friend remained to the free Aeneans? If the Ythrian was alive.

He stalked on. A pair of doorways gaped along his path. He flashed light into them, but saw just empty cham-bers of curious shape.

Then the floor slanted sharply downward, and he round-ed a curve, and from an arch ahead of him in the right wall there came a wan yellow glow.

He gave himself no chance to grow daunted, snapped off his beam and glided to the spot. Poised for a leap, he peered around the edge.

Another cell, this one hexagonal and high-domed, reached seven meters into the rock. Shadows hung in it as heavy, chill, and stagnant as the air. They were cast by a ponderous steel table to which were welded a lightglobe, a portable sanitary facility, and a meter-length chain. Free on its top stood a plastic tumbler and water pitcher, free on the floor lay a mattress, the single relief from iridescent hardness.

'Erannath!' Ivar cried.

The Ythrian hunched on the pad. His feathers were dull and draggled, his head gone skull-gaunt. The chain ended in a manacle that circled his left wrist.

Ivar entered. The Ythrian struggled out of dreams and knew him. The crest erected, the yellow eyes came ablaze. '*Hyaa-aa,*' he breathed.

Ivar knelt to embrace him. 'What've they done?' the

191

man cried. 'Why? My God, those bastards – '

Erannath shook himself. His voice came hoarse, but strength rang into it. 'No time for sentiment. What brought you here? Were you followed?'

'I g-g-got suspicious.' Ivar hunkered back on his heels, hugged his knees, mastered his shock. The prisoner was all too aware of urgency; that stood forth from every quivering plume. And who could better know what dangers dwelt in this tomb? Never before had Ivar's mind run swifter.

'No,' he said, 'I don't think they suspect me in turn. I made excuse to flit off alone, came back and landed under cover of dust storm, found nobody around when I entered. What got me wonderin' was letter today from my girl. She'd learned of Merseian secret agent at large on Aeneas, telepath of some powerful kind. His description answers to Jaan's of Caruith. Right away, I thought maybe cruel trick was bein' played. Jaan should've had less respect for my feelin's and examined – I didn't show anybody letter, and kept well away from Arena as much as possible, before returnin' to look for myself.'

'You did well.' Erannath stroked talons across Ivar's head; and the man knew it for an accolade. 'Beware, Aycharaych is near. We must hope he sleeps, and will sleep till you have gone.'

'Till *we* have.'

Erannath chuckled. His chain clinked. He did not bother to ask. How do you propose to cut this?

'I'll go fetch tools,' Ivar said.

'No. Too chancy. You must escape with the word. At that, if you do get clear, I probably will be released unharmed. Aycharaych is not vindictive. I believe him when he says he sorrows at having to torture me.'

Torture? No marks . . . Of course. Keep sky king chained, buried alive, day after night away from sun, stars, wind. It'd be less cruel to stretch him over slow fire.

Ivar gagged on rage.

Erannath saw, and warned: 'You cannot afford indignation either. Listen. Aycharaych has talked freely to me. I think he must be lonely, shut away down here with nothing but his machinations and the occasional string he pulls on his puppet prophet. Or is his reason that, in talking, he brings associations into my consciousness, and thus reads more of what I know? This is why I have been kept alive. He wants to drain me of data.'

'What is he?' Ivar whispered.

'A native of a planet he calls Chereion, somewhere in the Merseian Roidhunate. Its civilization is old, old – formerly wide-faring and mighty – yes, he says the Chereionites were the Builders, the Ancients. He will not tell me what made them withdraw. He confesses that now they are few, and what power they wield comes wholly from their brains.'

'They're not, uh, uh, super-Didonans, though . . . galaxy-unifyin' intellects . . . as Jaan believes?'

'No. Nor do they wage a philosophical conflict among themselves over the ultimate destiny of creation. Those stories merely fit Aycharaych's purpose.' Erannath hunched on the claws of his wings. His head thrust forward against nacre and shadow. 'Listen,' he said. 'We have no more than a sliver of time at best. Don't interrupt, unless I grow unclear. Listen. Remember.'

The words blew harshly forth, like an autumn gale: 'They preserve remnants of technology on Chereion which they have not shared with their masters the Merseians – if the Merseians are really their masters and not their tools. I wonder about that. Well, we must not stop to speculate. As one would await, the technology relates to the mind. For they are extraordinary telepaths, more gifted than the science we know has imagined is possible.

'There is some ultimate quality of the mind which goes deeper than language. At close range, Aycharaych can read the thoughts of *any* being – any speech, any species, he claims – without needing to know that being's symbolism. I suspect what he does is almost instantly to analyze the pattern, identify universals of logic and conation, go on from there to reconstruct the whole mental configuration – as if his nervous system included not only sensitivity to the radiation of others, but an organic semantic computer fantastically beyond anything that Technic civilization has built.

'No matter! Their abilities naturally led Chereionite scientists to concentrate on psychology and neurology. It's been ossified for millions of years, that science, like their whole civilization: ossified, receding, dying . . . Perhaps Aycharaych alone is trying to act on reality, trying to stop the extinction of his people. I don't know. I do know that he serves the Roidhunate as an Intelligence officer with a roving commission. This involves brewing trouble for the Terran Empire wherever he can.

'During the Snelund regime, he looked through Sector Alpha Crucis. It wasn't hard, when misgovernment had already produced widespread laxity and confusion. The conflict over Jihannath was building toward a crisis, and Merseia needed difficulties on this frontier of Terra's.

'Aycharaych landed secretly on Aeneas and prowled. He found more than a planet growing rebellious. He found the potential of something that might break the Empire apart. For all the peoples here, in all their different ways, are profoundly religious. Give them a common faith, a missionary cause, and they can turn fanatic.'

'No,' Ivar couldn't help protesting.

'Aycharaych thinks so. He has spent a great deal of his time and energy on your world, however valuable his gift would make him elsewhere.'

'But – one planet, a few millions, against the – '

'The cult would spread. He speaks of militant new religions in your past – Islam, is that the name of one? – religions which brought obscure tribes to world power, and shook older dominions to their roots, in a single generation.

'I must hurry. He found the likeliest place for the first spark was here, where the Ancients brood at the center of every awareness. In Jaan the dreamer, whose life and circumstances chanced to be a veritable human archetype, he found the likeliest tinder.

'He cannot by himself project a thought into a brain which is not born to receive it. But he has a machine which can. That is nothing fantastic; human, Ythrian, or Merseian engineers could develop the same device, had

194

they enough incentive. We don't, because for us the utility would be marginal; electronic communications suit our kind of life better.

'Aycharaych, though – Telepathy of several kinds belongs to evolution on his planet. Do you remember the slinkers that the tinerans keep? I inquired, and he admitted they came originally from Chereion. No doubt their effect on men suggested his plan to him.

'He called Jaan down to where he laired in these labyrinths. He drugged him and . . . thought at him . . . in some way he knows, using that machine – until he had imprinted a set of false memories and an idiom to go with them. Then he released his victim.'

'Artificial schizophrenia. Split personality. A man who was sane, made to hear "voices",' Ivar shuddered.

Erannath was harder-souled; or had he simply lived with the fact longer, in his prison? He went on: 'Aycharaych departed, having other mischief to wreak. What he had done on Aeneas might or might not bear fruit; if not, he had lost nothing except his time.

'He returned lately, and found success indeed. Jaan was winning converts throughout the Orcan country. Rumors of the new message were spreading across a whole globe of natural apostles, always eager for anything that might nourish faith, and now starved for a word of hope.

'Events must be guided with craft and patience, of course, or the movement would most likely come to naught, produce not a revolution followed by a crusade, but merely another sect. Aycharaych settled down to watch, to plot, ever oftener to plant in Jaan, through his thought projector, a revelation from Caruith –'

The Ythrian chopped off. He hissed. His free hand raked the air. Ivar whirled on his heel, sprang to stand crouched.

The figure in the doorway, limned against unending night, smiled. He was more than half humanlike, tall and slender in a gray robe; but his bare feet ended in claws. The skin glowed golden, the crest on the otherwise naked head rose blue, the eyes were warm bronze. His face was ax-thin, superbly molded. In one delicate hand he aimed a blaster.

'Greeting,' he almost sang.

'You woke and sensed,' grated from Erannath.

'No,' said Aycharaych. 'My dreams always listen. Afterward, however, yes, I waited out your conversation.'

'Now what?' asked Ivar from the middle of nightmare.

'Why, that depends on you, Firstling,' Aycharaych replied with unchanged gentleness. 'May I in complete sincerity bid you welcome?'

'You – workin' for Merseia –'

The energy gun never wavered; yet the words flowed serene: 'True. Do you object? Your desire is freedom. The Roidhunate's desire is that you should have it. This is the way.'

'T-t-treachery', murder, torture, invadin' and twistin' men's bein's –'

'Existence always begets regrettable necessities. Be not overly proud, Firstling. You are prepared to launch a revolutionary war if you can, wherein millions would perish, millions more be mutilated, starved, hounded, brought to sorrow. Are you not? I do no more than help you. Is that horrible? What happiness has Jaan lost that has not already been repaid him a thousandfold?'

'How about Erannath?'

'Heed him not,' croaked Ythrian to human. 'Think why Merseia wants the Empire convulsed and shattered. Not for the liberty of Aeneans. No, to devour us piecemeal.'

'One would expect Erannath to talk thus,' Aycharaych's tone bore the least hint of mirth. 'After all, he serves the Empire.'

'What?' Ivar lurched where he stood. 'Him? No!'

'Who else can logically have betrayed you, up on the river, once he felt certain of who you are?'

'He came along –'

'He had no means of preventing your escape, as it happened. Therefore his duty was to accompany you, in hopes of sending another message later, and meanwhile gather further information about native resistance movements. It

196

was the same basic reason as caused him earlier to help you get away from the village, before he had more than a suspicion of your identity.

'I knew his purpose – I have not perpetually lurked underground, I have moved to and fro in the world – and gave Jaan orders, who passed them on to Yakow.' Aycharaych sighed. 'It was distasteful to all concerned. But my own duty has been to extract what I can from him.'

'Erannath,' Ivar begged. 'It isn't true!'

The Ythrian lifted his head and said haughtily, 'Truth you must find in yourself, Ivar Frederiksen. What do you mean to do: become another creature of Aycharaych's, or strike for the life of your people?'

'Have you a choice?' the Chereionite murmured. 'I wish you no ill. Nevertheless, I too am at war and cannot stop to weigh out single lives. You will join us, fully and freely, or you will die.'

How can I tell what I want? Through dread and anguish, Ivar felt the roan eyes upon him. Behind them must be focused that intellect, watching, searching, reading. *He'll know what I'm about to do before I know myself.* His knife clattered to the floor. *Why not yield? It may well be right – for Aeneas – no matter what Erannath says. And elsewise –*

Everything exploded. The Ythrian seized the knife. Balanced on one huge wing, he swept the other across Ivar, knocking the human back behind the shelter of it.

Aycharaych must not have been heeding what went on in the hunter's head. Now he was shot. The beam flared and seared. Ivar saw blinding blueness, smelled ozone and scorched flesh. He bent away from death.

Erannath surged forward. Behind him remained his chained hand. He had hacked it off at the wrist.

A second blaster bolt tore him asunder. His uncrippled wing smote. Cast back against the wall, Aycharaych sank stunned. The gun fell from him.

Ivar pounced to grab the weapon. Erannath stirred. Blood pumped from among blackened plumes. An eye was gone. Breath whistled and rattled.

Ivar dropped on his knees, to cradle his friend. The eye

197

that remained sought for him. 'Thus God . . . tracks me down . . . I would it had been under heaven,' Erannath coughed. '*Eyan haa wharr, Hliirr talya –* ' The light in the eye went out.

A movement caught Ivar's glance. He snatched after the gun. Aycharaych had recovered, was bound through the doorway.

For a heartbeat Ivar was about to yell. Stop, we're allies! That stayed his hand long enough for Aycharaych to vanish. Then Ivar knew what the Chereionite had seen: that no alliance could ever be.

I've got to get out, or Erannath – everybody – has gone for naught. Ivar leaped to his feet and ran. Blood left a track behind him.

He noticed with vague surprise that at some instant he had recovered his flash. Its beam scythed. *Can't grieve yet. Can't be afraid. Can't do anything but run and think.*

Is Aycharaych ahead of me? He's left prints in both directions. No, I'm sure he's not. He realizes I'll head back aboveground; and I, whose forebears came from heavier world than his, would overhaul him. So he's makin' for his lair. Does it have line to outside? Probably not. And even if it does, would he call? That'd give his whole game away. No, he'll have to follow after me, use his hell-machine to plant 'intuition' in Jaan's mind –

The room of revelations appeared. Ivar halted and spent a minute playing flame across the thing within. He couldn't tell if he had disabled it or not, but he dared hope.

Onward. Out the door. Down the mountainside, through the sharp dust, athwart the wind which Erannath had died without feeling. To the aircar. Aloft.

The storm yelled and smote.

He burst above, into splendor. Below him rolled the blown dry clouds, full of silver and living shadow beneath Lavinia and hasty Creusa. Stars blazed uncountable. Ahead reared the heights of Ilion; down them glowed and thundered the Linn.

This world is ours. No stranger will shape its tomorrows.

An image in the radar-sweep screen made him look behind. Two other craft soared into view. Had Aycharaych raised pursuit? Decision crystallized in Ivar, unless it had been there throughout these past hours, or latent throughout his life. He activated the radio.

The Imperials monitored several communication bands. If he identified himself and called for a military escort, he could probably have one within minutes.

Tanya, he thought, *I'm comin' home.*

XXI

Chimes rang from the bell tower of the University. They played the olden peals, but somehow today they sounded at peace.

Or was Chunderban Desai wishfully deceiving himself? He wasn't sure, and wondered if he or any human ever could be.

Certainly the young man and woman who sat side by side and hand in hand looked upon him with wariness that might still mask hostility. Her pet, in her lap, seemed touched by the same air, for it perched quiet and kept its gaze on the visitor. The window behind them framed a spire in an indigo sky. It was open, and the breeze which carried the tones entered, cool, dry, pungent with growth odors.

'I apologize for intruding on you so soon after your reunion,' Desai said. He had arrived three minutes ago. 'I shan't stay long. You want to take up your private lives again. But I did think a few explanations and reassurances from me would help you.'

'No big trouble, half hour in your company, after ten days locked away by myself,' Ivar snapped.

'I am sorry about your detention, Firstling. It wasn't uncomfortable, was it? We did have to isolate you for a while. Doubtless you understand our need to be secure about you while your story was investigated. But we also had to provide for your own safety after your release. That took time. Without Prosser Thane's cooperation, it would have taken longer than it did.'

'Safety – huh?' Ivar stared from him to Tatiana. She closed fingers on the tadmouse's back, as if in

200

search of solace. 'Yes,' she said, barely audibly.

'Terrorists of the self-styled freedom movement,' Desai stated, his voice crisper than he felt. 'They had already assassinated a number of Aeneans who supported the government. Your turning to us, your disclosure of a plot which might indeed have pried this sector loose from the Empire – you, the embodiment of their visions – could have brought them to murder again.'

Ivar sat mute for a time. The bells died away. He didn't break the clasp he shared with Tatiana, but his part lost strength. At last he asked her, 'What did you do?'

She gripped him harder. 'I persuaded them. I never gave names ... Commissioner Desai and his officers never asked me for any ... but I talked to leaders, I was go-between, and – There'll be general amnesty.'

'For past acts,' the Imperial reminded. 'We cannot allow more like them. I am hoping for help in their prevention.' He paused. 'If Aeneas is to know law again, tranquillity, restoration of what has been lost, you, First-ling, must take the lead.'

'Because of what I am, or was?' Ivar said harshly.

Desai nodded. 'More people will heed you, speaking of reconciliation, than anyone else. Especially after your story has been made public, or as much of it as is wise.'

'Why not all?'

'Naval Intelligence will probably want to keep various details secret, if only to keep our opponents uncertain of what we do and do not know. And, m-m-m, several high-ranking officials would not appreciate the news getting loose, of how they were infiltrated, fooled, and led by the nose to an appalling brink.'

'You, for instance?'

Desai smiled. 'Between us, I have persons like Sector Governor Muratori in mind. I am scarcely important enough to become a sensation. Now they are not ungrateful in Llynathawr. I can expect quite a free hand in the Virgilian System henceforward. One policy I mean to implement is close consultation with representatives of every Aenean society, and the gradual phasing over of government to them.'

'Hm. Includin' Orcans?'

'Yes. Commander Yakow was nearly shattered to learn the truth; and he is tough, and had no deep emotional commitment to the false creed – simply to the welfare of his people. He agrees the Imperium can best help them through their coming agony.'

Ivar fell quiet anew. Tatiana regarded him. Tears glimmered on her lashes. She must well know that same kind of pain. Finally he asked, 'Jaan?'

'The prophet himself?' Desai responded. 'He knows no more than that for some reason you fled – defected, he no doubt thinks – and afterward an Imperial force came for another search of Mount Cronos, deeper-going than before, and the chiefs of the Companions have not opposed this. Perhaps you can advise me how to tell him the truth, before the general announcement is made.'

Bleakness: 'What about Aycharaych?'

'He has vanished, and his mind-engine. We're hunting for him, of course.' Desai grimaced. 'I'm afraid we will fail. One way or another, that wily scoundrel will get off the planet and home. But at least he did not destroy us here.'

Ivar let go of his girl, as if for this time not she nor anything else could warm him. Beneath a tumbled lock of yellow hair, his gaze lay winter-blue. 'Do you actually believe he could have?'

'The millennialism he was engineering, yes, it might have, I think,' Desai answered, equally low. 'We can't be certain. Very likely Aycharaych knows us better than we can know ourselves. But . . . it has happened, over and over, through man's troubled existence: the Holy War, which cannot be stopped and which carries away kingdoms and empires, though the first soldiers of it be few and poor.

'Their numbers grow, you see. Entire populations join them. Man has never really wanted a comfortable God, a reasonable or kindly one; he has wanted a faith, a cause, which promises everything but mainly which requires everything.

'Like moths to the candle flame –

'More and more in my stewardship of Aeneas, I have

come to see that here is a world of many different peoples, but all of them believers, all strong and able, all sharing some tradition about mighty forerunners and all unready to admit that those forerunners may have been as tragically limited, ultimately as doomed, as we.

'Aeneas was in the forefront of struggle for a political end. When defeat came, that turned the dwellers and their energies back toward transcendental things. And then Aycharaych invented for them a transcendence which the most devout religionist and the most hardened scientist could alike accept.

'I do not think the tide of Holy War could have been stopped this side of Regulus. The end of it would have been humanity and humanity's friends ripped into two realms. No, more than two, for there *are* contradictions in the faith, which I think must have been deliberately put there. For instance, is God the Creator or the Created? – Yes, heresies, persecutions, rebellions . . . states lamed, chaotic, hating each other worse than any outsider –'

Desai drew breath before finishing: ' – such as Merseia. Which would be precisely what Merseia needs, first to play us off against ourselves, afterward to overrun the subject us.'

Ivar clenched fists on knees. 'Truly?' he demanded.

'Truly,' Desai said. 'Oh, I know how useful the Merseian threat has often been to politicians, industrialists, military lords, and bureaucrats of the Empire. That does not mean the threat isn't real. I know how propaganda has smeared the Merseians, when they are in fact, according to their own lights and many of ours, a fairly decent folk. That does not mean their leaders won't risk the Long Night to grasp after supremacy.

'Firstling, if you want to be worthy of leading your own world, you must begin by dismissing the pleasant illusions. Don't take my word, either. Study. Inquire. Go see for yourself. Do your personal thinking. But always follow the truth, wherever it goes.'

'Like that Ythrian?' Tatiana murmured,

'No, the entire Domain of Ythri,' Desai told her. 'Eran-nath was my agent, right. But he was also theirs. They

203

sent him by prearrangement: because in his very foreignness, his conspicuousness and seeming detachment, he could learn what Terrans might not.

'Why should Ythri do this?' he challenged. 'Had we not fought a war with them, and robbed them of some of their territory?'

'But that's far in the past, you see. The territory is long ago assimilated to us. Irredentism is idiocy. And Terra did not try to take over Ythri itself, or most of its colonies, in the peace settlement. Whatever the Empire's faults, and they are many, it recognizes certain limits to what it may wisely do.'

'Merseia does not.'

'Naturally, Erannath knew nothing about Aycharaych when he arrived here. But he did know Aeneas is a key planet in this sector, and expected Merseia to be at work somewhere underground. Because Terra and Ythri have an overwhelming common interest — peace, stability, containment of the insatiable aggressor — and because the environment of your world suited him well, he came to give whatever help he could.'

Desai cleared his throat. 'I'm sorry,' he said. 'I didn't intend that long a speech. It surprised me too. I'm not an orator, just a glorified bureaucrat. But here's a matter on which billions of lives depend.'

'Did you find his body?' Ivar asked without tone.

'Yes,' Desai said. 'His role is another thing we cannot make public: too revealing, too provocative. In fact, we shall have to play down Merseia's own part, for fear of shaking the uneasy peace.

'However, Erannath went home on an Imperial cruiser; and aboard was an honor guard.'

'That's good,' Ivar said after a while.

'Have you any plans for poor Jaan?' Tatiana asked.

'We will offer him psychiatric treatment, to rid him of the pseudo-personality,' Desai promised. 'I am told that's possible.'

'Suppose he refuses.'

'Then, troublesome though he may prove — because his movement won't die out quickly unless he himself denounces it – we will leave him alone. You may disbelieve this, but I don't approve of using people.'

Desai's look returned to Ivar. 'Likewise you, Firstling,' he said. 'You won't be coerced. Nobody will pressure you. Rather, I warn you that working with my administration, for the restoration of Aeneas within the Empire, will be hard and thankless. It will cost you friends, and years of your life that you might well spend more enjoyably, and pain when you must make the difficult decision or the inglorious compromise. I can only hope you will join us.'

He rose. 'I think that covers the situation for the time being,' he said. 'You have earned some privacy, you two. Please think this over, and feel free to call on me whenever you wish. Now, good day, Prosser Thane, Firstling Frederiksen.' The High Commissioner of the Terran Empire bowed. 'Thank you.'

Slowly, Ivar and Tatiana rose. They towered above the little man, before they gave him their hands.

'Probably we will help,' Ivar said. 'Aeneas ought to outlive Empire.'

Tatiana took the sting out of that: 'Sir, I suspect we owe you more thanks than anybody will ever admit, least of all you.'

As Desai closed the door behind him, he heard the tadmouse begin singing.

Jaan walked forth alone before sunrise.

The streets were canyons of night where he often stumbled. But when he came out upon the wharf that the sea had lapped, heaven enclosed him.

Behind this wide, shimmering deck, the town was a huddle turned magical by moonlight. High above lifted the Arena, its dark strength frosted with radiance. Beneath his feet, the mountain fell gray-white and shadow-dappled to the dim shield of the waters. North and east stood Ilion, cloven by the Linn-gleam.

Mostly he knew sky. Stars thronged a darkness which seemed itself afire, till they melted together in the cataract of the Milky Way. Stateliest among them burned Alpha and Beta Crucis; yet he knew many more, the friends of his life's wanderings, and a part of him called on them to guide him. They only glittered and wheeled. Lavinia was down and Creusa hastening to set. Low above the barrens hung Dido, the morning star.

Save for the distant falls it was altogether still here, and mortally cold. Outward breath smoked like wraiths, inward breath hurt.

— Behold what is real and forever, said Caruith.

— Let me be, Jaan said. You are a phantom. You are a lie.

— You do not believe that. We do not.

— Then why is your chamber now empty, and I alone in my skull?

— The Others have won — not even a battle, if we remain steadfast; a skirmish in the striving of life to become God. You are not alone.

— What should we do?

— Deny their perjuries. Proclaim the truth.

— But you are not there! broke from Jaan. You are a branded part of my own brain, hissing at me; and I can be healed of you.

— Oh, yes, Caruith said in terrible scorn. They can wipe the traces of me away; they can also geld you if you want. Go, become domesticated, return to making shoes. Those stars will shine on.

— Our cause in this generation, on this globe, is broken, Jaan pleaded. We both know that. What can we do but go wretched, mocked, reviled, to ruin the dreams of a last faithful few?

— We can uphold the truth, and die for it.

— Truth? What proves you are real, Caruith?

— 'The emptiness I would leave behind me, Jaan.

And that, he thought, would indeed be there within him echoing 'Meaningless, meaningless, meaningless' until his second death gave him silence.

— Keep me, Caruith urged, and we will die only once, and it will be in the service of yonder suns.

Jaan clung to his staff. *Help me.* No one answered save Caruith.

The sky whitened to eastward and Virgil came, the

206

sudden Aenean dawn. Everywhere light awoke. Whistles went through the air, a sound of wings, a fragrance of plants which somehow kept roots in the desert. Banners rose above the Arena and trumpets rang, whatever had lately been told.

Jaan knew: *Life is its own service. And I may have enough of it in me to fill me. I will go seek the help of men.*

He had never before known how steep the upward path was.

But I pray you by the lifting skies,
And the young wind over the grass,
That you take your eyes from off my eyes,
And let my spirit pass.

—KIPLING

THE END

A SELECTED LIST OF SCIENCE FICTION IN CORGI

WHILE EVERY EFFORT IS MADE TO KEEP PRICES LOW, IT IS SOMETIMES NECESSARY TO INCREASE PRICES AT SHORT NOTICE. CORGI BOOKS RESERVE THE RIGHT TO SHOW AND CHARGE NEW RETAIL PRICES ON COVERS WHICH MAY DIFFER FROM THOSE ADVERTISED IN THE TEXT OR ELSEWHERE.

THE PRICES SHOWN BELOW WERE CORRECT AT THE TIME OF GOING TO PRESS (JUNE '78)

☐	10619 4	OX	Piers Anthony	85p
☐	10528 7	OMNIVORE	Piers Anthony	70p
☐	10506 6	ORN	Piers Anthony	75p
☐	09082 4	STAR TREK 3	James Blish	30p
☐	10315 2	STAR TREK: LOG FIVE	Alan Dean Foster	60p
☐	10673 9	STAR TREK FOTONOVEL 1: CITY ON THE EDGE OF FOREVER		
			Sondra Marshak and Myrna Culbreath	85p
☐	10580 5	THE PRICE OF THE PHOENIX: A STAR TREK NOVEL		
			Sondra Marshak and Myrna Culbreath	75p
☐	10661 5	DRAGONSONG	Anne McCaffrey	75p
☐	10773 5	DRAGONFLIGHT	Anne McCaffrey	80p
☐	10163 X	THE SHIP WHO SANG	Anne McCaffrey	75p
☐	10162 1	DECISION AT DOONA	Anne McCaffrey	75p
☐	10161 3	RESTOREE	Anne McCaffrey	70p
☐	10734 4	LOGAN'S WORLD	William Nolan	70p
☐	10507 4	NIGHT WALK	Bob Shaw	80p
☐	10605 4	MONSTERS	A.E. Van Vogt	70p
☐	10463 9	TO DIE IN ITALBAR	Roger Zelazny	

CORGI SF COLLECTOR'S LIBRARY

☐	09805 1	BILLION YEAR SPREE	Brian Aldiss	75p
☐	09533 8	THE SHAPE OF FURTHER THINGS	Brian Aldiss	65p
☐	09706 3	I SING THE BODY ELECTRIC	Ray Bradbury	45p
☐	09581 8	REACH FOR TOMORROW	Arthur C. Clarke	65p
☐	09473 0	THE CITY AND THE STARS	Arthur C. Clarke	40p
☐	09413 7	REPORT ON PLANET THREE	Arthur C. Clarke	40p
☐	09474 9	A CANTICLE FOR LEIBOWITZ	Walter M. Miller	45p
☐	09749 7	THE DREAMING JEWELS	Theodore Sturgeon	40p
☐	10088 9	THE MYSTERIOUS ISLAND	Jules Verne	50p
☐	10213 X	STAR SURGEON	James White	60p

All these books are available at your bookshop or newsagent; or can be ordered direct from the publisher. Just tick the titles you want and fill in the form below.

CORGI BOOKS, Cash Sales Department, P.O. Box 11, Falmouth, Cornwall.

Please send cheque or postal order, no currency.

U.K. send 22p for first book plus 10p per copy for each additional book ordered to a maximum charge of 82p to cover the cost of postage and packing.

B.F.P.O. and Eire allow 22p for first book plus 10p per copy for the next 6 books, thereafter 4p per book.

Overseas customers please allow 30p for the first book and 10p per copy for each additional book.

NAME (block letters)...

ADDRESS ....

(JUNE 1978) ....